LONG
TIME
GONE

LONG TIME GONE

A JACKSON GAMBLE NOVEL

GREGORY STOUT

For Carol, my biggest fan

Praise for Long Time Gone

"As always, Gregory Stout's intricate plot, clever sleuthing, and great dialogue kept me reading *Long Time Gone* a long time into the night. Fans and new readers of Stout's work will applaud his protagonist's willingness to take on a challenge, his determination in the face of impossible odds, and his loyalty to both his friends and his craft. If I were ever in a tight situation, I'd want Jackson Gamble on my side."—Skye Alexander, author of the Lizzie Crane mystery series

"Greg Stout has created an intricate, tightly written plot that splits open Nashville's underbelly; and he simultaneously intertwines the plot with protagonist Gamble's tenderly unconventional love story. Add to this Stout's clear-cut descriptions of places and people, a quirky humor that makes one burst out in laughter, and the reader is sure to call for more Jackson Gamble."—Libi Siporin, author of the Leah Contarini series

Chapter One

Say what you will about Tommy Mack, but from the time he was in grade school, he knew exactly what he wanted to be when he grew up. Other kids in his class talked about being astronauts, or firemen, or President of the United States. By the time they reached high school, those same kids daydreamed about becoming a hip-hop artist, or an airline pilot, or a professional athlete. Brainier kids saw themselves becoming doctors, or teachers or maybe a veterinarian. Not Tommy. He couldn't hit a baseball, or sink a free throw, and he was a lousy student, in part, as it turned out, because he suffered from dyslexia. And so, from his earliest years, he had only a single goal. Tommy's dream was to become a career criminal.

In retrospect, Tommy's vector shouldn't have come as much of a surprise. Tommy's father was killed in a military training exercise during the lead-up to the Gulf War when Tommy was just four years old. His mother, BeeBee Mack, never remarried, and as a single mom lacking even a high school diploma, she was stuck working shitty jobs that paid next to nothing. As a result, her primary resource for child care was the television set in her cramped apartment and a downstairs neighbor whom she depended upon to babysit her son three days a week. At about the same time, she took up with a series of no-account boyfriends, some of whom were abusive, and others who stole what little money she had, before disappearing into the Tennessee night.

BeeBee herself began staying away for longer and longer periods of time, until one night, she didn't come home at all. What remained of her bloated body was found several weeks later, floating in the Cumberland River near

Pegram. According to the medical examiner's report, the COD was manual strangulation. No suspect was ever apprehended nor even identified. After BeeBee's death, Tommy went into the system, bouncing from one temporary home to another, skipping a lot of school, and getting his primary education from re-runs of *Kojak*, *Dragnet* and *Hawaii Five-O* on cable TV. He always rooted for the bad guys, trying to figure out whether there was a way they might have gotten away with their crimes.

When it came to honing his craft, however, Tommy was an eager student, and he began working on it for real in high school, shaking down younger kids for their lunch money. On the street, just to see if he could get away with it, he tried his hand at riskier offenses, including vandalism, tagging neighborhood garages and businesses, keying cars, skipping classes, and staying out most nights after curfew. As he got older, to raise money, he took a shot at just about any penny-ante hustle you could think of: shoplifting, clouting vending machines, garage burglaries, selling street-corner drugs, and going door-to-door, rattling a collection can partly filled with gravel at his neighbors. Years later, he even took a shot at Internet crime, posting a bogus GoFundMe page where he was able to raise a few hundred dollars to pay veterinary bills for a nonexistent pet ferret. You name it, Tommy was willing to give it a go.

In the early days of his professional life, Tommy occasionally worked with a partner, usually someone who would act as either a lookout or a wheelman. Running with the crowd that he did, it was never much of a challenge to recruit accomplices, but then there was always the problem of how to split up the take. His partners wanted half, but Tommy felt that since he was the one who was actually committing the crime, the partner should be happy with less. And then, on one particular job, a late-night burglary at a small-time pawnshop, the partner, feeling justifiably underappreciated, turned up stoned and crashed the getaway car into a utility pole that he was absolutely certain hadn't been there a few hours earlier. The result was that Tommy suffered a fractured patella and a broken tibia and was unable to get away on foot. He was pinched, tried, convicted, and sentenced to a two-year jolt in the county jail. By the time he was released—after fifteen months, thanks to time off for good behavior—he had determined that in the future, his would be strictly a solo act.

The only problem for Tommy was that, despite his unswerving dedication to his craft, he simply wasn't very good at it. Over the years, he tried using a few aliases, including Tony Martin, Travis Maxwell, and Trevor Morris, mostly in the hopes that if he was arrested in one jurisdiction, his name wouldn't appear in some centralized database that would end up flagging him as a predicate offender. It worked for a while, but eventually, the Tennessee Department of Corrections modernized its recordkeeping system, and then Tommy, regardless of his alias, was easy pickings for local law enforcement. Not that he was ever very difficult to spot. He was a fidgety guy, small, easily intimidated, and a terrible liar under pressure.

And so, whether he committed a burglary or stole a car, sooner or later— usually sooner—he got caught. His early arrests, while he was still a juvenile, nearly always resulted in probation, or community service, or a three-month stay at a youth facility. Once, he even drew six months at a state-sanctioned honor farm called Crossroads of Life, which was run by a retired Army chaplain. The idea was to take at-risk young men and put them through a structured regimen of strenuous physical work, fresh air, academic studies, and a heaping helping of religious instruction. None of it took, and within a month of being released, Tommy was up to his old tricks, committing petty crimes whenever the opportunities presented themselves.

In his adult years, he never confronted anyone directly, because the one or two times he tried it, he ended up getting face-planted in the sidewalk. And because he never got picked up carrying a deadly weapon, he drew light sentences, mostly county time lasting no more than a year or two, and nearly always with time off for good behavior. Still, by the age of fifty, he had spent roughly half his life in one kind of custody or another. And then, on a warm spring night in late April, Tommy stepped over the line.

What started out as a no-brainer B&E at an upscale home in Mount Juliet quickly turned into a potential career-ender when he stole some antique jewelry that had belonged to the homeowner's grandmother. The homeowner in this case was one Robert Edward ("Just Call Me Red") Cherry, head of the largest organized crime family in the Mid-south. As luck would have it, two days later, Tommy was arrested on an old outstanding Davidson County warrant for some damn thing or other. And while he was in the tank awaiting his arraignment, he foolishly chirped to his cellie about a big score he thought he'd made as a result of a burglary he'd pulled off two nights earlier. Unfortunately, his cellie, looking to trade information for a sentence reduction, snitched. And by the time Fat Wally Sadler, the go-to guy of Nashville bail bondsmen, showed up to bail him out, word had already gotten back to Tommy through the jailhouse grapevine that "Just Call Me Red" had, in fact, paid for his bond and was eager for a word with him when he got out. Reading between the lines, the minute he hit the pavement, Tommy headed for parts unknown.

That was when I got the call.

I regularly did work for Fat Wally, and, as it so happens, tracking down bail skips is a big part of my business. I also find missing persons, runaways, and deadbeat ex-husbands. Once in a while, I provide 24-7 security for visiting celebrities, run background checks on prospective employees and marriage partners where a prenup is in the offing. Other times, I investigate identity theft and occasionally act as a bagman buying back stolen property, incriminating documents, and indiscreet photos and videos that surface at inconvenient moments. On the other hand, and although I've been asked on more than one occasion, I don't do divorce work, strongarm stuff, or murder for hire.

I had rounded up Tommy on a couple of other occasions, and from talking to people who knew him, I learned that when he took it on the run, he never went very far. The last time I found him, he was holed up with a former acquaintance from his juvenile detention days, now living just up the road in Goodlettsville. On the way back to the lockup, Tommy told me he'd never in his life been more than a hundred miles from the place he was born, which was in an older neighborhood just north of the river. He didn't give me any trouble after I scooped him up, and in fact, I found him to be affable and charming, to the point that he even sprung for lunch before I handed him back to the cops. Perhaps for that reason, I was happy to accept Fat Wally's call, figuring I wouldn't have to go very far to pick him up and that there wouldn't be much risk involved in bringing him back.

And so, I started looking.

I found out Tommy had only one living relative, an older sister. But she lived in California with her husband, a Marine top-kick, currently billeted at Miramar. I doubted Tommy would travel that far, and if he did, I was equally certain he wouldn't be welcomed with open arms. I had to make a few telephone calls, but I was able to learn the identity of Tommy's cellmate while he was in the city lockup. The guy's name was Cletus Duffy, and with almost no effort at all, I managed to get the go-ahead to see Cletus on visitor's day. Since Cletus was on his way to Trousdale Turner Correctional Center in Hartsville for a parole violation, and since the corrections officers knew me, and also knew I wasn't there to orchestrate a jailbreak, I was permitted to meet with him in an ordinary interview room. I brought along a carton of cigarettes and a box of Mr. Goodbars, items I knew Cletus could use to trade for protection, or for money to use in the vending machines in the common room once he was back in stir.

When we met, Cletus was handcuffed and shackled and dressed in a jailhouse orange jumpsuit and a white t-shirt. Like Tommy, he was a little guy, a bit under five-six with stringy blond hair and a couple days' growth of patchy beard. I was already sitting down when a CO escorted him into the room. Since his cuffs were attached to a chain around his waist, I didn't offer to shake hands.

"The fuck are you?" he said, giving me a look that I guessed was supposed to be scary, but mostly just looked like he was squinting into a bright light. Some guys never get it right.

"My name is Jackson Gamble," I told him. "I'm a PI, and I'm trying to get a line on Tommy Mack. Also, I brought you some swag."

"I get it," he said brightly, as if he had just discovered the cure for cancer. He snatched the Marlboros and the Mr. Goodbars over to his side of the table. "You're working for that fat fool what threw his bail."

"No flies on you," I said. "I just figured since you guys were cellies for a few days, he might have said something about where he'd be likely to go when he got out."

He leaned back in his chair and gave me a look that I guessed was supposed to convey that he was wise to my game. "Why should I tell you anything? I don't know you."

"Couple reasons. One, I'm a nice guy, and I brought you candy bars and some smokes. They're good as gold in here. You already know that, and you ought to be grateful. Two, snitches get stitches—which you also know. Red Cherry may appreciate that you ratted Tommy out, but I'm guessing some of your other besties here at the lockup may not be so pleased to know you're a squealer. I've got one or two contacts hereabouts, and I'd be happy to let them know you've updated your resume." I paused to let that sink in. "That happens; you're going to want to ask for protective custody, at least until you get back to Hartsville."

He hemmed and hawed for a few minutes, but finally, he gave me the names of a couple people Tommy said he was tight with, including the friend in Goodlettsville where he had holed up the last time. I made a few notes, thanked Cletus, and went on my way. Unfortunately, the leads proved to be dead ends, as none of the contacts panned out. And so, after a couple more days of looking, with no results, I called Fat Wally and told him I hadn't been able to track down his guy, but that I'd keep looking.

Back in the old days, when a John Dillinger, a Baby Face Nelson, or a Pretty Boy Floyd could simply slip across a state line to evade capture, Tommy Mack might have been able to disappear without too much trouble. In today's world of electronic surveillance, what Tommy was trying to do—take it permanently on the lam from both the cops and the crooks—was, for all intents and purposes, simply not possible. Nowadays, to stay under the radar, a fugitive would have to give up his car and his phone (both have GPS); not use any credit cards; not get sick enough to require a doctor's care; stay out of airports, bus terminals, and passenger rail stations (all have CCTV); don't cross any toll bridges, or use any tollways, or stop at a gas station (that pesky CCTV again); don't return to any former residences, or old-school hangouts; don't contact any old lovers, friends or family, because somebody will eventually give you up for the reward money. Somewhere deep in the Nevada desert or the hills of Appalachia, there may be a safe haven, but at what cost? Better to plea-bargain your way into protective custody, or, if you have accomplices, rat them out and cut some kind of a deal to get into witness protection. In Tommy's case, this time around, the only party that wanted him badly was the one that likely also wanted to put him in the ground. And in Tommy's mind, that did not make for a promising outcome.

Chapter Two

It had been a week or so since I had put my search for Tommy Mack on the back burner,

and nearly two weeks since he had waltzed out of the city lockup and into the trees. Fat Wally was calling me regularly, sometimes twice a day, asking whether I had turned up any leads, and when I told him I hadn't, threatening to take his business elsewhere. And although I knew he wouldn't, I couldn't really blame him if he did. Tommy's court date was coming up, and if he didn't turn up before then, his bond would be forfeited. That meant Wally would have to make good on the whole amount, in this instance, seventy-five thousand dollars. I knew good and well he was insured for it, but I also knew his premiums would take a significant jump when it came time to renew.

* * *

It was just past three o'clock on a Monday afternoon. I was sitting at my desk playing games on the computer and not really thinking about Tommy Mack when I heard the door to the outer office open and then close again. I got up to see who it was, thinking that maybe Wally had decided to stop by to give me another pep talk, in person this time. It wasn't Wally, though. It was a woman, tall, attractive, dressed for success in navy-blue slacks with matching pumps and shoulder bag, an ivory-colored blouse with three-quarter-length sleeves, and a lemon-yellow scarf around her neck. Her hair was chestnut brown with lighter highlights. Her nails and lipstick were a bright shade of red, and her makeup was impeccably applied. Her perfume, which reminded me of the scent of irises, was pleasant without being overpowering. A snappy pair of Tom Ford sunglasses was propped on top of her head. If I had to guess, I would have placed her somewhere north of forty, south of fifty, and judging from how she was dressed, reasonably well-off. Taken together, it seemed to be a good groove for her.

She paused momentarily in the outer office, looking first at the furnishings, and then through the open door to the inner office at me, as if she were trying to decide whether she had come to the right place.

I said, "Can I help you?"

"I hope so," she said. "Are you Mr. Gamble?"

"Yes, I am," I told her. "Would you like to sit down?"

"Thank you." She took a seat in one of the visitor's chairs. She was nervous. She glanced around the office. In no particular order, she would have spotted a second-hand computer together with a printer on a rolling stand, a couple of battered green filing cabinets, a mini-fridge, a microwave, a metal bookcase crammed with paperback novels I keep on hand for slow days, and a coffee pot that hadn't been put to use in over a year. I watched as she crossed her legs, then uncrossed them, and crossed them again. She retrieved her sunglasses from their perch atop her head, folded them, and placed them in her handbag. I waited. She twirled a strand of hair around her finger. I opened my desk drawer and took out a pad and pencil. It took another moment before I was able to catch her eye.

"Ready now?"

She was having trouble sitting still. She bounced her leg up and down. She rubbed her hands together. She fiddled with her hair some more.

"Well. I'm not sure where to start."

"Right. How about if you tell me your name?"

"Of course, I'm sorry." She went back to fiddling with her hair. "It's Bergman. Sarah Bergman."

"And would that be Miss, Mrs., Ms., or none of my business?"

"It's Mrs. Bergman. Mrs. Isaac Bergman."

"Okay, well, Mrs. Bergman, before we get started, I should tell you right up front, I don't do matrimonial work, if that's why you're here."

"It's not that, Mr. Gamble. It's…I need you to find my husband. Maggie said you could help me."

"Maggie Totten? My Maggie?" I raised my eyebrows at that. Maggie is Margaret Totten. Maggie and I have been informally, but monogamously, together for several years, and I still haven't found quite the right word to describe my relationship with her. "My girlfriend" sounds like we're in high school, and calling her "my woman" comes across like I ought to be dressed in an animal skin and dragging her around by her hair.

I met Maggie Totten during an investigation I'd taken on a few years back. That time, I was hired to track down a runaway fourteen-year-old girl, a student at the high school where Maggie was working as a guidance counselor. She was coming off a bad divorce, preceded by a miscarriage, the result of being thrown down a flight of stairs by a couple teenaged boys who were trying to steal her purse. Since then, like many people who somehow find each other at a time when they have no one else in their lives, we connected and have become solidly committed, but minus marriage vows or any plans to make them. Instead, we make do with regular sleepovers, movies, and dinner dates, occasional trips to an indoor gun range, and most weekends together.

"Maggie said you used to be a policeman. Is that right?"

"It is. I started out as a uniformed patrolman, same as every other cop. Eventually, I made detective. I did that for three years, and then I left the force and went into business for myself."

When she didn't serve up any other questions about my career path, I said, "Can I ask how you know Maggie?"

"I'm sorry, I should have said. Maggie and I used to work together, before she got transferred to that awful high school. After that, we gradually lost touch, but not before she told me about you."

The "awful high school" Sarah Bergman was referring to was called Woodcrest, a blackboard jungle located in a sketchy part of the city. The district transferred Maggie from a more middle-of-the-road school to Woodcrest after the incident, which caused her multiple injuries and the miscarriage. The district hoped she would quit, but instead, she took on an assignment as a guidance counselor, the position she held at the time I first met her. Unfortunately, the transfer to Woodcrest was only the beginning of Maggie's problems with the school district.

A year or so after Maggie and I started seeing one another, the district, as a cost-cutting move, decided to outsource their counseling services. Because Maggie had tenure, she was given the choice of remaining on the payroll as a classroom teacher or signing on with the new company and continuing to do counseling as a gig worker. Instead, she allowed herself to be terminated and used her severance to return to school, where she earned a doctorate in sociology from Vanderbilt. These days, she works for the Tennessee Department of Family Services as a crisis counselor. I'd call it a tossup which one of us has the shittier job.

Sarah Bergman said, "When Maggie first started seeing you, she told me you were a private investigator. She said you were honest and very good at what you do. We haven't really kept in touch, I'm sorry to say, but I wrote your name down in case I ever decided I might want to see my husband again. And now…well, here I am."

"Meaning your husband is not around, and now you do, in fact, want to see him again?"

"That's right. Do you think you can find him for me?"

"Possibly, although I think sometimes Maggie overestimates my abilities. What's your husband's name?"

"Isaac. Isaac Bergman."

"Okay." I wrote that down. "And when was the last time you saw your husband, Mrs. Bergman?"

She hesitated just for a moment. "It's been…well, it's been a little more than four years ago."

I put my pencil down. "Four years."

"Yes."

"Mrs. Bergman…" I began.

"I know what you're going to say. Four years, that's a long time. You probably can't help me."

"Well, you're right. Four years is a long time, and without something more to go on, I probably can't help you. But just to be sure, why don't you let me get a little more information, and then let's see if we can figure something out."

"Fine, ask away. Whatever you need."

"Okay. The last time you saw your husband, as far as you can remember, was everything all right? I mean, were you considering splitting up, or was he contemplating a career change, or a move to another city? Anything at all like that?"

She hesitated for just the briefest moment. "No. I mean, everything seemed to be fine. I would have said we were perfectly happy the way things were."

"Was he in trouble with the law?"

"Why would you ask that? He's not a criminal, you know."

"I'm not implying anything, Mrs. Bergman. I'm just trying to get a clearer picture of your situation."

"Oh. Well. Then, no."

"Any financial problems? Impending bankruptcy? Gambling debts?"

"Again, no."

"Any chance he was seeing another woman?"

"Definitely not. I would have known."

"You're sure?"

"Absolutely."

She didn't sound sure, but I let it pass. "Okay. Mrs. Bergman, do you and your husband have any children?"

"Does that matter?"

"Maybe. I was thinking he might have gotten in touch with one of them." She shook her head. "Sorry, no children."

"How about family? Does your husband have relatives here in Nashville?"

She shook her head no. "Madison, Indiana. Isaac has a sister there. We kept in contact for a while after Isaac left, but then it just dropped off. I think she got tired of asking me the same questions, and I got tired of not having any answers for her."

"I understand. Do you remember her name, by any chance?"

"Leah. Leah Bergman. She's a pediatrician. As far as I know, she never got married."

I made a note of that. "Let's try something else. Was your husband in the military reserves, or did he have a job that required him to travel a great deal?"

"He was a professor at Saint Bernadette University, here in town."

I said, "Saint Bernadette is a Catholic university, Mrs. Bergman. Forgive me for saying so, but with a name like Isaac Bergman, your husband doesn't sound like a Catholic."

She sat up straight in her chair. "All Catholics aren't named Dugan or O'Malley, Mr. Gamble. And anyway, my husband taught classical languages. Hebrew, Latin, and Greek, to be exact, so what difference does his ethnic background make?"

I tried to look sheepish. "Point taken, Mrs. Bergman. I apologize. And I realize it was a long time ago, but on the day you last saw him, did you speak with your husband, or did anything unusual happen?"

"Like what?"

"Like, for instance, when he left for work in the morning, did you have a fight? Was he planning a trip? Did he take a suitcase, or an overnight bag? Anything at all to suggest he might be spending the night away from home?"

"Don't you think I would have mentioned something like that?" There was the smallest hint of irritation in her voice.

"I'm just trying to be thorough. You wouldn't believe the things people forget to mention in circumstances like this."

"Oh, well then, no. It was like any other day. I saw him in the morning, and then he telephoned in the afternoon. He said there was a language department meeting that night that might run late, and that he'd tell me about it when he got home. But then—but then, he never came home, and I never saw him again."

"Just like that? No calls, nothing?"

"Not a thing. Of course, I telephoned the university, but they said there were no meetings scheduled and that perhaps he had his dates mixed up."

I thought about that. "Off the top of your head, would you happen to remember just what was the date of the meeting?"

"Do you think I'd forget something like that? It was April the second, four years ago."

I wrote that down. "And did he say what the meeting was about?"

"Well, he didn't come right out and say it, but I'm sure he was hoping this might be the year the university was going to extend a tenure offer. I know I hoped it was. But neither one of us specifically mentioned it. I think we were both afraid we might just be setting ourselves up for disappointment if it turned out to be something else."

"And since then, you haven't had any contact at all? No calls, no letters, nothing?"

"Nothing at all."

I said, "Let me ask you this. So far, we've determined that your husband taught classical languages by day."

"That's right."

"Okay, then, what else did he do?"

"I don't understand. Are you asking whether he had a second job?"

"Not specifically, but did he? I mean, I'm guessing a non-tenured professor at a small, private school doesn't earn a particularly high salary."

"We were comfortable." Her tone was icy, and I wondered whether I had touched a nerve.

"Okay, then, think about this. What did your husband like to do when he wasn't working? I mean, he gets up in the morning, showers, maybe has breakfast or a cup of coffee, and then goes to work. At the end of the work day, did he always come straight home, or did he sometimes stop for drinks with his co-workers? In the evening, did he ever go out by himself? I don't know, was he in a bowling league, or did he go to an Elks club meeting, or get together with his buddies for a poker night? And on the weekends, what then? Did he like to go fishing, or play golf? Anything like that?"

"Oh, I see. Well, most semesters, his last class ended around the middle of the afternoon, so he would sometimes stay in his office at the university and take care of administrative stuff. You know, tinkering with lesson plans, grading student work, that kind of thing. Plus, a couple of afternoons, he kept office hours, so if any of his students needed to meet with him, he'd be there."

"And then what? Home by six or six-thirty, have dinner, watch TV, and then go to bed?"

"Most of the time, yes, that's pretty much how it went." She paused, remembering, I guessed. "Doesn't sound like much of a life, does it?"

"Sounds pretty much like everybody I know."

"Well, he did spend a lot of time on his computer. He said he was doing research for a book he was planning to write. Sometimes, he'd head out to one of the other university libraries to work on it."

I thought about that. "What kind of a book was it? Did he ever show it to you?"

"No. He said it wasn't ready for anyone to see it yet."

"Right. So, when your husband didn't come home, I assume you contacted the police."

"Of course."

"And what did they tell you?"

"They asked a lot of questions, same as you, and took a lot of notes. They said they'd do whatever they could and that they'd stay in touch. After that, I talked to them a few more times, but nothing ever came of it. Then, nothing. It turned into—what do they call it on television? A cold case." She shifted uncomfortably in her chair.

I could sense she was getting agitated. It's a common affliction among people who occupy my customer chair. It's never easy pouring out the sorriest parts of your life's story in front of a total stranger. I said, "Mrs. Bergman, would you like some water? Or I can run down the hall and get you a soft drink if you prefer. I'm afraid I don't have any coffee."

"Thank you, Mr. Gamble. I'm fine."

"Okay." I waited until she got settled again. "So. You talked to the police."

"Yes. And the last time I spoke with them, which was about a year and a half ago, they said they had contacted the state police and the TBI, you know, to widen the search. But after so much time had passed with no word at all, they said I should consider that perhaps he didn't want to be found and that I should get used to the idea that unless either somebody recognized him, or he decided to come home on his own, it was possible I might never see him again."

I put a sympathetic look on my face. "That must have been very upsetting for you."

"Yes, it was. I mean, the police aren't supposed to just give up on an investigation, are they?"

"They don't really give up. It's just that there are new cases coming through the door almost every hour of the day. And if none of their original leads pan out, after a while they just have to move on and hope they catch a break somewhere down the line. You'd be surprised how often it seems to work out that way."

When she didn't say anything, I went on. "Mrs. Bergman, you didn't say, but can I ask why, after all this time, you still want to find your husband?"

She gave a small shrug. "Because, as you say, he is my husband. I still love him. I've been living in an empty house for four years. I'm tired of that. I want him back in my life."

I leaned back in my chair. "Well, then, if you really want to go ahead with this, here's what we're going to have to do. Before we talk about my fee, I need to get contact information from you. Let's start with your telephone number." She rattled off a string of digits, which I wrote down on my pad.

"Is that your home or your work number?"

"It's my cell."

"And what's your work number?"

"Are you wondering whether I have a job? So that I can pay you for your services?"

"No," I said, annoyed at the implication. "I just need to be able to reach you in case something comes up."

"All right. Well, then, since COVID, I mostly work from home. The number I gave you is good any time of the day."

"That will help. Do you have a photo of your husband you can leave with me?"

"Nothing very recent, obviously. I have some from a few years ago. Will that be of any use to you?"

"It's better than nothing. Unless he's taken steps to change his appearance, it's possible I'll run across somebody who might have seen him."

"Well…I didn't bring one with me, but you can stop by my home any time and pick one up." She gave me her address, which I wrote down next to her telephone number.

"How about your husband's cell number? Do you still have that?"

"Yes." She gave me the number, which I wrote down below hers.

"Couple more things," I said, "and then we're done for now, although I'll almost certainly have more questions later."

"Go ahead."

"Mrs. Bergman, did you and Isaac have separate bank accounts, or were they jointly held?"

"They were joint accounts."

"Okay, good, and this is important. After you husband disappeared, was there any activity in any of your accounts that didn't originate with you? Checks, PayPal, debit card charges, ATM's, anything like that. Do you understand what I'm asking?"

"I understand, and the answer is no. There were no checks written, no savings withdrawals, and no transactions on our debit card. Nothing."

"All right, I think that covers it for now. But just to let you know, my fee is five hundred dollars per day, prorated, plus expenses. Normally, I like to get a couple days in advance. But before we do that, let me make some telephone calls, just so I'm not running around wasting your money if it turns out there isn't anything I can do. I have to tell you, though, after all this time, it's entirely likely that your husband has moved out of the area. He may even have established a new identity someplace else. And if he has, he may be happy where he is and not want to come home again."

"Is that even a possibility?"

"Without knowing anything more than what you've told me, I couldn't say. But if I do find him and it turns out that he's settled in somewhere else, you'll have to decide how you want to proceed, because unless there's an outstanding court judgment of some kind, there isn't anything I can do legally or otherwise to compel him to come back. At that point, you'll need to think about retaining an attorney to find out what are your options going forward.

"I understand," she said. But she didn't sound convinced.

"I have a few contacts within law enforcement, and once I have a photo, I can do an Internet search and maybe ask around in a few other places. It's possible I'll be able to come up with something, but after all this time, I'm afraid your original assumption is probably correct. I very likely can't do much to help you."

"Do your best, Mr. Gamble. That's all I can ask." And with that, she rose from her chair and walked out, trailing behind her a faint fragrance of irises.

After Sarah Bergman was gone, I looked back over the few notes I had taken during our conversation. Something wasn't quite right. I thought I knew what.

When adults go missing, they're usually not that hard to find. As Tommy Mack was undoubtedly discovering, no matter where they go, adults leave a trail of credit card charges, airline or train reservations, CCTV videos, phone records—you name it. And in our increasingly paranoid world, there are video cameras on the street corners of just about every major city in the country. Also, in the case of a lot of people who go missing, they don't really want to disappear forever. They just need to get away for a while to sort out whatever the problem is that's got them feeling lost, lonely, or alienated from their present situation. Maybe it's an abusive or alcoholic spouse, or it's financial difficulties, or maybe they're on the run from the law, or a business failure. Whatever the case, after a while, they're either found, or else they come home on their own. In any of these situations, after four years, Isaac Bergman should have turned up. That he hadn't did not bode well for a successful outcome.

* * *

Before I left the office, I tried calling the number Sarah Bergman had given me for her husband's cell. Not surprisingly, I got a recording telling me that the number was no longer in service and that no further information was available. After that, I did an Internet search for a Doctor Leah Bergman, M.D., in Madison, Indiana. I called the number indicated and got yet another recording, this time informing me that the Southeast Indiana Pediatric Clinic was closed for the day, and that their regular hours were 8:00 A.M. to 4:30 P.M. Then I remembered that part of Indiana is on Eastern time, so I'd need to try back the next morning.

With nothing more to do, I left the office around four-thirty. I drove home, showered, and then went out again to meet Maggie at a downtown restaurant she liked. As always, she looked terrific in a gray blazer over a soft green dress. And despite that I had changed into a clean shirt and a sport jacket, by comparison, I still looked as though I picked out my rig from the clearance rack at a Goodwill outlet. Over cocktails, and between the salad course and the entrees, she got around to asking whether I had met with Sarah Bergman.

"I did. She came by this afternoon."

"You know," she said, taking a sip of her appletini, "I don't think I've spoken with Sarah in more than a year. Then, yesterday morning, out of the blue, she called. She said she wanted to talk with you, but that she first needed to make sure you were still doing whatever it is you do."

"And what did you tell her that was?"

"Looking for lost puppies. That is what you do, right?"

"That's it. Did you tell her anything else?"

"That you're still doing it. I said you were the best and that if anyone could help her, you could." She gave me an impish grin. "You are the best, aren't you?"

"I found you, did I not?" I took a long drink of my Stella and twirled my finger in the air to signal the waiter to bring another round. "And when Sarah called you, did she say what she wanted?"

"She started to, but then she got another call. She said she'd call back later, but she never did. I thought maybe she'd forgotten all about it."

The second round of drinks arrived along with our entrée courses, chicken

Milanese for Maggie and pan-seared halibut for me.

I said, "How long have you known Sarah?"

She took a bite of her chicken. "This is very good. Would you like to try some?"

"I'm good, thanks."

She took another bite. "Sure?"

"Yes."

"Well, then, to answer your question, I met Sarah during the time before I got into guidance work, when I was still a classroom teacher. So, what does that make it? Maybe ten or twelve years ago." She helped herself to a forkful of my halibut. "This isn't bad. Maybe next time I'll try it." She always did that.

"Glad you like it," I said. "We were talking about Sarah Bergman. Did you ever meet her husband?"

"Once or twice. He seemed nice enough, if your type runs to men who wear corduroy sport coats with suede elbow patches. Also, as I remember it, he had a little ponytail. Is that why she came to see you?"

"She says she wants me to find him."

"Oh, my. Whatever did you tell her?"

"I said that after four years missing, the likelihood I'd be able to turn anything up was pretty close to zero."

"That must have been disappointing. Did she give you any money?"

"No. I told her to hold off on that until I had a chance to do a little checking around. I didn't want to take any of her money until I had a better idea what I'm up against."

"You're such a sweetheart," Maggie said, giving me a smile that could melt a block of ice inside a deep freeze. "I don't know how any woman is able to keep her hands off you."

Chapter Three

The next morning, Maggie and I slept late, and then she made us breakfast at her condo. Stanley, her psychopathic pet cat, was nowhere to be seen. Stanley, an oversized gray tabby of indeterminate age, belonged to the teenaged girl I had been hired to find a few years earlier. At the conclusion of the case, Stanley became Maggie's cat after she rescued him from death row at a nearby animal shelter. Stanley took to Maggie like they had been best friends forever, but in his occasional dealings with me, he was crankier than a wolverine in a trap. Most times, when he saw me, he arched his back and hissed and then ran out of the room to hide until he was sure I was gone. Once or twice, I tried making nice with him, but all that ever got me was bitten, or clawed, or both. This particular morning, he was nowhere in sight, which was just fine with me.

I helped Maggie clean up the breakfast dishes. Then, before heading out to pay a visit to Saint Bernadette University, I took another stab at getting Isaac Bergman's sister, Leah, on the phone. At first, the pediatric clinic's receptionist was reluctant to put my call through, saying that Dr. Bergman was just about to meet with a patient. Could she take a message and have the doctor return my call?

"If it's no trouble, could you please tell her I'm calling about her brother, Isaac? I can hold."

It took a minute or two, and then Doctor Bergman came to the phone. "Yes?"

"Doctor Bergman?"

"This is Leah Bergman. Who am I speaking to?" There was an edge to her voice, but it wasn't excitement I was hearing; it was something else. More like the way a person sounds when he or she has answered a telemarketer's sales call by mistake.

"Doctor Bergman, thank you for taking my call. My name is Jackson Gamble. I'm a private investigator, calling from Nashville, Tennessee. I've been retained by Isaac's wife, Sarah, to look into his disappearance."

There was a pause. "And?"

"And, as I understand it, your brother went missing more than four years ago. And to be completely honest, I want you to know that I have very serious doubts that I'm going to be able to find him. I want to be clear about that right up front, so that I don't raise your expectations without cause. I also want you to know that this isn't some kind of a hustle. I'm not selling anything, and I don't want any money from you."

"Then why are you calling?"

"Because I'm hoping that maybe since the time he disappeared, you might have heard from him. Perhaps he called, or texted you, or sent an email. Really, anything that might give me a place to start looking."

"Mister...Gamble, is it?"

"Yes."

"Mr. Gamble, I'm afraid I have absolutely no idea where Isaac might be. I hadn't spoken with him for at least two years before he wandered off, and I certainly haven't heard from him since. If I had to guess, I'd say he found some younger woman who could wind him up tighter than Sarah was able to do, and so he went off someplace with her to try to recapture his youth. I understand that's a common wet dream for men his age."

"Is that something he would have been likely to do?"

"More than likely. I'm surprised Sarah stayed with him as long as she did."

"So then, no love lost there, Dr. Bergman?"

"That might be putting it a bit harshly, Mr. Gamble. Isaac is my brother, and he's not a bad person, exactly. But he is also an overgrown adolescent who has wasted his productive years chasing after graduate degrees in nonsensical disciplines. After he acquired them, he found himself a spot where he could be surrounded by pretty young women who thought he was a dashing, romantic figure, like some Byron of the Bible Belt. As far as I'm concerned, Sarah is better off without him. I told her that then, and I'm telling you that now. My advice? If Sarah has given you any money to conduct your investigation, give it back and tell her you're sorry, but it's hopeless." When I didn't say anything, she said, "Now, if there's nothing else, I have patients waiting." And she hung up.

The Byron of the Bible Belt. I'd have to remember that.

* * *

Saint Bernadette University is named in memory of a young French woman named Marie, later Marie-Bernarde Soubirous. In 1858, while on an outing with friends to gather firewood, Marie is believed to have seen a vision of the Virgin Mary in a grotto located near a small stream. According to Catholic tradition, the vision appeared to Marie no fewer than eighteen times. During one such occurrence, the vision declared to her, "I am the Immaculate Conception," and asked that a chapel be built on the site. Moved by the experience, Marie subsequently joined the convent of the Sisters of Mercy, where the Mother Superior gave her the name Marie-Bernarde. Never in good health, Marie-Bernarde died in 1879 at the age of thirty-five. In the present day, the grotto and the stream are part of a church called the Sanctuary of Our Lady of Lourdes. The water in the stream is believed to have healing powers, so the church and the grotto have become an important site for religious pilgrimages. Marie-Bernarde was canonized by Pope Pius XI as Saint Bernadette in 1933.

Back in Middle Tennessee, Saint Bernadette University is a small, private institution located on the far south side of the city. Originally founded as a Roman Catholic theological seminary, Saint Bernadette greatly expanded its curriculum after World War II. It did so primarily to take advantage of the anticipated enrollment surge brought about by the passage of the GI Bill and the number of returning veterans pursuing the seemingly boundless employment opportunities opening up to newly-minted university graduates. And so, in the present day, enrollment at Saint Bernadette is open to persons of all faiths and continues to offer a wide variety of professional and liberal arts degrees. Theological instruction is still a big part of the curriculum, but it is conducted at a separate campus located in Franklin—once a small town that these days an up-market community of about eighty thousand, located twenty or so miles south of the city.

When I got to the university, I drove slowly around the campus, not sure what I was looking for, but for just a moment or two, I didn't care. The tree-lined boulevard, with imposing-looking academic buildings on either side, the sidewalks crowded with fresh-faced students convinced they would soon have the world by the tail, and the general carefree atmosphere all took me back to my own undergraduate days at a middling, compass-point school in southern Missouri, where I majored mostly in beer-swilling and minored in cutting classes. When I came to a crosswalk, I rolled down the car window and called out to a couple of coeds, who may have been on their way to class, or perhaps back to their dorm or sorority house. When they approached, I asked whether they could tell me where I could find the administration building.

"Nice ride," said one of the girls, for the moment ignoring my question. She was a pretty brunette with a wide smile and a splash of freckles across her cheeks and her nose. She was dressed in fashionably torn and faded jeans and a sweatshirt emblazoned across the front with three identical Greek letters. The ride she was referring to was the car I'm driving these days, a nearly-new, blood-red Porsche Panamera, something that, in truth, I could never afford and have no business owning.

The Porsche came to me by way of a stunningly beautiful woman whom I had quite literally allowed to get away with murder. The woman's name was Audra Lambert. She had been involved with a newspaper reporter named Albert Glass in a scheme to swindle a political action committee out of several million dollars. The scam worked, and once she had the money securely in hand, she shot and killed her erstwhile partner and high-tailed it out of the country. I could have easily stopped her and handed her over to the cops, but for reasons I still don't fully understand, I let her go. Maybe because someone gifted with that much mental toughness and physical beauty doesn't belong in a cage behind stone walls. And when she was settled in another part of the world, she mailed me the title and the keys to the car as a parting gift. In the same package was a note that read "call me," accompanied by a telephone number for, I guessed, a throwaway cell phone. I still have the number squirreled away in a file folder in my office. On occasion, I have been tempted to call, just to see who might pick up, but up to now, I haven't quite gotten the nerve.

"You an instructor here?" the girl asked me.

"Hope to be," I said. "Underwater basket weaving."

"Tri-Delt," she told me, pointing her finger to her chest, in case I missed the association. "If you decide to call, ask for Molly. I'm there most weeknights. Administration is at Corbin Hall, next block, halfway down, on the left."

I left her and her friend, whose name I didn't get, in the crosswalk, and headed down the boulevard. I was hoping to talk to somebody in human resources who might be able to give me a little something to go on to help track down Isaac Bergman. I parked in an open space in front of the building. I was pretty sure getting my hands on the information I was looking for would take some time. However, I wasn't interested in walking the two blocks from the public parking area, and I was hopeful the campus cops wouldn't notice I was in a 15-minute loading zone—not that my new ride was by any means easy to overlook.

I walked up a dozen wide limestone steps and entered Corbin Hall through a set of heavy glass and metal doors that might have weighed a quarter-ton apiece. The reception area was high-ceilinged, with a terrazzo floor and walls trimmed with what looked like oak wainscotting. A pretty young woman behind the reception desk looked up from her laptop and gave me a tentative smile.

"Can I help you?"

"I hope so," I said, giving her my sincerest smile in return. "I'd like to speak to someone in your HR department, if that's possible."

"Oh," she said, wrinkling her nose as if a day didn't go by without some job-seeker or other walking through the door, resume´ in hand. "Did you want to fill out an employment application? Because if you do, you have to first apply online and attach a copy of your CV and a list of references. Plus, we do initial interviews on Skype." And just like that, I realized that if I ever needed to look for a real job again, I wouldn't have the slightest idea how to go about finding one.

"Don't need a job." I took out my wallet and showed her my identification and PI license. "I'm a private investigator. I need to get in touch with someone who used to work here who's gone missing. I was hoping I could get some information that might help point me in the right direction."

"A missing person, really? That sounds exciting. What's the person's name?"

"Isaac Bergman," I told her. "I don't suppose there's any chance you'd know him?"

She shook her head. "Nope, sorry." Then, "Just a minute." She got up from her chair and disappeared through a doorway behind the reception desk. I could hear her talking to somebody, but with the door partly shut, I couldn't make out what was being said. Then, the door opened again, and I heard her say, "Okay, thanks, I'll tell him."

She returned to the counter and gave me another smile, this one definitely apologetic. "Mister Gamble, thank you for waiting. I spoke to Mrs. Ellis, our director of human resources, and she said she remembers Professor Bergman, but that he no longer teaches here, and, in fact, has been gone for several years. She says she's sorry, but after that much time, we wouldn't have anything in our active records that would be of any use to you."

"Okay. What's your name, can I ask?"

"Caitlin."

"Well, Caitlin, maybe I could talk with Mrs. Ellis. I'll only take a minute."

She shook her head doubtfully. "I don't know. She's pretty busy."

I said, "Do I need to make a stink?"

"I guess that's up to you." She raised her eyebrows. "Do I need to call security?"

I walked around behind the reception counter. "Give me ten minutes. Then you can call the National Guard if you want to."

It didn't take ten minutes. I was in and out in five. I thanked Mrs. Ellis and exited her office with a name, an address, and—I hoped—a useful lead.

27

Chapter Four

The address Evelyn Ellis gave me was on a quiet, residential lane just off West End Avenue. Walking distance from Vanderbilt, but a good forty-five-minute drive from the Saint Bernadette campus, if you were in a hurry. An hour if you weren't, and then you still had to find a parking space. The contact's name she gave me was Professor Emeritus Robert Joshua Levy, recently retired from the classical languages department at Saint Bernadette. Mrs. Ellis warned me that Professor Levy was quite elderly and not in the best of health, although, she assured me, his mind and memory were both as sharp as ever.

"He was doing fine up until a couple of years ago. Still teaching a full schedule of classes. But then, he had a heart attack, and right after that a minor stroke. After all that, he went downhill pretty fast. So, if he starts to look tired, you might offer to come back another time."

I said I understood, thanked her for her time, and headed back toward the city.

Robert Levy's house was a well-kept red brick bungalow with white shutters and a flagstone front walk bordered on either side by thick clusters of red and orange phlox. My ring on the doorbell was answered by a pretty, plump woman of approximately sixty years. I noticed that she had some kind of a brace on her left leg, and when she walked, she used a blue-tinted aluminum cane for support. She caught me looking, and said, "Knee replacement, about four weeks back. The tell me it'll only be another week or so of therapy, and then I'll be able to get around without it. After that, they say the knee'll be good as new."

I showed her my identification and asked whether the professor might be available to answer a couple of questions about a former colleague.

"Oh, the professor is expecting you," she told me. "He's excited. Evelyn, from over to the university, called and said you might be heading our way."

"Are you Mrs. Levy?" I asked.

She made a noise that could have been a laugh. "Lord, no. My name is Roseanne Burgess. I come by every day to do a little cleaning and to cook the professor's lunch and supper. Mrs. Levy passed away many years ago, and since he's been retired, it's just been the professor and me. He doesn't get around so good anymore, so once in a while, I stay a little bit after, and we play some gin rummy. 'Course, he thinks he's just the best card player ever, but the truth is, most times, I let him win."

"You are a wise woman," I said.

Walking a bit gingerly and leaning on her cane, Roseanne Burgess ushered me through the house and into a three-season room in the back that looked out on all sides at an immaculately kept yard surrounded by a six-foot-high wooden privacy fence, the kind more commonly found in California or Arizona. Near the fence was a low berm planted with flowering crabapple trees and rosebushes in a riot of colors. A light breeze was blowing through the yard, creating a kind of kaleidoscopic effect, with reflected sunlight rippling against the flowers and blossoms as they danced in the wind. Inside, all of the windows were closed, so that the room I was in was very warm from the mid-day sun. Light classical music was coming softly from somewhere I couldn't see. I couldn't tell if it was Brahms or Bach, since my knowledge of classical music is limited to whatever is playing on the classic rock station on our local FM dial. But it was a pleasant sound all the same, *apropos* to the surroundings.

Seated near one of the windows was a man in a wheelchair. The man was wearing khaki slacks and a blue and black flannel checkered shirt, both of which seemed several sizes too large. He had a white beard, thick wool socks, and brown leather slippers on his feet, and a brightly colored knit *yarmulke* on his head. I would have said he had been tall once, but was now stooped over, perhaps from arthritis or from some other degenerative spinal disorder. He was very pale and very thin, and I guessed that whatever was wrong with him would soon run its course, and he would be joining his late wife in whatever afterlife he put his faith in. At that, though, his voice was strong, as was his handshake, and his eyes still held an inquisitive light.

"You must be Mr. Gamble," he said by way of greeting. "I've been looking forward to meeting you since Evelyn called to say you might be coming over."

"Professor," I said. "Thank you for seeing me on short notice."

"Wouldn't miss it, sir. I don't get many visitors these days." He paused for a moment and then waved me into a chair opposite where he was sitting. "Would you like some tea, or maybe a soft drink? Perhaps something stronger? We have just about anything you might want."

"I'm good, thanks."

"Very well, then, let's get to it. Evelyn said you had some questions about Isaac Bergman. I'll be happy to tell you what I can, but first, tell me something about yourself."

"Excuse me?"

"Well, you already know something about me. I'm a retired university professor. I taught classical languages for more than forty years, and nowadays, I'm clearly most of the way through the back nine of my life. I have grown children who never telephone, and my wife died many years ago. After that, I never remarried, except perhaps to my job as a teacher. I suppose I never found much time for anything else." He sighed, as if reflecting on the wisdom of his life's choices. "So, Mr. Gamble, what about you? What's your CV?"

When I gave him a blank look, he said, "Your *curriculum vitae*. Your resume, in other words, expressed in Latin, as is the custom in academic circles. What exactly is it you do?"

"Well, okay." I took a moment and gave him a capsule summary of my work history, including my time with the police and then on my own as a PI.

"I'm forty-seven years old, and I'm as honest as I can be, given my line of work. Also, I'm very good at what I do."

"Which is what?"

"Pretty much whatever comes my way. But mostly, I find people who've gone missing."

"Like Isaac Bergman." It wasn't a question.

"Yes, like Professor Bergman, and maybe you can save a lot of time for both of us if you can tell me where I should be looking for him. I gathered from Mrs. Ellis that you and Bergman worked closely during the time he was here."

"Back to business, then." He paused, as if to gather his thoughts. "Isaac was my graduate assistant for a few years. Later on, I was his dissertation advisor. As I recall, the title of his paper was something like *"Ars Amatoria and the Banishment of Publius Ovidius Naso by the Emperor Augustus."*

I said, "I'm sorry?"

"The Roman poet, Ovid. He was—he still is—very famous. Catullus wrote racier stuff, some of it even pornographic by current standards, but he was gone from the scene by the time Augustus was at the throttle. Anyway, Ovid is best known for a poem he wrote called *Ars Amatoria—The Art of Love*, in English. Unfortunately, for some reason, it offended the sensibilities of the emperor Augustus Caesar, so he ran Ovid out of Rome and exiled him to Tomis. These days, in case you're wondering, Tomis is called Constanta, in Romania. There are lots of translations of Ovid's poem, if you'd care to read it." His tone of voice was sincere, but there was a twinkle in his eye that said he might be putting me on.

"Professor…"

He made a small movement with his hand. "Personally, I wouldn't bother reading the dissertation, or the poem, for that matter. You can get a lot more interesting sex from the 'Song of Solomon.' Or, if you prefer, Sylvia Day or Maya Banks. According to my younger colleagues, they are all the rage these days."

"Never read them, either," I told him. "Or Ovid, as far as that goes."

"You haven't missed anything. And anyway, just between you and me, most of these dissertations are nothing but bullshit. I mean, give credit where it's due. Doctoral dissertations represent the culmination of a long and tedious process, and the candidates themselves are both intelligent and highly motivated. Happily, for lazy old humbugs like me, they are also an inexhaustible source of cheap research assistants and instructors for entry-level freshman courses. But let's face it. In the real world, nobody really gives a fig whether Alcibiades was a traitor to Athens, or why Octavian kicked Ovid out of Rome. For all we really know, Ovid could have been *shtupping* Scribonia." When I gave him a blank look, he quickly added, "She was Octavian's second wife. However, she had already been married several times herself, so she may have been a bit of a round-heels in her own right."

"Fair enough," I said. "But I've seen guys in a bar beat one another bloody over whether Ali could have taken Joe Louis when they were both in their prime, or if Michael Jordan could have dunked over Wilt Chamberlain."

"Good point," the old man said. "But to get back to your reason for being here, you're looking into Isaac Bergman's disappearance. May I ask why?"

"Simple enough. His wife hired me to find him."

His eyebrows shot up. "Sarah? Really? Why in the world would she want you to do that?"

"Well, I don't know, except that she says she loves him. She misses him, and she wants him back in her life."

"After, what has it been, five years? You can't be serious."

"She says four." I leaned back in my chair. "Professor, I gave up a long time ago trying to figure out people's motives. Maybe the guy has a pile of CDs that mature this year, or maybe she wants to haul his ass into court to charge him with desertion. I don't know. At the moment, all I know is she wants me to find him."

"And you believe after this much time, you will actually succeed." It wasn't a question.

"Actually? Actually, no, I kind of doubt it. He's been gone much too long, and he may very well be dead, or living in another part of the world under an assumed name."

"Then, if you don't mind my asking, why did you tell Sarah you'd take her case?"

"Good question. I guess I'm just a sucker for a love story. And anyway, finding people is how I make my living, and as I said, I'm very good at it. So, if it's possible to find Isaac Bergman, as long as he's alive, that's what I'm going to do."

Chapter Five

"So. Now that we've got the preliminaries out of the way, what can I tell you, Mr. Gamble? How can I help you bring your search to fruition?"

"Well, my understanding is that the night Bergman disappeared, he telephoned his wife earlier in the day and told her he would be late getting home because he had to attend a faculty meeting. Only then, when he failed to come home at all, Sarah Bergman telephoned someone here at the university and was informed that no such meeting had been scheduled."

"I'm aware of that, yes. At the time, I assumed he got his dates mixed up. You know what people say about academics. They're always wandering around lost in the fog inside their own heads."

"Yes, sir. Sarah said whoever she spoke with when she called told her the same thing, only that doesn't explain where he did go. Or why."

"No, I suppose it doesn't."

"I'm thinking out loud now. Did Bergman have a class that day? On the day he disappeared, I mean?"

"I'm not certain, but I imagine he did. Beginning foreign language classes usually meet daily. You need repetition to get the basics down quickly, you see."

"And would you have any idea what time his last class would have been dismissed?"

"No idea." The old man shook his head. "Why does that matter?"

"In a minute. First, tell me. If there had been a faculty meeting, what time would it have started?"

"That I can tell you. We always tried to start at seven o'clock. That way, nobody would have to miss their evening meal."

"Okay, so here's the question, then. If Professor Bergman actually believed there was a meeting and that it started at seven, what would he have likely been doing between whatever time he dismissed his last class and the time the meeting was supposed to have started? Grading papers? Or would he have gone to dinner someplace, or maybe met a colleague for a drink? And if he did, would anyone on campus have seen him or talked to him during that time?"

"I wouldn't know. I suppose any of those things are possible. Perhaps you could ask someone in the registrar's office to look up his class schedule."

I made a mental note to ask Sarah Bergman what time Isaac had called to tell her he would be late. I said, "Professor Levy, you were Isaac's dissertation advisor. Now, I never got far enough in college to even think about writing a dissertation, but I can imagine that a doctoral candidate and his advisor must spend a lot of time together. They would have to get to know one another pretty well. So, can you tell me anything about Isaac's frame of mind around the time he disappeared?"

He wrinkled his forehead, as if in thought. "I can tell you he would not have been particularly happy, because the university had informed him that it would not be offering him tenure. Furthermore, he was told that his contract would not be renewed at the end of the term."

"So then, he was being fired?"

"'Fired' is not a term commonly used in academia. Let's say he was not invited to return for the fall semester."

"Well, that's not what his wife led me to believe. She was under the impression that the purpose of the meeting was specifically to extend Bergman a tenure offer."

"No, no, that's not how it's done. It's not like pledging a fraternity. He would have met with the chancellor in a private session."

"So, then, he knew before the supposed meeting that he wouldn't be returning to the university for the fall semester. That's new information," I said. "Do you happen to know the reason why he was being? What was it?

Dismissed?"

"Reasons, you mean. Of course I do. For one, he hadn't published anything of any consequence during his time here. A couple of peer-reviewed articles in academic journals were about it."

"And how long was his time here?"

"I don't recall right off. Eight or nine years, something like that. That should have been plenty of time for him to come up with something worthwhile. It's an old adage, but it's true. Publish or perish. It sounds harsh, I suppose, but that is the reality. Tenure-track teaching positions are very competitive, even in a small school like Saint Bernadette."

"Okay, so he didn't publish anything important. You said there were other reasons."

"Yes. There were rumors. And a complaint or two."

"About what?" I asked. But I remembered my brief conversations with Bergman's sister and Molly, the Tri-Delt, and I was pretty sure I already knew the answer.

"Mister Gamble, I did my undergraduate work at NYU, back in the late fifties and early sixties, a few years before the era of free love, or sex, drugs, and rock and roll. But even then, New York City had a reputation as being rather, what shall we say, casual in its attitudes toward sexuality. So, sleeping around occasionally, or even frequently, would not necessarily raise any eyebrows as long as you were discreet. Well, with that in mind, there were certain men on campus who were referred to as what, in polite company might be called 'ladies' men' or 'skirt-chasers'. At my fraternity, Zeta Beta Tau, we called them *khamer eyzl*. That's a Yiddish term that could be loosely translated as 'cock-hound.'"

I had to laugh at that. "I see. And Isaac Bergman brought his breezy style with him to Saint Bernadette, I suppose."

"He did. He was a good-looking man, and a lot of the young women were quite taken with him. I don't think it would be a stretch to say he was just as taken with them. Of course, it was a different time. By the time he got here, we'd already had one American president who had admitted to committing extramarital sex acts in the Oval Office. Same-sex marriages were legal in any number of states, and pornographic movie channels—though not necessarily good ones—were included in your basic cable package. But even so, Isaac Bergman was a married man, and Saint Bernadette is, at its core, still a faith-based institution, so it didn't take long before rumors began. Professor Bergman was cautioned any number of times, but no official action was taken until the time came to decide whether to grant tenure."

"'Cautioned.' You mean, like warning shots."

"Just so."

"And so, all at once, he didn't just quit. He also vanished."

"Well, yes and no. He didn't quit, as you put it. He was given the opportunity to resign, which he did, but it was not effective immediately. He was still under contract through the end of the term, you see. Even knowing he would not be invited back, walking out on a contract before the end of the semester would have been tantamount to professional suicide."

"Did he clean out his office before he left?"

He shook his head. "You know, I don't believe he did."

"Doesn't that suggest to you that, wherever he went, he thought he'd be back the next day?"

He nodded slowly. "I suppose I'd have to say that is a reasonable assumption."

"All right, then. What did happen to his belongings?"

"Well, as I recall, his wife came and collected his personal effects. Wall hangings, his diplomas, things like that. Anything that was property of the university is probably archived someplace, if it hasn't been thrown out or recycled."

"And as far as you know, no one here at the university heard from him since the time he left."

"Not a word, that I'm aware. Of course, he was a frequent topic of conversation at faculty meetings and social gatherings for a few weeks, but then the term ended, and most everyone went home for the summer. When we returned in the fall, the university had hired a replacement. Professor Bergman's disappearance just didn't seem to come up very often, and after a while, people more or less forgot about it."

"Okay," I said. "Just a couple more questions, and then I'll be on my way."

"Take your time, Mr. Gamble. I'm sure I don't have to tell you; my calendar is not particularly crowded these days, and I'm enjoying our conversation. I don't get all that many visitors anymore. At my age, I've outlived just about all my contemporaries."

"Well, let's try this, then. When Isaac Bergman left, are you aware of anyone else who either disappeared around the same time, or who might have dropped out or quit? I'm thinking specifically of either female faculty members or students who might have been the objects of his attention."

"You mean, did he go middle-aged crazy and take off with a younger woman?"

"I'm just fishing now, Professor."

"Off the top of my head, I wouldn't know. Remember, I taught classical languages, which, as you might imagine, meant that I only came into contact with a small percentage of our student body. It's not a course of study that's in wide demand, in case you haven't guessed. I suppose you could check with Caroline Feldman in the registrar's office. After we're finished here, I'll call and ask her to provide you with whatever information you need. We're old friends. I'm sure she'd be happy to help you in any way she can."

"Thank you. Then I just have one more thing. Can you think of any other members of the faculty Professor Bergman might have been friends with? Specifically, I'm wondering about people he would have been close enough with so that they might have some idea of what was going through his head about that time."

"You mean, besides being angry at not being granted tenure."

"Besides that, yes. I'm wondering whether there might have been some family issues or health problems. Things that would not necessarily have been common knowledge."

He appeared to give that some thought. "Well, a lot of people knew him, of course. Saint Bernadette is not a big university, and faculty friendships are far from uncommon. But, as far as close friends, the only two I can think of off the top of my head are Phillip May and Caroline Feldman, whom I mentioned before. Phillip teaches chemistry and meatball physics here at

Saint Bernadette."

I said, "Meatball physics?"

"It's what we call introductory physics for freshmen who didn't take a course in high school. They learn about gravity and magnetism and the laws of motion, and they read about Newton and Einstein. It helps meet the science requirement for a degree in any of the liberal arts."

"I see."

"Anyway, Phillip and his wife were good friends with Isaac and Sarah. Of course, the Mays were divorced a few years ago, and I think Phillip's wife moved away, so these days, he lives by himself. Caroline Feldman works in the admissions office. I'm sure either of them would be happy to talk with you. I don't have either of their telephone numbers handy, but you can go online to the Saint Bernadette website and find what you need. Feel free to do a little name-dropping if you think it will help at all."

I said I would do that. Then I thanked Professor Levy for his time and walked back outside into the sunshine of a perfect late spring afternoon.

* * *

When I got back to the car, I called the number Sarah Bergman had given me, to ask her whether it would be convenient for me to come by her home later that evening to pick up the photos of Isaac that she had promised me. However, when I got her on the line, she said something had come up and she would be busy that evening. Would tomorrow night be all right? I said that was fine and that I'd try to stop by around eight o'clock. I confirmed her address, and we made a date for the following evening. Then I wished her a pleasant evening and said I would see her tomorrow. That left me free to spend the evening with Maggie and to think about things other than Isaac Bergman and Tommy Mack.

Chapter Six

Instead of going straight home or back to the office, I drove downtown to the Nashville *Times* building at Eleventh and Broadway. As I had explained to Robert Levy, back in the days before I hung out my PI shingle, I was a freshly minted detective on loan from the Nashville PD to the Davidson County district attorney's office. During a routine investigation on an unrelated matter, I stumbled over some information that led me to believe that a senior circuit court judge named Boyce Ozburn was handing down questionable directed verdicts in certain civil cases, usually where a politically connected litigant was involved. When I was sure I had my story straight, I took the matter to the district attorney, a man named Roger Seacrist. I was told in no uncertain terms that this particular investigation was off-limits, due in large part to the fact that we were in an election year, and Judge Ozburn was headed for an appointment to the appellate court, provided he survived the upcoming retention vote.

I thought about it for a day or two. Then I decided the matter was too important to just let slide, so I took what I had to a reporter at the *Times* named Dick Dohrn. It wasn't a lot, and Dick was skeptical at first, but eventually he began asking questions of his own. In the end, the story was front-page news in the paper, and Boyce Ozburn fell short in his bid to be retained on the bench. It didn't take long for the higher-ups to figure out how the *Times* got the story, and I was given an unsatisfactory performance review and tagged for a reduction in grade back to a uniformed patrolman. Before the paperwork went through, I resigned from the force and went into business for myself. In the years that followed, Boyce Ozburn made a fortune in real estate, Roger Seacrist came within a few thousand votes of being elected governor of Tennessee, and Dick Dohrn became senior editor at the *Times*. Fast-forwarding to the present day, Boyce Ozburn was living the good life in Costa Rica, Dick was still at the *Times*, and Roger Seacrist was taking another run at elected office, this time running for the United States Senate.

Truth be told, I was a bit hesitant to ask Dick for any favors. The last time he had cooperated with me on an investigation, a reporter on his staff named David Quail had wound up taking a bullet in the back of his head because he was getting too close to what would turn out to be the resolution of the case. I never got the sense that Dick blamed me for his man's killing, but I was also unsure whether he would be willing to commit himself or his newspaper to giving me a hand with another one of my cases. On the other hand, I thought, not to ask is not to receive.

I found Dick where he always seemed to be, sitting behind his desk in the *Times* city room. I hadn't seen him in the year or so since my other case had gone sideways, but his appearance didn't seem to have changed much, except that his hair was a little thinner, and it looked as if he had gained a pound or two. He wore wire-rimmed glasses and a white, short-sleeved dress shirt, open at the collar. As was his habit, he was rolling a mint-flavored toothpick back and forth from one corner of his mouth to the other, the remnant of what had been a two-pack-a-day habit, and muttering darkly to himself about something on his desk that he was reading.

I rapped on his door frame and gave a wave of greeting when I walked into his office.

"Good Lord, do my eyes deceive me?" he said, rising to extend his hand. Then, just as quickly, his eyes narrowed, and he pulled his hand back again. "Wait a minute, what am I thinking? You want something, don't you? What is it this time?"

"Just a minute of your time," I said, "and maybe a short walk down memory lane."

He glanced pointedly at his watch. "I can give you five minutes. Then I'm due in a meeting that'll take about a half hour."

"Fair enough, then. Let me get right to it. I'm wondering what you can tell me about a guy named Isaac Bergman."

"Is he any relation to Ingrid? Or maybe Ingmar?"

"Neither one, I'm afraid. He was a teacher, or rather a professor, of classical languages at Saint Bernadette University. He disappeared about four years ago, so far without a trace. I was thinking you might remember something about it."

Dick said, "Four years ago. After four years, people remember things like shaking hands with the President, or getting sick from eating a bad oyster on a Caribbean cruise." He shook his head. "But Isaac Berman?"

"Bergman," I corrected him.

"Bergman, then. Why do you care about this guy, anyway? Oh, wait, let me guess. Somebody's paying you an outrageous sum of money to find him, right?"

"His wife. She misses him, and she wants him back."

"Why? Did he win a Power Ball Lottery somewhere?" I had a wisecrack ready, but he didn't give me an opening.

"Look, I really don't have time right now to hash this out with you, but I can tell you, if we did a story on this guy, I don't have any recollection. But just the same, you know the drill. I'll call downstairs and get you set up in the archives. Just type in the guy's name and see what comes up. And be sure to let me know what you find. You know, just in case there's a lawsuit later. Or, God forbid, an actual story."

I promised I would, and we said goodbye.

* * *

Ten minutes later, I was in the *Times'* basement archive, breathing air that smelled like stale coffee, cigarette smoke, and black mold, and tapping away with two fingers at a computer keyboard. It took a little digging, because a single missing person investigation only attracts so much attention. That is a roundabout way of saying that, unless the gone man or woman has a fairly high profile, nobody much gives a shit, other than friends and family, and the handful of cops assigned to the case.

With regard to Isaac Bergman, there was a half-column article on page six of a *Times* edition dated four years and two months earlier. The article said that Metro police had undertaken an investigation to determine the whereabouts of Professor Bergman, "a popular and highly respected teacher of Latin, Greek, and Hebrew at Saint Bernadette University." It also mentioned that he had been on staff for eight years and had published a couple of articles in such online professional journals as *Teaching Classical Languages, Classical World,* and *Byzantine Studies.* An unnamed spokesman for the university was quoted as saying Professor Bergman gave no indication that he was planning to take a leave of absence, or otherwise departing before the end of the term. The spokesperson, perhaps arising from a sense of delicacy, did not go on to say that Bergman had already been given the heave-ho, and, in any case, would not be returning at the beginning of the fall semester. The police, meanwhile, said that although there was no indication of foul play, they were devoting every available resource to finding out where he might have gone.

I also found a follow-up article, dated ten days after the first. Professor Bergman's car, a red 2015 Dodge Challenger, had been found thirty feet off the shoulder of Highway 41, wrapped around a hundred-year-old oak tree that seemed none the worse for the encounter. According to the county sheriff's office, the best guess was that the car had been stolen by a person or persons unknown, who took it for a joyride and somehow lost control, resulting in its being wrecked. It was assumed that whoever had stolen the car had survived the crash and simply walked away. The article didn't say anything about what happened to the Challenger after it had been found wrecked, but I was pretty sure I knew where it went next.

From my time with the cops, I was aware the city had a longstanding contract with a salvage yard in nearby LaVergne. I decided, first chance I got, to drive out and take a look at the car—assuming, of course, it was still there. Not because I expected to find any leads the police had overlooked. Mostly, I was just curious. The police might have been looking for evidence relating to possible grand theft auto. My own interest was in discovering whether anything about the car might give me an insight into Isaac Bergman's personality, or perhaps his state of mind at the time of his disappearance. It was a long shot, I knew, but sometimes it's those long shots that can make or break a case. And at the moment, I didn't have much else to go on.

* * *

I gathered up my notes and rode the elevator back upstairs to the third-floor city room. Dick Dohrn was back from his meeting, so I stuck my head in the doorway to thank him for giving me access to the archives and to let him know what I had turned up.

"Which sounds like basically nothing," he told me after I filled him in. "From what you're telling me, for whatever reason, the guy got the hell out of town as fast as he could and abandoned his car somewhere. It probably sat for a while, and then somebody clouted it, stripped it for parts, and ditched the hulk in some wrecking yard."

"Was that before or after running it off the road and smashing into a tree?"

"Okay, you got me there. I don't suppose Bergman's body was stuffed into the trunk."

"Apparently not, but if you were Bergman and you were trying to make a quick getaway, why would you leave your car behind?"

"Good question. Maybe he got a ride."

"What?"

"Well, you know. Maybe wherever he was going next, he wasn't going alone. Maybe he fell in love with some sexy trust-fund co-ed, and the two of them split for parts unknown in her car. That kind of thing does happen once in a while, you know."

Chapter Seven

When I got back to the office I called Maggie, hoping to get together with her later, but she said she had made arrangements with one of her work friends to have dinner and then take in a movie. That meant I was on my own for the evening, and with nothing better to do, I got on the computer and looked up an English translation for the *Ars Amatoria.* It turned out to be a fairly lengthy poem, written in the year 2AD. It consisted of three books, generally organized around the topics of how a man can find a woman, how a man can keep a woman, and, in the third book, helpful hints on how a woman can find and keep a man. I was especially intrigued by Ovid's advice to men regarding how to find a woman:

> *Neatness pleases, a body tanned from exercise: a well-fitting and spotless toga is good. No stiff shoe-thongs, your buckles free of rust, no sloppy feet for you, swimming in loose hide: don't mar your neat hair with an evil haircut: let an expert hand trim your head and beard. And no long nails, and make sure they're dirt-free: and no hairs, please, sprouting from your nostrils. No bad breath exhaled from an unwholesome mouth.*

And just in case she needs a bit more persuasion:

> *And tears help: tears will move a stone: let her see your damp cheeks if you can. If tears (they don't always come at the right time) fail you, touch your eyes with a wet hand. What wise man doesn't mingle tears*

with kisses?

It seemed like good advice, even in the present day, especially the part about sprouting nose hair. In the last section of the third book, entitled "And So to Bed," Ovid describes to his female readers how to catch and hold a man. Then he describes the payoff:

> *Let each girl know herself: adopt a reliable posture for her body. She who's known for her face, lie there face upwards: let her back be seen, she whose back delights. She who has youthful thighs, and faultless breasts, the man might stand, she spread, with her body downwards.*
> *There's a thousand ways to do it: simple and least effort, is just to lie there half-turned on your right side.*

Hot stuff, even for the notoriously libidinous Romans, and good advice all around, although for whatever reason, it seemed to have gotten Ovid kicked out of Rome. It made me wonder whether I ought to read it to Maggie. Then I decided that it might not be such a good idea, though I could see how a smooth-talking professor with suede elbow patches and a jaunty ponytail might be able to use it to sweep a less experienced coed off her feet. It also made me wonder whether, in a #MeToo world, such a read-aloud might not only be enough to get the professor canned, but also to get him killed.

Later that night, I fell asleep on the couch, dreaming of women with youthful thighs and faultless breasts, all of them wearing Tri-Delt sweatshirts.

* * *

The next morning, I got a call from Sarah Bergman. She said she had managed to put her hands on a few photos of her husband, Isaac, and that I was welcome to stop in any time to pick them up. She also said she had found an old address book of his and wondered whether that might be helpful tracking down leads. I could have that, too, if I wanted. But there was a catch.

"I was thinking, if you came by this evening, you could bring Maggie with you. I haven't seen her in ages, and I know she works during the day. I could fix us some cocktails and snacks, and maybe the three of us could visit for a while." I told her that would be fine and that we'd be there about seven.

After I hung up with Sarah Bergman, I put a call in to Metro police headquarters. I asked to speak to a missing persons cop I knew there named Carl Sutton. Carl and I had a relationship that went back to the days when I was a newly-minted detective, and he took me under his wing after a fashion, acting as a part-time mentor. In the years since I had gone private, our relationship had occasionally gone through some stresses and strains, largely due to the fact that the flow of information between us, more often than not, went from him to me, rather than the other way around.

As it turned out, Carl was on medical leave, arising from some complication or other having to do with his diabetes, which I knew, given his weight and his age, he struggled to keep under control. So, instead of Carl, I ended up talking to another detective named Calvert. Over the telephone, he sounded less than enthusiastic, as if I was taking him away from something he'd rather be doing. But he agreed to meet with me and said he'd be in the office the rest of the morning if I wanted to come right over.

Unlike Carl Sutton, Marvin Calvert did not have a private office at the Metro Public Safety Building. Instead, he occupied a fabric-covered cubicle, just large enough for his chair and desk, a three-drawer file cabinet, and a visitor's chair wedged into a corner. Calvert himself looked to be in his early thirties, suggesting that his detective's shield was a fairly recent acquisition. He was tall, red-haired, and clean-shaven. He wore gray slacks, a short-sleeved white dress shirt, and a red and silver diagonally-striped tie. His desktop was neat, with only a pad of paper and a cup filled with ballpoint pens. After the cool reception I got during my earlier telephone call, I expected to get five minutes of his time, followed by a quick brush-off. But instead, he surprised me.

"Mister Gamble," he said. "Pleased to meet you." He rose from his chair, gave me a smile, and extended his hand for me to shake. Usually, when I make a call at police headquarters, I'm received like a carrier of some communicable and ultimately debilitating disease. Calvert, with his amiable greeting, made me wonder whether I had unknowingly stumbled into an alternate universe, one where cops and keyhole peepers actually got along with one another.

"So, Mr. Gamble," Calvert said, waving me into his visitor's chair, "you said something over the phone about a cold case. How can we help you?"

Are you for real? I wanted to ask. *You're seriously interested in helping?* Instead, I said, "Cold case is one way to put it. I've been asked to try to track down a critical missing person named Isaac Bergman."

Calvert leaned back in his chair and clasped his hands together behind his head. "Missing since when?"

"A little more than four years." It took about ten minutes while I filled him in as best I could on Bergman's disappearance, beginning with my visit with Sarah Bergman and continuing through my conversations with Robert Levy and Dick Dohrn. I also told him about how Bergman's car had turned up stripped in a local salvage yard around the same time as he went missing.

"Did robbery-auto theft ever run that down, do you know?"

"No idea," I told him. Everything I've been telling you dropped into my lap just about forty-eight hours ago."

"Okay, how about this?" he said, sitting up straight in his chair and making a few notes on his pad. "Let me look into this for you. And you're right, four years is a long time. Plus, as of this moment, I know absolutely nothing about this case beyond what you've just told me. I'll ask around, check the files, and see what I can come up with. Why don't you call me back tomorrow afternoon? By then, I should know something, and if I come up empty, I'll let you know that, too. That sound fair?"

I said it did. I handed him one of my business cards, we shook hands, and I left. Back in my car, I thought about what had just taken place and asked myself why a young detective would want to get involved with a case like Bergman's. And then it came to me that maybe, just maybe, if he was able to crack the case, it might put him closer to the head of the line when it came time to pass out promotions.

Enlightened self-interest, I realized. Adam Smith called it "the invisible hand."

***

Sarah Bergman's home was located a couple of blocks from where Robert Levy lived. It was a tree-shaded, older neighborhood that had been well-maintained since the time the homes were built back in the early 1950s. It was a smallish, red brick bungalow with gray shutters, flower boxes beneath the windows, and a single-car garage at the end of a driveway just long enough to accommodate a second vehicle without the rear bumper hanging over the sidewalk—provided, at least, that it wasn't one of those locomotive-sized pickup trucks that everyone seems to be driving these days. Taken as a whole, it was the kind of place that seemed eminently suited to a young associate professor and his wife, him aspiring for tenure and the prestige and financial security that came with it.

I parked the car at the curb and let Maggie walk ahead of me to the front entrance. After a moment, Sarah opened the door, gave a squeal of delight, and embraced Maggie as if she were a long-lost relative, just returned from ten years' sequestering in a cloistered convent.

"Mister Gamble," she said, "thank you for coming. And for bringing my dear friend. Maggie, how are you? It's been simply ages since we've had a chance to get caught up."

I started to say something like, "She has a phone, you know," but Maggie shot me a look I'd seen before in similar situations. Roughly translated, it meant keep-a-lid-on-it-if-you-know-what's-good-for-you.

We went inside, and Sarah sat us down in a living room that was very floral and very feminine, with a sofa upholstered in a blue-green-white satin material that featured what appeared to be hibiscus, or possibly clematis, print. I couldn't be sure, although if they'd been dandelions, I'd have recognized them without any problem at all. In front of the sofa was a glass-topped cocktail table flanked on either side by comfortable-looking occasional chairs covered with a contrasting floral print. An iced pitcher of what looked like margaritas and three glasses with salted rims, along with a bowl of lime slices, sat on a tray in the center of the table. A plate of cheese and crackers, some oversized red grapes, and green apple slices rounded out the presentation.

I said, "Mrs. Bergman, before we get started here, I wanted to let you know I spoke with the police earlier today, and I think they might be interested in revisiting your husband's case. No promises, either from them or from me. But sometimes, a fresh set of eyes can see something that could have been overlooked earlier."

"Well, that should be a big help," Maggie said brightly. Then, to Sarah Bergman, she said, "I told you, didn't I? He's the best."

"Then, here's something else that I hope will help you." Sarah Bergman handed me a brown manila envelope. "These are the photos of Isaac you wanted. You can share them with the police if you think it will help. I thought there were more, but he never much liked having his picture taken. There may be some others tucked away someplace. If I run across them, I'll give you a call."

"Thank you," I said. "These will at least get me started." I set the envelope on the floor next to where I was sitting.

"Well, aren't you going to look?" Maggie asked.

"Later is fine," I said. "I know you two would like to do some catching up."

"Okay, then," Sarah Bergman said. "Should we have a drink?"

Maggie nodded. "Absolutely."

Sarah poured three glasses to the top, then raised hers. "To old friends," she said, clinking rims with Maggie. "And to new ones." She reached across the table and clinked mine.

"You have a lovely home," I said, just to be saying something. "I feel like I'm inside a greenhouse."

"Maggie knows I love flowers. My husband used to buy me roses every Friday night on his way home from the university."

"That was nice of him," I said, "considering." I helped myself to a slice of apple.

"Considering?"

I knew right away that I should have kept the last part of that comment to myself. I wanted to say something like, *You mean, considering it was widely known on campus that he was a skirt-chaser*, but once again, Maggie shot me a look that stopped me cold.

"Considering," Maggie said, deftly bailing me out, "that most associate professors at small universities are notoriously underpaid."

"Yes, that's true, I know. And Isaac and I used to worry about that. We had to watch our expenses closely. But that would have all changed once he was granted tenure. More money wouldn't have come all at once, but at least we would have had security. We had all kinds of plans." She gave Maggie and me a small smile.

I said, "Tenure?"

"Yes. I'm sure I mentioned when we spoke earlier that Isaac was up for tenure at the end of the semester when...well, when he left."

That reminded me of something. I said, "The day your husband went missing. You said he called to tell you he had a meeting that evening. Do you remember, by any chance, what time he called?"

"It was...it was in the middle of the afternoon, I think."

"So, he would have been between classes, then."

"No, after. Isaac's last class that semester ran from one until one fifty-five."

"Then he would have had the rest of the afternoon free."

"Yes, I suppose so. Why?"

"Just wondering," I said. "I'm trying to reconstruct his day in my mind. See if there's anything else I should be looking at."

There was a pause. This time, Maggie would have had to retrieve the Remington .380 she carried in her purse and shoot me where I sat to stop me from saying what I had to say.

"Mrs. Bergman," I began.

She looked at me over the rim of her glass. "Please, call me Sarah. We're all friends here."

"All right, then, Sarah. I remember when we spoke earlier, you told me you thought the meeting your husband was planning to attend had something to do with a tenure offer."

"Well, yes, that's what we were hoping, anyway."

"Did he tell you that was the purpose of the meeting?"

"Well, no. But we were hoping."

"Sarah, I'm sorry to have to be asking you this, but since the time he went missing, hasn't anyone told you that your husband had been advised that he would not be offered tenure? And, what's more, that he had been informed of this several weeks before the day he disappeared?"

"What? No! Where did you hear that?" Sarah Bergman's surprise was genuine. "That was the whole reason for the meeting he was supposed to attend that afternoon. The dean of the university was going to extend tenure offers to Isaac and some of his colleagues."

"I'm sorry, Sarah, I thought you knew. There was no meeting. I spoke with Robert Levy yesterday and he told me the university had decided that your husband would not be offered tenure. He also said that Isaac had been informed sometime earlier that his teaching contract would not be renewed for another year. I'm sorry to be the one telling you this, especially after all this time. But Professor Levy was quite clear on the issue."

Her face collapsed like a spoiled souffle. "I...I don't know what to say. Did Professor Levy have any idea why Isaac wasn't going to be offered tenure?"

I did my best to keep my tone even and my response non-judgmental. "Levy said something about how your husband hadn't published a great deal of whatever it is that academics get published. He implied that the few things your husband wrote that did find their way into print was—well, he just didn't publish enough. The university expected more. Again, I'm sorry to be the one telling you this. I assumed you knew."

The temperature in the room seemed to drop about twenty degrees, along with Sarah Bergman's tone of voice. "I see. And did that old bastard also tell you that my husband had a reputation for being, what shall we say, attractive to the young women on campus?"

"I don't recall anything like that," I lied, not wanting to make the situation any worse than it already was. "Professor Levy's emphasis was more on your husband's publishing history. Publish or perish was the term he used."

Maggie raised her eyebrows ever so slightly. I recognized that as a warning sign, not unlike a rattlesnake's rattle, and changed the subject. "Sarah, if I may, on another matter, Professor Levy did tell me that shortly after your husband went missing, you came to his office and removed his personal effects."

"Yes."

"Can I ask, do you still have them?"

She nodded. "In the garage. There are a couple of cardboard boxes stacked in the back corner. I looked through them right after I got them home, but I didn't see anything that might explain where Isaac had gone." Anticipating my next question, she said, "You can take them with you if you think there might be something there that will help your search. I can show you where they are if you'd like."

Maggie said, "Let's have another drink first."

That turned out to be a bad idea. Sarah Bergman got suddenly quiet, and then, about halfway through her second margarita, tears started forming in the corners of her eyes. A moment after that, she was full-on bawling. I couldn't tell whether she was overcome at having to relive her husband's disappearance all over again, or if she was just a weepy drunk, though I would have thought it should have taken more than one margarita and part of a second to set her off.

Maggie slid over to Sarah's side of the sofa and hugged her, which prompted an even more copious torrent of tears. That was my cue. I excused myself and got up from my chair. I walked through the kitchen and out into the garage. After a few minutes fumbling around in semi-darkness—the overhead light was burned out—I found the boxes Sarah was talking about and carried them back into the kitchen. By that time, Sarah had stopped crying and was dabbing at her eyes with a tissue.

I said, "If it's all right, I think it might be easier if I took these. Then I won't have to take up any more of your time sitting here. Depending on what turns up, I'll bring them back in a day or two, and if I have any questions, maybe you can answer them for me."

She didn't say anything, just nodded, so I gathered up the envelope with the photos, said goodnight, and went outside to put the boxes in the back seat of the car. Maggie followed me as far as the end of the driveway.

"What?"

"I'm going to stay for a bit. Maybe see if I can get Sarah settled down. I'll call an Uber later."

"You don't have to do that. Just call me when you're ready, and I'll come pick you up. I'll probably be up late, anyway. I want to look through this stuff she gave me."

She shook her head. "No. I might be here a while."

"Sure? I can come back and get you. It's no trouble."

"Thanks, I'll be fine. And Gamble, it was sweet of you to lie to Sarah just now. You know, about Isaac being a tomcat. I don't know if she was fooled, but all the same, it was a good effort."

I said, "What makes you think I was lying?"

"You have a tell. I always know when you're lying. It's one of the reasons I fell for you."

Chapter Eight

After I got home, I took a quick look through the photos of Isaac Bergman given to me by his wife. Taken as a whole, I would have said he was a fairly unremarkable-looking individual. There were six images altogether, including a wedding picture showing the happy couple cutting into a three-layered cake with a be-ribboned knife. Another showed Isaac by himself, seated at his desk in what I supposed was his office, presumably at Saint Bernadette University. There were stacks of books and papers on his desk, and he wore a contented smile, as a man is apt to do when he is comfortable in his own skin and expecting nothing but good things to come his way. Still another showed Isaac posed for what I assumed was a yearbook photo, or perhaps a graduation program. He wore doctoral regalia, including a black robe trimmed in red, a doctoral hood, and a black velvet tam with a gold tassel.

The last one—date and location not shown—was a close-up. The head-and-shoulders shot showed Isaac, now in his late forties or early fifties, wearing glasses with red frames and a tiny diamond stud in his left earlobe. All in all, very with-it, I thought, and sure to cause many a coed to swoon. He had light-colored hair that hung slightly over his ears and a short, neatly trimmed beard that matched the color of his hair. He wore a broadcloth dress shirt with a button-down collar and a knit necktie that might have been dark gray or blue. I was particularly interested in his eyes to see whether there was any hint of discomfort or uncertainty, the way a man might look if he thought he was about to lose his position on the faculty of a small but well-regarded university. But if there was, I couldn't see it.

I was looking through the photos a second time, trying to decide whether there was anything in any of them that might help me get inside Professor Bergman's head, when my phone rang. It was Maggie.

"I'm going to stay the night with Sarah. After you left, she went completely to pieces, and it took me almost an hour and the rest of the margaritas to get her settled down and into bed. I'll sleep in the guest room, and then she can give me a lift home in the morning."

I told her that was probably a good idea and that I'd see her tomorrow. I thought about starting to take a look through the two boxes of Isaac Bergman's personal stuff I had brought home with me, then decided I'd done enough for one night, and tomorrow would be soon enough. The guy had been gone for four years. I decided one more night wouldn't make any difference one way or the other. One hour and two bottles of beer later, I fell asleep in front of the television, watching an old black-and-white, Jacques Tourneur-directed mystery/horror picture called *The Leopard Man* on our classic movie channel.

** * **

I got to the office just about nine the next morning. When I walked in, the telephone was ringing. I thought it might be Maggie, primed and ready to give me a blow-by-blow of her sleepover with Sarah Bergman. And if not Maggie, then it had to be Fat Wally, wanting to know whether I'd managed yet to find Tommy Mack.

To my surprise, it was neither.

"Good morning, Mr. Gamble. This is Robert Levy calling."

"Professor Levy. What can I do for you?"

"Well, I was wondering whether you'd had a chance to talk further with Sarah and if she'd been able to give you any more information that might help you locate Isaac."

"I did, but I didn't learn very much, I'm afraid. She gave me a few photos, which might be useful, and a couple of boxes of personal files and whatnot that she retrieved from his office after he disappeared. I don't know if any of it will be of any use."

"I see. And have you had a chance to look at it?"

"Not yet, no. Shortly after we began talking, she got very upset. Apparently, she was unaware that her husband would not be offered a contract for the upcoming year, and I'm sorry to say she didn't take it very well. So, I took the boxes and left. My lady friend promised to stay the night with her and make sure she was okay, but I haven't heard from either one of them this morning."

"Interesting." He paused for a moment. "Mister Gamble, this might seem like an unseemly request, but I wonder if I could ask you to keep me apprised of your progress finding Isaac? I understand that I am not your client, and I also know I told you Isaac and I weren't exactly close. But I was his advisor, and I did get to know him reasonably well, and, well, I'd appreciate it if you would do that for me."

I picked up my pencil and began drumming it on the top of my desk. "As you say, Professor, and with all due respect, you're not my client. And unless Mrs. Bergman asks me to keep you in the loop, I really can't discuss the specifics of my investigation with you. My suggestion would be that you communicate directly with her. I'm sorry, and I appreciate your concern, but that's just how this business works."

"I understand completely. So then, you're saying you wouldn't have any problem if I called Sarah and asked her to keep me informed?"

"That's entirely up to you and Sarah. Maybe if you put your heads together, one of you will remember something that might jump-start the investigation. But before you go, if you don't mind, I have a question for you. Something that came up last night that has me curious."

"And that is?"

"Just this. Why, in all the time since Bergman disappeared, did no one ever tell Sarah that there was no tenure offer forthcoming, and that, in fact, he would be let go at the end of the semester? She was under the impression that his being offered tenure was pretty much a done deal."

There was a pause. "I have no idea. I suppose nobody mentioned it to her because it was assumed she already knew. That was something Isaac should have told her right away, so they could start making other plans. Obviously, from what you said earlier, he did not do that."

"Obviously."

"Well, perhaps the answer to that question is the key to why he went missing."

* * *

After I hung up with Robert Levy, I began thinking about why, after four years, he had suddenly developed an interest in what had happened to Isaac Bergman. Apparently, Bergman's disappearance hadn't bothered him at the time, or at any time later on. I also wondered, not for the first time, why his wife had suddenly decided she wanted him back. Maybe it was true she still loved him and wanted him back in her life. Or maybe it was something else. But what? Something having to do with money, like, say, an insurance policy that Sarah needed to make sure he was dead in order to collect? To do that, she would have to have him declared legally dead, and if I were to run across his body during the course of my investigation, that would make having to take legal action a moot point.

I had to admit, at that moment, I had nothing at all definite to go on. Which led me to another consideration. At the time I first met with Sarah, I had said I'd look around for a bit to see whether there was even a case worth pursuing. For that reason, I hadn't asked her for a retainer. But after two days of poking around, I hadn't come up with anything that seemed likely to move my investigation along. I decided to give it one more day, and if I still was without any promising leads, I'd tell her that she should either give it up, or consider consulting a larger firm that would have more resources than I did.

That meant, even with my self-imposed deadline, I still had work to do, starting with an examination of the two boxes of material that Sarah had retrieved from her husband's office. I didn't have much hope of finding anything useful, but since the boxes were all I had, I figured I might as well take a look. I began by unloading and setting off to the side all the items that didn't require any action, such as a stapler, paperweight, pens, pencils, a box of paper clips, several "World's Greatest Teacher" coffee cups, a magnifying glass, a letter opener, and a calculator. I couldn't see where any of that would lead me one step closer to finding my man, or, failing that, figuring out what might have happened to him.

Next up were his diplomas, all elegantly and expensively framed. One was from the University of Notre Dame, a B.A. in philosophy, and two more, *cum laude*, from Boston University, in classical studies. Whatever else Isaac Bergman might have been, he evidently knew his stuff. After that, I began leafing through several manila file folders. I wasn't able to find much except some personal correspondence, including a congratulatory letter from the office of the dean of the college of fine arts, commending him on an article he'd gotten published in some professional journal. Unfortunately for Bergman and his career, there did not seem to be a second congratulatory letter to be found.

In another file, I found what looked like outlines and rough drafts of articles that he might have been planning to submit for publication. In still another, I found some handwritten notes, evidently from students, thanking him for time he'd spent giving a little extra help, or telling him how much they'd enjoyed his class. What I didn't run across was anything that suggested somebody wanted to kill him, or run off with him to a desert island, or threatening to expose him for some sexual escapade or other.

And then I found something a bit more interesting. It was an ordinary calendar book, dated four years earlier. When I opened it, there was a two-page spread for each month of the year. It was the kind of book someone might have in order to keep track of meeting dates and times, student appointments, lunch or dinner dates, or other events such as doctor or dentist visits. I began flipping through the pages, mostly finding nothing more than notations of Bergman's daily activities, such as "faculty meeting, 700P" for a date in February or "lunch w/Phil, 1130" for another day in late March. Most of the entries were like that, involving meetings, lunches, dinners, parties, or university events.

But, there were several others that I couldn't quite make sense of, such as

"MB/730/750" or "RE/900/600," and other initials such as LK, GR and RW. Paging through the calendar, I realized that all of the notations I couldn't make sense of were either for a Friday or a Saturday, and they appeared at least three times every month. Some weeks, there was a double entry, so that it appeared Bergman was conducting two meetings with the same person during the same week. I tried working backward from the weekend dates, and, sure enough, in each instance, there was a meeting scheduled earlier in the week that read something like "MB 930A," or "SS 415P." So, using "MB" as an example, he met with that individual during the early part of the week and then again on either Friday or Saturday, though I couldn't guess what the second set of numbers might indicate. Also, and perhaps tellingly, none of these meetings, or conferences, or whatever they were, were scheduled during the summer months, or over spring or Christmas breaks, suggesting that, whatever was going on, it likely involved either students or other faculty members during the times classes were in session.

And then I had a thought. When I first interviewed Sarah Bergman, she had said that the day her husband disappeared was April second. However, checking his calendar, there was no entry for a faculty meeting, or any other appointment indicated for that date. That meant that whatever Isaac was planning to do that evening, it did not appear to involve attending a meeting at the university.

He had other plans. But to do what?

Frustrated for the moment, I put the calendar aside and went back to rummaging through the boxes. I found manila file folders with what looked like lecture notes, others with Bergman's own meeting minutes. Another file contained copies of magazine articles related to his field of instruction, some with titles so esoteric that I had no idea what they might be about. There were some travel expense forms, group insurance booklets, and even the outline of a spy novel he was apparently getting ready to begin writing. It looked to have something to do with a university professor who doubled in his spare time as an amateur secret agent. In the story, it appeared the fictional professor was using his knowledge of ancient languages to expose a clandestine organization intent on discrediting the teachings found in the

Christian Bible. For some reason, it struck me as something I'd already read, and in any event, the premise of the story didn't seem like one that would help get Bergman back onto the tenure track at a place like Saint Bernadette.

Chapter Nine

It took another couple of hours before I finished sorting through the boxes Sarah Bergman had given me, and the only other item of interest I was able to put my hands on was Isaac's personal telephone directory. Without actually counting, I estimated there must have been at least a hundred names, addresses, phone numbers, and, in some cases, email addresses, of people he kept in contact with, either personally or professionally. I hoped the case wouldn't come down to actually having to contact every single one of them to find out what they knew. I did remember, however, that Robert Levy had given me the names of a couple of people Isaac was close with, Phillip May and Caroline Feldman. I decided I might as well start with Caroline Feldman.

When I dialed Ms. Feldman's number, her voicemail informed me that she was out of the office all day, but if I would leave my name and number, she would get back to me. I left my office and cell numbers and a short message, outlining in a general way what I wanted to talk to her about, and hung up. I had better luck with Phillip May. He was in his office, apparently with time on his hands, and said if I wanted to come by, he had the rest of the afternoon free to talk. I told him I could be there inside of an hour. He gave me his office address and told me where I could find a parking space that wouldn't require me to walk halfway across campus to get where I needed to go. Forty-five minutes later, I was sitting across the desk from him.

If I had to guess, I'd have said Phillip May was somewhere around forty-five years old, with brown eyes, a light complexion, a fashionably trimmed beard, and an incipient bald spot that he had made a game, but not altogether successful effort to conceal with an elaborate comb-over.

"So, Mr. Gamble," he said after we shook hands, "what can I do for you?" He waved me into a chair in front of his desk.

"Well, as I mentioned when I called, I've been asked to look into the disappearance of Isaac Bergman. I spoke with Robert Levy earlier in the week, and he indicated to me that you and Professor Bergman were friends. I realize he's been a long time gone, but I was hoping you might be able to tell me a little bit about him."

"Like what, for instance?"

"Things like, what did he do in his spare time? Did he have any hobbies?"

"I think he was working on a book. Some kind of a spy thriller, he told me. He never showed it to me, though."

"I know about that," I said. "Anything else?"

"Again, like what?"

"Like, I don't know what. Was he keeping another woman on the side, or was he running off to a casino on the weekends gambling away his paycheck?"

The suggestion seemed to surprise him. "Why would you think that?"

"No reason, except that he vanished one day without a trace, and he didn't talk to anyone about any plans to do that. Now, I don't know how it is in academia, but in my world, when somebody disappears for no apparent reason, it usually means the person is either on the run from something he greatly fears, or else he's dead in a shallow grave somewhere."

"Or, he could be running toward something." He leaned back so far in his chair I thought it might tip over backwards, and propped his feet up on the top of his desk.

"Well, to answer your question directly, I was as surprised as the next guy when he just, what shall we say, vanished into thin air. At first, we all figured there must have been some family emergency, but then when he didn't come back the next day, or the day after that, and he didn't call, we didn't know what to make of it. Still don't."

"Did the police talk to you?"

"Oh, for sure. They talked to everybody. His wife, obviously, but also me and my wife—that was before we were separated—as well as a number of his students and some of his faculty colleagues. I don't think they were able to come up with much, or if they did, I never heard what it might have been."

I decided not to mention that I was working on getting the police to reopen their own investigation. "Okay, but if what Robert Levy said about you and Isaac being good friends is correct, I have to ask whether he gave you any indication that he was thinking about his situation here at the university, or that he was considering leaving."

"You're talking now about the fact that he wasn't going to be offered tenure?"

"Yes. Was that common knowledge around the campus?"

"Well, it wasn't generally known, if that's what you're asking. I mean, the other members of the classic lit and languages department might have been aware. And, of course, I knew about it, since Isaac and I were friends. As you might imagine, he was pretty upset. But as far as the wider university community was concerned, I'd have to say no. Decisions regarding hirings and firings are personnel matters and are kept confidential."

"So then, would the same thing be true about his contract not being renewed for the coming year? Was that kept confidential as well?"

"Yes, it was. The faculty wasn't told about that until after his disappearance, because, of course, we had to hurry up and find other instructors to take over his class load."

"Okay, but then, that brings up another point. Since you and Isaac were friends, and since you knew he was leaving before any of his other colleagues were informed, did he say anything to you about what he planned to do next? I mean, there are a dozen other colleges here in Nashville. Do you know, was he thinking about applying for a position with any of them?"

"Not that I know of."

"Or elsewhere? University of the South, or Lane College? Someplace like that?"

"If he was, he didn't say. I think he was probably still in shock over losing his position here, and wasn't thinking that far ahead." He paused, as if to gather his thoughts. "Look here. Isaac has been gone for, what, four years now?"

"That's right."

"So, why this sudden interest now?"

"If you're talking about me, that's simple enough," I said. "I'm interested because it's my job. It's how I get paid."

"And who are you working for? Robert Levy?"

"Why would you think that?"

"Well," he swung his legs back off his desk and placed his feet flat on the floor. "Because, for one thing, from what you've told me so far, he's the only person you seem to have spoken with."

"And for another?"

"And for another, and I shouldn't be telling you this, I think there may have been some kind of trouble between Levy and Isaac. Did Levy talk to you about that?"

I let his question slide. "What kind of trouble?"

"I don't know. I mean, it wasn't even something I knew for sure. It was just an impression I got. Maybe it was some kind of legal trouble having to do with Isaac's being let go, or maybe Levy was involved in some action or other between Isaac and the university."

"Involved how? The story I got was that Isaac was being let go at the end of the semester. He didn't have tenure, and from what I know of such things, Saint Bernadette was well within its rights to terminate Isaac for any reason, or for no reason at all. And as far as Robert Levy is concerned, Bergman didn't work directly for Levy. He was employed by the university, so unless Isaac was involved in some kind of illicit activity that Levy knew something about, I don't see where there would be any grounds for any kind of legal action."

He gave a small shrug. "Well, then, maybe I'm wrong about that. Maybe the two of them were getting along just fine, and his leaving had to do with something else altogether."

I said, "Professor May, Isaac's wife turned over a number of his personal effects that she retrieved from his office, including a date book. When I looked through it, I noticed that he had scheduled a lunch date with you the week before he went missing."

"So?"

"So, I'm wondering. You said that you were aware Bergman had been told he wouldn't be returning in the fall, but apparently, he never informed his wife that he'd been let go. Can you think of any reason why he would have kept that from her? I mean, doesn't it seem odd that he would have talked to you, but not Sarah?"

He pretended to think about that. "Well, maybe he thought there was still an opportunity to save his position, and he didn't want to upset her until he was sure he'd exhausted every opportunity to get his job back. You know, maybe he planned to appeal to the board of regents, or, as I've already suggested, threatened a wrongful discharge lawsuit."

I said, "I guess that's possible. Let's try something else. Would you happen to know whether he was having any other kind of trouble? Maybe he and his wife weren't getting along, or maybe he had money problems of some kind?"

"I wouldn't know anything about that. Isaac was never very forthcoming about his private life. If he was having the kinds of difficulties you're suggesting, he never would have said anything to me about it."

"So then, what did you talk about?"

"Mister Gamble, you're asking me to remember a conversation that took place more than four years ago, and with that in mind, I'd have to say I really can't recall. If we talked about anything, it was probably something to do with students. You know, kids who might have been struggling, or who looked to have a good chance of getting into a graduate program."

"And that's it?"

"Probably. And anyway, what difference does it make? It was a long time ago, and nobody has seen or heard from Isaac since then. Do you really not have anything better to do with your time than chasing after a ghost?"

"Sure," I said. "I could go fishing, or maybe wash my car, but the only thing I'm getting paid to do right now is finding out what happened to Isaac, whether he's alive or dead, and if he's alive, letting my client know where he is. If you can help me with that, I'd appreciate it. If not, then I'm sorry to have taken up your time. I'm sure you're very busy."

"You know, you're right." He made a show of looking at his watch. "I've already said too much, I'm afraid, and I just remembered I have a meeting with a student beginning in a few minutes. I'm sorry, but we'll have to wrap this up."

And just like that, our conversation was over.

Chapter Ten

I walked out of my meeting with Phillip May, feeling I had missed something important, but I had no idea what it might have been. In my previous conversations with Robert Levy, he had said nothing about any lawsuits involving Isaac Bergman, or even that there had ever been any animosity between the two men. And then I wondered whether I was looking at what May had told me the wrong way around. Maybe Bergman's lawsuit had nothing to do with Robert Levy directly. Maybe he was planning to sue the university over being denied tenure. That was a long shot, I knew. Public school teachers are granted tenure more or less automatically after a set number of years, but university tenure is discretionary. But then, why file suit and then just disappear?

There was no point in asking his wife about it, since she was apparently in the dark about her husband's problems with the university. So, when I got back to the office, I began checking the names in Isaac's telephone directory against the attorneys listed in the telephone directory. Owing to the number of people Isaac had listed and the number of lawyers in the yellow pages, it took nearly an hour to match up a man named Luther Fanning with a law firm called Morse, Kaplan, and Jamison. I telephoned the firm and was informed by the receptionist that Mr. Fanning was out of the office and would not return until Monday. Saying only that the matter I wished to discuss was a personal one, I made a ten o'clock appointment for the morning of his return.

***

For all of the times he had found himself in front of a judge, Tommy Mack had never actually had an attorney he could call his own. Whenever he got arrested, the best he was able to do was to get some public defender to persuade the judge to knock his sentence down to time served. Most often, this worked out to anywhere from one to six months, which was usually about the same length of the time he'd spent in the county lockup waiting for his case to come to trial. Generally, he drew short sentences, since he was not a violent offender, didn't carry a weapon, and never entered a residence or a business when anyone else was on the premises. That meant the top charge was second-degree burglary, a class D felony, two-and-a-half years, tops. Sometimes, his public defender was able to get the charge reduced to unlawful entry, rather than the much more serious offense of home invasion, which could get him an industrial-strength jolt of up to thirty years in a state facility.

Over the years, I had gotten to know Tommy a little. He had tried on a couple of other occasions to skip his bail, so that I had to find him and bring him back to the city. Once, when one of his cases looked like it might go to trial, I had even been called as a character witness, though I didn't have the slightest idea what I could say that would be of any help to him. As it turned out, I never got the chance to testify, because his case pleaded out before I was able to take the stand. I supposed I could have said Tommy was very personable and interesting to talk to. He could tell lots of stories about the various petty crimes he'd committed over his twenty-odd years on the wrong side of the law and seemed happy to do so. However, his most recent caper at the home of Red Cherry, while it did have the makings of an entertaining story, was not one that was likely to include a happy ending.

After Red Cherry threw Tommy's bail and presented the bond certificate at the city jail, Tommy was fitted with an ankle bracelet that contained a GPS transmitter. That way, his whereabouts could be tracked twenty-four-seven. But instead of walking out the front door and into the waiting arms of Red Cherry, Tommy played it smart. He excused himself to go to the men's room and then beat feet out the back door of the Downtown Detention Center, where he was able to flag a cab. His first stop was a hardware store a few blocks away, where he bought a Buck folding knife and a serious wire cutter to cut through the nylon ankle strap and remove the monitoring device. Next, he had the cab take him to an apartment complex near the airport. There, he knocked on a certain door in a certain way and waited until a certain individual opened that door. After a brief negotiation, Tommy came away with a small vial of liquid ketamine, also known as Special K, which is a general, fast-acting anesthetic that is sometimes used in emergency surgery. However, like Rohypnol, it can also be used in small doses as a recreational hallucinogenic, or in slightly larger doses as a date-rape drug. The downside of Special K, which Tommy knew all too well, was that too large a dose of ketamine could be fatal.

His last stop for the evening was a downtown bar frequented by middle-aged singles. Most of the time, these folks were looking for nothing more complicated than a little conversation, perhaps some networking, or maybe an exchange of telephone numbers, and, once in a while, a discrete hookup. Tommy, however, wasn't looking for anything as ordinary as that, and he wasn't looking for a woman he could sexually assault. He was looking for a quick way out of town.

Tommy took a seat at the bar, nursing a diet ginger ale and scanning the patrons until he settled his gaze on a woman about his age. She was by no means stunning, but attractive enough, sitting by herself on a stool at the opposite end of the bar. He observed her for about twenty minutes, during which time, she checked her makeup in a compact she had in her purse. After that, she took out her phone, checked the time, and then, he supposed, checked for messages. By then, both Tommy and the woman had both figured out that she had been stood up. He waited another moment, then got up from his seat and walked over to where she was sitting. Tommy introduced himself as Michael Emery, a name he had used once or twice in the past when he was running phony investment scams. Before long, the two were chatting away as if they had known each other all their lives, so Tommy/Michael offered to buy his new friend a drink. Her first instinct was to tell him to buzz off, but as everyone up and down the justice system knew, Tommy did not in any way come across like a threatening individual. And so, sensing that the evening might not be a total loss after all, she accepted.

As the bartender was delivering the drinks, two cosmopolitans, the woman, whose name was Abigail Crowley, excused herself and went off to the ladies' room, perhaps to check her hair and her makeup in better light. While she was gone, Tommy dosed her drink with the ketamine, not enough to knock her cold, but enough to make her drowsy and inattentive. By the time she returned, Tommy had relocated himself and the drinks to a booth against the far wall. They shared some small talk for a while. Abagail told Tommy she worked in the accounting department at one of the recording companies over on The Row. Her job, she said, was payroll and cutting quarterly royalty checks to the recording artists. Tommy said that sounded more interesting than his own job, working as a salesman at a local Ford dealership.

"It used to be more interesting," he told Abigail. "But, nowadays, all anybody wants to buy is either a pickup truck or some big-honker SUV. Where's the fun in that? I mean, give me a hot Mustang any day."

It took a few more minutes of car talk mixed with music industry talk, but then Abigail's speech began to slur, and, finally, she just dozed off, right there in the booth where she was sitting. Tommy saw that as his opportunity. After checking to make sure nobody was paying any attention, he reached underneath the table and retrieved Abagail's purse from the seat where she was sitting. In another minute, he had her car keys and was out the door.

The key fob had the four-intersecting-rings Audi logo impressed on it, so it took practically no time at all to locate the car, a triple-black A5 cabrio of fairly recent vintage, parked in a lot across the street. Idly, Tommy wondered how much an accounts payable-slash-payroll clerk at a recording company got paid that she was able to afford an expensive ride like that. He wondered, but he did not waste time thinking about it. In no more time than it took to adjust the seat and the mirrors, Tommy was on his way out of town, heading north on Interstate 65.

Chapter Eleven

I was hoping, when I got back to the office following my meeting with Phillip May, that there might be a message from Marvin Calvert, the missing-persons detective I had spoken with the previous afternoon. No such luck, and when I checked my email, there was no message there, either. That meant I could call him and potentially make a nuisance of myself, or I could be patient and wait for him to get back to me. I decided to wait. Isaac Bergman had been a long time gone already, and so far, I hadn't actually spent any of my client's money looking for him. So, instead, I put in a call to a woman I knew who I thought might be able to come up with something that I could use. Her name was Wanda Beaudry, and in a former life, like me, she had been a Metro police detective.

Back in the days when we were on the job, Wanda and I were assigned to the district attorney's office for a time as investigators. That job isn't anywhere nearly as interesting as it sounds. Mostly, it consists of verifying police reports, serving subpoenas and search warrants, taking statements from witnesses and defendants, and sometimes arranging for extraditions. That was then. These days, although we are still friends, Wanda is no longer a cop. She is the proprietor, if that's the right word for it, of a shelter for battered and abused women.

I called the number of the shelter, and, in keeping with their standard procedure, was asked to leave my name and telephone number. My call was also recorded. This was done to avoid the staff and the residents having to talk to the abusers who put the women there in the first place without having the chance to screen the call first. It made perfect sense, and I was happy to comply. Wanda called me back about ten minutes later.

"So," she said when I picked up. You must really have nothing to do, calling me."

"Actually, I do have something to do. I just don't know how to do it."

"Tell me."

So, I filled her in on my non-starter investigation into the disappearance of Isaac Bergman. I mentioned that I had talked to a few people who had worked with him, and that I might have gotten a young missing-persons detective interested, but that so far, nothing seemed to be generating any leads.

"Well, he's sure enough not here at the shelter, if that's where you're going with this. I'd say after all this time, he's either started a new life with a new identity, or else he's dead and buried someplace you're not likely to find him." There was a pause. "That's what this call is about, isn't it? You want me to run this guy through NCIC."

NCIC, the National Criminal Identification Center, is operated by the Department of Justice. It was created in 1967 as a national database of criminal records that allows local and state law enforcement agencies to search for information about stolen property, missing or wanted persons, and domestic violence protection orders. Except on a superficial level, however, it is not accessible by the general public—or private investigators, for that matter. To be able to do a deep dive, you need to be employed by a state or local police department, and you need to have a password. Unlike me, Wanda, through some oversight when she left the Metro PD, still retained hers.

"Okay, give me the guy's name again." I spelled it out for her, and then she said, "How's that lady you've been seeing? You know, the one you almost got killed? She dumped you yet?"

"Not yet," I said. "Matter of fact, you both are in the same kind of business. She's got a doctorate now, and she works as a crisis counselor. I think you'd like her."

"Well, then, bring her around sometime. We might be able to put her to work. Strictly as a volunteer, of course. We're not made out of money.

Meantime," she said, "let me see what I can find on this Bergman guy. I'll call you back in a day or two, unless you're in a hurry."

"No hurry at all," I said. "He's been gone four years. He can be gone a little longer."

Chapter Twelve

That evening, I had an early dinner out and then went back to my house to watch a Robert Mitchum-Jane Greer-Kirk Douglas movie called *Out of the Past.* It was originally released in 1947 and is widely regarded as one of the signature films to come out of the post-war *noir* era. The plot generally revolves around the ultimately futile attempt of a former private detective who is trying to make a break from his prior life by opening a gas station in a small town in California. Of course, it doesn't work out for him, and before the end of the first reel, he's been drawn back into his old line of work, once again fighting for possession of his very soul. I wondered if there was a message somewhere in that for me.

It was just getting to the part where Mitchum and Greer, thinking to escape a murder rap, are driving toward a police roadblock that will end up with both of them being killed, when the telephone rang.

Maggie was calling. There was a problem.

"Have you heard from Sarah today?"

"No," I said. "Was I supposed to?"

"I don't know. I've been trying to reach her all day, but her phone keeps going to voice mail. I'm worried something's happened to her."

"Because she isn't answering her phone? Maybe she made another pitcher of margaritas."

"Because I haven't heard anything from her since I left her this morning."

"Was she supposed to check in with you?"

She sighed into the mouthpiece, the way she does when something I've said has annoyed her. "She was still sleeping when I left her house. I left a note asking her to call and let me know she was all right, or if she needed me to do anything for her." There was a pause. "I think we should go back to her house, just to make sure she's okay."

I looked at my watch. Eight fifty-five. Not late enough to beg off until tomorrow. I said, "Do you want me to meet you there, or should I pick you up on the way?"

"I'm already in my car. I'll meet you there."

"Works for me," I told her. "I'll be there in twenty minutes."

* * *

I had just parked in front of Sarah's house when Maggie drove up behind me in her silver Volvo station wagon. I got out of my car and walked back to meet her. I couldn't have said exactly why, but all at once, I got an uncomfortable feeling that things were about to go very, very wrong. The lights were on inside the house, and Sarah's car was in the driveway, but even standing in the street, I could see the front door was slightly ajar, maybe an inch, maybe two.

Not good.

I told Maggie to stay put near her car and call Sarah's number. She started to give me an argument, but I cut her off with a wave of my hand. "Just do it," I said. "And stay here until I can figure out what's going on."

Then, I turned and walked up to the front porch. Without touching the doorbell button or the doorknob, I nudged the door open a bit further with my foot to take a look inside.

Sarah's phone was on the side table next to the sofa, and I could hear the ringtone from Maggie's call. And Sarah was home, sure enough, but she wasn't able to pick up the phone, not then, and not ever again. I found her face down on the living room floor, right in front of the sofa. There was still damp blood in her hair, on the side of her face, and on the carpet around her head, suggesting that she had been struck with great force by an object of some kind on the side of her head. One of her shoes was off, lying on the floor about two feet from her body. There was no blood on her hands, so that, whatever was the impact that killed her, it was hard enough that she lost consciousness immediately, with no chance to even try to protect herself against any following blows, if there had been any. More out of force of habit than anything, I pressed my finger to her throat, to see if I could feel a pulse. Nothing, and her skin was cool to the touch, indicating she had been dead for at least a couple of hours.

Once, near the beginning of my time as a Metro PD detective, I briefly side-kicked with a senior homicide detective whose regular partner was on vacation. One night, we caught a case involving a shooting at a home in an up-market residential area. When we arrived on the scene, we found a woman and her three children, all dead from a single, small-caliber gunshot wound to the chest. It was as if the shooter was making sure that the bodies would not be damaged in such a way that they would not look good in repose at their respective funerals.

We found the shooter in another part of the house, missing most of the left side of his head. When he took his own life, instead of a small-caliber pistol, he positioned the barrel of a twelve-gauge shotgun under his chin and pulled the trigger. My partner surmised that the man had decided that, in his final moments of life, as a macabre form of paying his penance forward, he wanted to make sure that his would be a closed casket. That way, he would not be seen in the company of his wife and children, whose lives he had so brutally ended during a fit of unfathomable violence.

As the story unfolded over the ensuing days, it turned out that the man had lost his high-paying executive position with a local manufacturer of aircraft components and had been out of work for several months. Unable to find comparable new employment, by degrees, he became more and more depressed and more and more angry and abusive. Finally, his wife let him know that she had had enough. She was leaving and taking the kids with her. And so, on that particular night, he decided to end it all for all five of them.

The old cops, the ones who have been there the longest and seen all there is to see, will tell you that after a while, you get used to the sight of death. I never did. On this occasion, after finding Sarah Bergman lying dead on the floor of her living room, I said a silent prayer, in hopes that she would find peace in whatever afterlife she believed in. It took me less than thirty seconds to do that, just long enough time for Maggie to get out of her car, come up the walk, and enter the room.

So much for staying put.

I have to hand it to her. Maggie is not easily thrown off her game. She didn't scream. She didn't faint, and she didn't rush to where Sarah's body lay on the floor. She just stood next to me and stared. Finally, she looked at me. The expression on her face was one that suggested she thought perhaps there was something I could do to make things right.

"Gamble?"

I shook my head. "Nothing we can do. She's been dead for some time. The police need to be notified, and you need to not be here."

She started to argue with me, but now was not the time. "I know you want to help, and I know Sarah was your friend, but until we have some idea of who did this to her and why, it would be better all the way around if you weren't involved. So, right now, I want you to get in your car and go home. I'll call the police and wait for them to get here. By the time the uniforms show up, and then the detectives, and then somebody from the medical examiner's office, if they don't arrest me with murder, it'll likely be after midnight before I can get away. I'll call you when they're finished with me, and we can figure out where we want to go from there. But I promise, we will find whoever did this and make them pay."

She looked at me. I said, "Do you believe me?"

"Yes."

"Then go. Do it now."

I waited until Maggie was down the road, and then I called the cops. Since I had a little time, and without touching anything, I took a quick look around the house, hoping I might find something the killer might have used to bash in Sarah Bergman's skull. I supposed he could have used a fireplace tool, but there were no bloodstains or strands of her hair on the shaft of either the poker or the shovel. Finding nothing, I went into the kitchen, the only other place I thought there might be something heavy enough, like a cast-iron skillet, to do the job. But there was nothing that looked out of place. A perfunctory trip through the garage also yielded nothing. There was a lawn mower, a weed whacker, and a plastic bucket filled with gardening tools. My instinct was to do a more thorough search, but I was worried the cops would show up before I finished poking around. That, I knew, would have set off a round of questioning I didn't want to have to deal with. So, instead, I went back outside to my own car to sit tight until the police arrived.

It took about ten minutes for the uniforms to make their appearance, lights but no siren. I knew that first-on-the-scene cops tend to be a little bit edgy, especially since there's always a possibility that the perp is still nearby. With that in mind, while I waited, I removed my shoulder rig and locked it in the trunk of my car. I am licensed to carry, but it didn't seem like a good idea to involve a couple of beat cops in a discussion about what reason I might have for running around armed in a residential neighborhood after dark, especially when there was a body not fifty feet away.

When the uniforms finally did show up, there were two of them, one young, one older, driving a standard blue-and-white MNPD prowl car. When they pulled in behind me, I got out of the car and stood still, holding my hands well away from my body. The older of the two, a sergeant and a training officer, I guessed, was a black man, mid-forties, broad across the chest, with imposing biceps and sergeant's stripes on his sleeves. The other cop was a younger white guy who looked to be not more than a month or two out of the academy. His hat, I noticed, seemed to be a size too large for his head. In another era, he could have been Barney Fife.

"You the one called this in?" the older cop asked.

"I found the body, yes."

"So then, are you saying she was alive when you found her?" the younger cop asked me.

"Yeah," I said, "that's exactly it. I found her alive. But I didn't have all night to wait around, and I knew you'd get here faster if she was dead, so I just went ahead and finished her off so we could move things along." I turned and stared at him in disbelief. "What the fuck is the matter with you?"

"New guy," the old cop said. "You got some I.D.?"

"I'm a licensed private investigator," I told him. "I'm going to reach inside my jacket and remove my license and identification, which I will then hand over to you. I'm telling you this now so there's no misunderstanding about what's happening here."

"Right." The big cop nodded and placed his right hand on his weapon. "You armed?"

"In the trunk of my car. I don't want anybody getting nervous for no reason."

"Appreciate that." I handed him my PI license, identification, and carry permit. He studied all three for a moment, then handed them back.

"You say there's a body."

"Inside," I said. "Ready to go take a look?"

While his partner waited by the car, the officer, whose name was Carroll, and I entered Sarah Bergman's living room. I said, "The door was partly open when I got here. I haven't touched anything, although I was visiting her last night, so there are probably a few of my prints here in the living room. I can tell you the victim's name is Sarah Bergman. I had another appointment with her this evening."

"An appointment to do what?" His tone left little doubt as to what he thought the answer would be.

"She had a job she wanted me to take on. Something belonging to her went missing. She wanted me to try to locate it for her. When I got here, the front door was open. I found things just the way they are now."

"Got it," he said. "Let's go back outside and wait for the detectives. You can sit in your car if you want. But first, give me the keys."

By the time we got outside, a small crowd of neighbors had gathered in the street and on the sidewalk in front of Sarah's home. Several people were pointing and staring at me, likely on the assumption that whatever had happened inside the house, I had something to do with it. And in a way, I guess maybe I did.

It didn't take long for the homicide detectives to show up, and, as it sometimes happens, I knew them both. The senior man was former Sergeant, now Lieutenant John Spillner. I knew him from back when I was still on the job, and we had crossed paths a few times since then. He was an okay guy as cops go, tall, lanky, several years north of fifty, and long since eligible for retirement. He was wearing a yellowish-tan suit that could have used a pressing, a yellow shirt, and a red-and-brown striped tie pulled loose at the collar. His partner was a black woman named Lorraine Proctor. She was tall, like Spillner, and dressed in dark gray slacks, an ivory-colored blouse, and black leather Sketchers work shoes. She also wore a .40 caliber Glock on her right hip. I had only met her two other times, once when I was cooling my heels in a temporary lockup and once when we were working separately on an investigation that had left a number of people dead before it finally reached a conclusion.

"Mister Gamble," she said when she spotted me. "As I live and breathe. What sort of mischief have you gotten yourself into this time?"

Carroll, the big uniform, said, "We got a body. A woman named," he paused to check his notebook, "Sarah Bergman. Your friend Mr. Gamble here says he found her already dead and called it in. Says he had an appointment with the victim. According to him, when he got here, the door was open, so he went inside. Also says he didn't touch anything."

He flipped the cover of his notebook shut and put it back in his pocket. "It appears she was struck from behind, but there doesn't seem to be any sign of a struggle, so maybe the killer took her by surprise. We took a look around, but we didn't see anything that looked like it could have been a murder weapon."

"Anything seem like it might have been taken? Television, computer, anything like that?"

"Doesn't look like it," Carroll said. "'Course, the killer coulda been careful, wiped everything down before he left."

"So probably not a burglary. And no nine-one-one call, either. I'm guessing whoever did this was somebody she knew, so she let him in," said Spillner. To Sergeant Carroll, he said, "How about you and your partner poke around a little outside the house. Maybe talk to the neighbors, find out if anybody noticed anything. Rest of us, let's go on inside and visit for a little bit. See what we can figure out."

Spillner and Proctor followed me into the house. Spillner waited while Detective Proctor took a quick tour through the rest of the house. She was gone about five minutes. When she returned, she went over to Sarah Bergman's body, knelt down on one knee, and placed the palm of her hand on Sarah's forehead. Then she leaned over and said something in a voice too low for me to hear. After that, she stood up and walked back over to where Spillner and I were standing.

"I didn't see anything right off that looks out of place," she said. "It could be a home invasion gone bad, I guess, but there are no open windows, and the back door is locked. It's hard to say whether anything's missing, but the usual stuff all seems to be where it belongs." She turned to me. "The officer says you told him you had an appointment with the victim. Said you told him she lost something she wanted you to find. You mind telling us what that was all about?"

"Not at all. Mrs. Bergman was a client. Her husband went missing a while back, and she asked me to look into it. I was just stopping by to bring her up to date on my investigation so far."

Spillner said, "Missing how?"

I shrugged. "How many ways are there? Isaac Bergman was a professor at Saint Bernadette University. He went to work one day and never came home. He'd called his wife earlier that same day to say there was a meeting and he'd be late, only there was no meeting. He just went off someplace, and nobody has heard from him since. A short time after that, his car turned up, wrecked, in a salvage yard in LaVergne."

"Interesting. And just exactly how long has this guy been missing?"

"Four years."

There was a beat. "Wait a minute," said Spillner, "you're saying this guy has been gone four years, and his wife was just now getting around to asking you to look for him?"

"I said the same thing when I first talked to her. If you're asking why I think she waited all this time, I haven't got the first idea. She said she still loved him and wanted him back in her life. That's about the best I can tell you."

"That's very touching," said Spillner. "How about if you take it from the top and lay this out for us? What you've been telling us so far doesn't make a whole lot of sense."

So, I walked the detectives through the case so far, starting with my visit from Sarah Bergman earlier in the week and continuing through my discussions with Robert Levy, Phillip May, and Detective Marvin Calvert. I didn't go into detail about how eager Calvert seemed to be to help out, thinking that information might not sit too well with his higher-ups. I also left out the part about Maggie being friends with Sarah Bergman, or her being with me when we found the body.

"You know, Mr. Gamble," Lorraine Proctor said, folding her arms across her chest. "I've met people who collect baseball cards, or stamps, or antique Christmas tree ornaments. But you? It looks to me like what you collect is dead bodies. You might want to think about finding another hobby."

"You're probably right," I told her. "But she wasn't dead when she first came to me."

"Cute. Any idea why she picked you and not somebody else?"

"Friend of a friend," I said. "I get a lot of referrals."

"And does this friend have a name?" Lorraine Proctor asked.

"I asked," I lied. "She didn't want to tell me."

"I see. And so far as this missing person case is concerned, up to now, it sounds like you've got nothing, is that right?"

"An hour ago, I would have said so. But the fact that somebody wanted Sarah dead tells me that there's something more to this story than what I just got finished telling you. As I understand it, missing persons looked into the disappearance at the time, but they weren't able to come up with anything concrete."

Spillner said, "So, what? You're an outraged taxpayer now?"

"No. I'm sure they did their best. But now, with Sarah getting killed right after she asked me to take another look at the case, that tells me that there was, and may still be, something else going on with her husband's disappearance."

"Something like what?"

"I don't know, but I'd say whoever killed her doesn't want anybody to find out what it is. Now, we've got a dead woman, and it's your job to find out who killed her. I'll help you any way I can with that. But Sarah hired me to find out what happened to her husband, and that's what I intend to do."

"Noble of you," said Lorraine Proctor. "Did Mrs. Bergman pay you any money?"

"No, she didn't. I told her I wanted to make a few inquiries first."

"Well, from what you've told us so far, you did that, and you've come up empty." She paused to let that sink in. "I guess for the time being, you're free to do whatever you want, but I want to remind you, in case it might have slipped your mind, that you are no longer a police officer, and you are certainly not on the homicide desk. Other than that, you can look for this missing husband to your heart's content, as long as it doesn't get in the way of our investigation. But the way I see it, under the present circumstances, you no longer have a client."

After that, we waited until a team from the medical examiner's office arrived, together with the Metro CSI unit. It took another two hours until all the crime scene photos were taken, and the doorknob, the window sills, and the hard-surfaced furniture in Sarah's living room all were dusted for prints. Then Sarah's corpse was placed in a body bag and rolled out the door on a gurney and into a waiting ambulance. I agreed to show up at police headquarters the next morning to make a statement and then to drop by the morgue with the detectives to make a formal identification. By the time we were finished and I was heading for my car, a crew from one of the local television stations was on scene and shoving a microphone and a camera into the face of every neighbor who might be looking for a few moments of fame.

* * *

My plan was to wait until I got home to telephone Maggie and let her know how it went with the cops. But as it turned out, I didn't have to, because she was already there, waiting for me. When I unlocked the front door, I found her asleep on the living room couch with the television tuned to one of the high cable channels that plays music. I used the remote to turn the TV off, then shook her awake.

"They didn't arrest you?" she asked. Her voice was thick with sleep. "I was looking forward to taking a selfie with you in an orange jumpsuit."

"Not tonight anyway, but don't lose hope just yet, because they're going to want to talk with me again in the morning. I have to make a statement and then a formal identification at the morgue."

"Tell me what else."

So, I gave her a blow-by-blow recounting of my conversations, first with the uniformed cops and then, later, with Detectives Spillner and Proctor. I made it a point to emphasize that I had left her name out of both discussions, but cautioned her that they'd inevitably start looking through Sarah's address book and dump her phone, and after that it was a sure bet that they would get around to talking with her.

"When they do," I said, "just remember that as far as tonight is concerned, you were never there."

Chapter Thirteen

Not surprisingly, my telephone rang early the following morning. The call was from Dick Dohrn at the *Times*, wanting to know the details about how I found the body of Sarah Bergman. "We want to run the story on page one."

"Above the fold, or below?"

"Below, what do you think? We're not talking about Stringbean Ackeman here. And I guess I should start by asking whether you're a suspect," he said.

"No, and at this point, I don't think the cops have one, either." So, off the record, I walked him through the sequence of events that took me to Sarah Bergman's home on Tuesday evening and how I found her front door partially open and her lifeless body on the living room floor. I also gave him the names of the two detectives, Spillner and Proctor, to make his follow-up a little simpler. I figured I owed him something in exchange for the help he'd extended to me over the years. On the other hand, I left out any mention of Maggie being there with me when I discovered the body.

"Any idea how she was killed?"

"Not yet. The guys from the M.E.'s office showed up while I was still there. The only thing they found right off was that she'd suffered a blow to the head. There was blood on the carpet where she fell, so I guess that must have been what it was."

"Okay." He was quiet for a moment, and I thought I heard him tapping his pencil on his desktop.

"Let me ask you something, Jackson. Based on our earlier conversation, do you think her murder had something to do with the disappearance of her husband, what was it? Four years ago?"

Now, it was my turn to be quiet. I said, "This is strictly off the record, but I think it's possible there's a connection, either because somebody thinks she knew something, or because they were afraid something would come to light as a result of my investigation."

"Well, okay, but if that's the case, wouldn't it have been simpler just to kill you?"

* * *

An hour later, the murder of Sarah Bergman was all over the television news. According to the report, Maggie and I watched over a breakfast of English muffins—mine was spread with crunchy peanut butter and a Diet Coke to wash it down. Maggie opted for regular butter with grape jelly and a glass of orange juice—the story was that the body had been found sometime late the previous evening and that homicide detectives had been alerted by "a close friend of the deceased." Sarah was described in the report as a single woman living alone who was self-employed as a family services counselor. At that point, the report went on to say, the police had no leads, no witnesses, and no motives for what was described as "a brutal attack." Oh, and, no surprise, all her neighbors described her as "a lovely person who didn't have an enemy in the world." Except, of course, for the individual who killed her.

Maggie picked up the remote and turned off the television. "Are you happy or upset that they left your name out of it?"

"You mean, as opposed to a 'close friend of the deceased'? Probably better they didn't mention me. I doubt it would be good for business for prospective clients to learn the guy they're thinking of retaining has a talent for tripping over dead bodies."

She sat quietly for a moment, sipping her orange juice. "Gamble? I know Sarah wasn't exactly a close friend, but she was a good person, and I liked her."

"I understand."

"Last night, you told me you'll find out who killed her and why. Do you think you can do that?"

"Honestly?" I said. "Probably not. I have no police power, and I only worked a homicide case one time when I was on the job. I'll do what I can, but if anybody finds the killer, it'll almost certainly be the police. They have far more resources than I do, and they can elbow their way into places I can't. Also, I know those two detectives. They're very good at what they do."

"But will you at least try?"

"Yes."

She put down her glass and folded her hands on the table. "Can I ask you something else?"

"Anything."

"If it was me instead of Sarah, lying dead on the floor with my throat cut, or a knife in my chest, would you still just try?"

At first, I thought she was just putting me on, but the look on her face said her question was a serious one. And I realized she was still not completely over the experience she had a few years earlier when she came very close to being just another murder victim on her own living room floor.

"If it were you, I would buy the biggest gun I could find, and then I would kill every son of a bitch that I thought had even a remote chance of being guilty, just to be sure I didn't overlook anybody."

She smiled as if she was the happiest person in the world. "That's what I like about you. You always know just the right thing to say."

* * *

Part of the arrangement Maggie and I have is that we each keep a necessary amount of extra clothes and toiletries at one another's places of residence to make our semi-regular sleepovers more convenient. In my case, that means I have a clean shirt and clean underwear, plus deodorant, toothpaste, a toothbrush, and a disposable razor at her place. In Maggie's case, that means a sufficient number of blouses, shoes, skirts, hosiery, slacks, and outerwear, plus underwear, cosmetics, and personal hygiene products to keep her going for at least a week. However, mine is a small house with only one bathroom, so I waited and read the morning paper for the better part of an hour while Maggie got set to go to work. The story about the murder of Sarah Bergman had not made the morning edition.

On my way downtown, as promised, I dropped by police headquarters, where I spent a couple of hours with Spillner and Proctor in an interrogation room equipped with video and audio recording equipment going back over my version of the events of the previous day, leading up to, and concluding with, the death of Sarah Bergman. At no point did I lie about anything that had happened, although I did leave out a few facts, including that Maggie had been with me at the time I found the body. I was pretty sure the omission might cause me a bit of trouble down the road, once the cops found out about her being there. But I figured nothing much would ultimately come of it since her presence didn't affect the circumstances of Sarah's death. On my way out, I ran into a couple of uniforms, frog-marching what appeared to be a very drunk and disorderly individual through the entrance doors. As I stepped aside to clear their path, the guy looked at me and said, "The fuck you looking at?" and tried to kick me, but the two unis pulled him back before he was able to connect.

All in a day's work, I thought.

After that, I reported to the medical examiner's office, where I formally identified the body of Sarah Bergman. The viewing area was cold and dimly lit and separated from where Sarah's body was laid out by a gray cinder block wall with a wide window that was covered by a curtain. After a moment, an attendant opened the curtain to reveal a body completely covered by a sheet. I nodded my head and the attendant pulled back the sheet to reveal the face of the woman on the table. It took me a minute to recognize that the body beneath the sheet was the same vivacious woman who had hired me only a few days earlier. Her face had been washed clean of makeup and was without expression so that she looked more like a wax effigy than a real person. I stared at her for a moment, then nodded my head. Yes, that was Sarah. Then I signed a couple of forms and took my leave, my official duties complete.

* * *

It was close to noon by the time I finally got to the office, where I found I had a small stack of mail, three telephone messages, and a surprise visitor waiting for me. The calls and the mail could wait, I decided. My visitor could not. I found him sitting on the couch I keep in the outer office, thumbing through a year-old copy of *Guns and Ammo*. If I hadn't known better, I would have said he was just another prospective client in need of whatever service I might have been able to provide. But in this instance, I did know better, and the individual waiting in my office was not just another customer. His name was Robert Edward Cherry, and he was someone who definitely needed to be taken seriously—and not kept waiting.

Red Cherry and I had crossed paths once before, about a year earlier. At that time, he was indirectly involved with a group that was backing my old boss, former Davidson County District Attorney Roger Seacrist, as a candidate for the governor's office. I was working on what started out as an unrelated investigation that had accidentally revealed that a substantial portion of the money the campaign had raised had come by way of a contribution from Cherry. To keep that information out of the newspapers and hence far away from public scrutiny, I had been offered a cushy job with the Seacrist campaign. I turned the offer down, which was just as well, since Roger lost the election in a squeaker.

What made Red Cherry's contribution problematical was that he was not just another political brown-nose, snuffling after an appointment to some mid-level state government post after Roger took office. In fact, Red, like Tommy Mack, was a career criminal, only on a scale Tommy couldn't even begin to dream of.

Interestingly, Red was not a native of Tennessee. In fact, he started out hundreds of miles away, as an apprentice wise guy, part of a loosely-organized outfit that operated all along the Gulf Coast, from New Orleans to Pensacola. The Mississippi Mafia, also known informally as the "Corn-pone Cosa Nostra," traced its origins to the late 1960s, and was initially headquartered in Biloxi, a town with a rich outlaw heritage of its own. In fact, crime was so rampant in the area that the FBI at one time designated the Harrison County sheriff's department as a criminal enterprise.

The Mississippi Mafia specialized in gambling, prostitution, loan-sharking, drug dealing, murder-for-hire, and intimidation of public officials. Taken together, it was a combination that all but guaranteed that any high-ranking member would be able to avoid being convicted of anything, either by a hung jury or an outright acquittal. It was also alleged to have been responsible for the murder of Buford Pusser, the one-time sheriff of McNairy County, Tennessee, whose story was immortalized in the movie *Walking Tall*.

Unlike the actual Cosa Nostra, the Mississippi Mafia was never united by ethnic heritage, or a blood oath of any kind. It did, however, have one unbreakable rule, "Thou shalt not snitch to the cops." It also took great pains not to interfere with the business activities of one Carlos Marcello, at the time the head of a real Mafia crime family based in New Orleans. Red Cherry, meanwhile, through a combination of cunning, determination, and eye-popping ruthlessness, eventually worked his way to the top of the organization. In one particularly gruesome instance, one of his victims was found impaled on a steel pipe in his own front yard. His hands and feet had been hacked off, and his genitals were found stuffed down his throat. The message in that instance was clear: Red Cherry was not a man you wanted to screw around with.

In the chaos that followed in the wake of Hurricane Katrina, the Mississippi Mafia more or less disintegrated, but not before Red was handed a twenty-five-to-life jolt for the assassination of some ADA in New Orleans who had been sniffing a bit too enthusiastically around his crew. It took a while, but eventually the organization's attorneys got the conviction overturned on some technicality or other, and Red was granted a new trial. However, before a second jury could be impaneled, the body of one of the two key witnesses in the case was discovered by a couple of fishermen floating face-down in Bayou Sauvage, a National Wildlife Refuge in New Orleans. The other witness, who was already in witsec, met an equally suspicious death when the vehicle he was driving inexplicably collided with

Amtrak's *Empire Builder* passenger train at an unsignaled grade crossing somewhere in eastern Washington State.

With no other witnesses available, the judge in the case had no choice except to dismiss the murder charge against Red for lack of evidence. That left him free as a bird to resume his life without so much as a speeding ticket on his record. Not long after that, he relocated his operation to Nashville.

Since getting settled in his new hometown, Red Cherry lost no time becoming something of a local celebrity. And his sketchy resume notwithstanding, he quickly emerged as a popular and frequently sought-after guest at certain Music City society functions. To all appearances, he is outwardly charming and accessible and is widely celebrated as a contributor to such worthy local organizations as the Performing Arts Center, the Middle Tennessee Historical Society, and even the National Organization of Women. More recently, he's gotten behind the Black Lives Matter movement in a big way, though not without eyebrows being raised in certain quarters.

And now here he was sitting in my office. And I couldn't imagine why.

Appearance-wise, he hadn't changed much in the year or so since I'd last seen him. For a man in his mid-fifties, he looked exceptionally fit, as if a rigorous workout was part of his daily routine. He had a million-dollar tan and was dressed like a man who had both money and taste and didn't care who knew it. Today, he wore a maroon silk shirt, no tie, a gray, four-thousand-dollar Brunello Cucinelli suit with lighter-gray pinstripes, and calfskin Paul Parkman casual loafers.

Just to get the conversational ball rolling, he said, "I suppose you're wondering what I'm doing here, right?" He spoke in a clear, unaccented voice that could have landed him a job as an anchor at any network newscast.

"It's as if you read my mind," I told him. "And now I guess you're going to tell me."

"I am. But first, let me ask you a question." He took a notepad and a Sharpie out of his inside jacket pocket and wrote something on the top sheet.

"If it's not too personal, how much money do you make in a typical year?"

When I didn't say anything, he went on. "I guess that means it's personal."

He tore off the paper and passed it across the desk.

"Does that look about right?"

It was a depressingly small, familiar number. "If you already know, why ask?"

"Just making sure. How would you like to make more? I'm talking quite a bit more."

I said, "Tell me this isn't heading where I think it is."

"Maybe it is, maybe it isn't. You're still working for that idiot bail guy, Sadler, right?"

I shrugged. "Hard to say. I don't think he's very happy with me right now."

"Because of that Tommy Mack thing, am I right? So how about on this one, you work for me instead?" He wrote down another number and showed it to me. "How would you like to make that much? All at one time, in cash, and off the books if you want it that way. It would take you six months to earn that much doing what you do now, and then you'd still have to pay the taxes. You can even have it in advance, today, right now, if you want."

I again looked at the number he had shot me. Just thinking about it was enough to bring tears to my eyes.

"I'm not going to clip the guy, and I'm not going to set him up so one of your guys can clip him, either, if that's what you're wanting me to do, Mr. Cherry. I don't do that kind of work."

"Call me Red," he said. "Listen, I know you've got this other thing you're working on, this university guy that went missing a few years ago. What I want is for you to forget about that case. Mister Chips is gone for good; take my word for it." He paused meaningfully. "And anyway, I just saw on the news that the woman who hired you to find him got killed, so I'm pretty sure she doesn't care whether you find him or not."

"What, did you talk to the cops?"

"I have a lot of contacts. Word gets around. So, how about if you let that one go, and spend all your available time finding the little bastard that broke into my house. When you do find him, you don't need to bring him in, or whatever it is you do when you locate a skip. Just call this number." He paused and wrote down a telephone number. "And let whoever answers know where he is."

"That jewelry he took is really that valuable?" I asked.

He made a noise that could have been a laugh. "Far from it. My grandparents never had any real money. That stuff he took is worth about as much as the scrap value of the stones and the gold. Hardly anything. But guys like Tommy Mack, they need to understand they are not welcome in my home without an invitation. That is something I need to impress upon him in the strongest possible way."

"Right," I said. "And just out of curiosity, how likely is he to walk out of the meeting in one piece? Or even walk out at all?"

He shook his head. "Not something you have any reason to worry about." He got up to leave. "If you need to, think about my offer for a day or two, then let me know. You can call that same number and let me know what you decide. I'm really hoping we can do business together."

* * *

After Red Cherry left, I went out into the hall, and walked the length of it and back again. I didn't have anywhere I needed to be, I just needed to burn off the adrenaline-fueled jitters brought on from my last conversation. I knew I wasn't in any personal danger from Red. I certainly hadn't done anything to incur his ire, unless you counted my inability up to this point to locate Tommy Mack. Still, spending part of a morning with a jungle cat, even a tame one on its best behavior, is enough to get anyone's pulse racing.

When I returned to the office, I checked the phone messages in my voicemail. One was from Phillip May, asking if I could call him back when I got a chance. Remembering that my first conversation with him had ended somewhat abruptly, I thought maybe he had decided there was some additional information he was willing to share with me. I wrote down the number and set it aside to listen to the other two messages.

The second call was from Marvin Calvert, the missing persons detective I had spoken with on Tuesday afternoon. He said he was sorry it had taken so long, but that he had some information for me, although he didn't think it would be of much help. The third was from Wanda Beaudry. I hoped she was calling to let me know she had turned up something on Isaac Bergman. But I knew it might also be for another reason. I hoped I was wrong about that.

Before returning telephone calls, I took a moment to look through the mail. Most of it was junk, including an offer for a walk-in bathtub and a couple of solicitations asking for donations to the Humane Society and to the Save the Whales organization. Mixed in with all of that was a handwritten envelope with a return address that I recognized right away. When I opened the envelope, I found a check for three thousand dollars—six days' work—made out to me and signed by Sarah Bergman. It was dated the day before her death.

That meant I had a client, after all.

Chapter Fourteen

eading north on Interstate 65 in the black Audi he had stolen from Abigail Crowley, Tommy Mack decided his best chance to get clear of Red Cherry once and for all was to drive to Chicago and get lost among the more than eight million people living between Gary and Milwaukee. In fact, he only got as far as Bowling Green, Kentucky, before he began to get homesick. He also noticed that there was only about a half of a tank of gas left in the car, and he knew if he stopped at a filling station along the I-state, there would almost certainly be security cameras at the pump islands. And before long there would also be a BOLO—be on the lookout—for the Audi, meaning the cops would be looking. And so, in the small hours of the morning, at the interchange at I-65 and U. S. Highway 68, he turned around and started back toward Nashville. When he got into town, he drove the Audi through a car wash before dropping it back in the same lot where he had stolen it earlier in the evening. Then he wiped down the steering wheel, the shift lever, and any other surfaces he might have touched to ensure he'd left no prints.

Ever the gentleman, he left a short note that included both a thank-you and an apology on the front seat, along with twenty dollars to pay for the overnight parking and the gas he used. He fished a ballpoint pen out of the glove compartment and copied down an address he found there on the palm of his hand. Then he locked the car, threw the keys into the trunk, closed it, and started walking. On foot, it would take him well into the afternoon to get to where he was headed next.

***

After Red Cherry took his leave, the first call I made was to Phillip May. He picked up on the third ring.

I said, "This is Jackson Gamble, returning your call."

"Mister Gamble, thanks for getting back to me." There was a pause. "I wanted to apologize for being short with you the last time we spoke. I'm afraid I was having a difficult day, and, well, I don't know where my manners went. Anyway, I'm sorry for that."

I waited.

"Also, I was wondering if you could come by my office sometime this afternoon. My last class is at one-thirty, so any time after, say, three o'clock would be good. That is, if it's not too much trouble."

"No trouble at all," I said. I promised to be there and hung up.

My second call was to Marvin Calvert. As he had indicated in his voice message, he had some information for me.

"Okay, thanks for getting back to me. First things first. I poked around a little to see what I could find on your man Bergman, and most of it you already know. His wife reported him missing when he failed to return home after what he said was a regular faculty meeting. She didn't call missing persons right away, she said, because sometimes those meetings ran late, and when they did, he would just go ahead and sleep in their guest bedroom rather than wake his wife. So, it wasn't until the next morning that she actually noticed he hadn't come home. That's when she contacted us."

"Did she say whether that was a usual thing? Not coming home, I mean."

"The case notes don't say, but I imagine if it was a regular thing, she probably would have waited until later that day to call us rather than first thing in the morning."

"Makes sense. What happened after that?"

"Well, the case was assigned to a couple of detectives, Nolan and Sutton. You know either one of them?"

"Sutton, I do. Don't know the other guy."

"Right. Well, to keep it short, it looks like they made the usual rounds.

Talked to people on the campus, including somebody named Phillip May and another guy named Robert Levy. Also, a lawyer named Gannaway."

That name rang a bell, loud and clear. I ran across James Gannaway during the course of a previous investigation involving the sale of a record company called Black Strap Music to a firm called Talent Management Associates. On the surface, it was all very up-and-up, except that the sole shareholder in TMA, as it was called, was one Robert Edward Cherry, the same gangster who had been sitting in my office not fifteen minutes earlier. The financial arrangements of that sale were handled by one James Gannaway, Esquire.

"Anything else?"

"Well, like I said, you already know the rest. Which is to say, there's nothing else to know. The robbery and auto theft detectives checked out the Challenger without finding out anything, except that by the time they got to it, it was in some wrecking yard, pretty well smashed up and missing most of its useable parts. I guess the city went ahead and sent it out for scrap. Apparently, there's some kind of a contract between the city and the yard, and that's where all the unclaimed wrecks end up."

"Okay," I said. "Thanks anyway."

Before I could hang up, Calvert said, "There's one more thing. I was talking with a couple of homicide detectives in the break room yesterday. I mentioned you had called looking for information about somebody named Bergman. Well, it turned out they had just caught a case involving somebody else named Bergman. So, of course, I asked if there was a connection."

"Sarah Bergman," I said. "She was Isaac Bergman's wife."

"Right, that's what I found out. They also said the honest taxpayer who found the body was you. Just out of curiosity, is there anything more to it than that?"

"You mean, did I kill her and then call it in? No."

"Didn't think so. Anyway, I thought as long as I was looking into the earlier case for you, you might want to hear about the medical examiner's preliminary report on this one."

"What is there to hear? Somebody bashed her in the head."

"That's correct. Several blows were struck from three-quarters behind with some kind of a cylindrical object. From the look of it, once when she was seated and several more times after she was on the floor. From the shape of the wounds, it looks like the weapon was a piece of pipe, or a broom handle, or the end of a pool cue. Something like that. But if it was wood, it must have been damn hard wood, because there were no wood splinters buried in her scalp."

"Okay."

"But that's not what killed her."

I sat up straight in my chair. "Then what?"

"According to the ME's report, it was hypoglycemia. Insulin poisoning. Either she committed suicide, or somebody helped her on her way, but suicide doesn't seem too likely considering she probably didn't hit herself on the head either before or after she injected the insulin. Anyway, it was a massive overdose. It sent her into a diabetic coma. If she'd gotten a glucose injection within a reasonable time, say two or even three hours, the doc here says that probably would have saved her. As it was, the TOD was around five in the afternoon, and I guess there was no one there to help her. If only somebody had gotten there sooner."

"Yeah," I said. "If only."

* * *

Before heading out to see what Phillip May wanted, I returned the call I had received from Wanda Beaudry. After the customary leave-a-message-and-wait, she called back.

"I wanted to let you know I checked on that Isaac Bergman character you asked about."

"And?"

"I came up empty. NCIC's got nothing, except for the original report that he had gone missing. Other than that, *nada*. There were no records of arrests, criminal complaints, weenie-wagging, not one thing. We also tried Facebook, LinkedIn, Snap Chat, Tik Tok, X, and every other shitty social media outlet we could think of. He didn't turn up in any of them. If he's still around, my guess is he's either changed his name or left the country."

"Or else he's dead," I said, "with no burial record."

"Looks that way, Jackson. Sorry I couldn't do more."

"Don't worry about it. I owe you one."

Yeah, well, about that." There was a pause. "We have a situation here that needs taking care of. I was going to call you anyway, so if now is a good time…."

I felt my heart sink. Any time Wanda asks me for help, it means that one of her clients at the shelter has arrived at the door in a bad way. Most of the time, these women have been abused—mentally, physically, sexually, or some combination of all three. Depending upon the degree of mistreatment, Wanda sometimes feels the need to make amends in kind. When that happens, she takes me along just in case things don't go as planned and she needs backup. So far, nobody has gotten killed. It was my job to make sure it stayed that way.

As she related the story to me, a young *Latina* woman showed up at the shelter several months earlier. She was pregnant at the time and had been badly beaten around her face and on her body. A doctor who donated her time to the shelter was called, and although she determined that the young woman's injuries were not fatal, she lost the baby she was carrying. The police were notified, but the woman, whose name was Rosaria Perez, refused to say anything other than that she had fallen down a flight of stairs. The cops, of course, had seen situations like this one a hundred times before and didn't believe a fall down a flight of stairs had caused her injuries. However, no matter how hard they tried to get at the truth, Rosaria stuck to her story. Under the circumstances, there was no choice except to suspend the investigation. However, they left the case open in the event further evidence turned up, or Rosaria changed her story. Not long after, Rosaria left the shelter and returned to her home, an apartment on the west side of town.

Nothing more happened after that until Rosaria showed up at the shelter for a second time about a week ago. She had been beaten up again, only this time, instead of claiming she'd walked into a door, she opened up to Wanda about what had happened and who was responsible. Rosaria said the man who beat her up, a gangbanger named Victor Robles, was a member of *Los Reyes del Crimen*, or, as it was known on the street, LRC. Rosaria told Wanda she was afraid that if she told the police, the LRC would come after her and kill her. That meant no cops. Wanda said she understood and promised Rosaria that she would not involve the police. Instead, she called me.

"I need to track this bastard down," she told me. "I'll let you know when I find out where he's living.

"And then?"

"Then we'll go and talk to him. Privately. Find out what he has to say. Maybe persuade him to turn himself in. Or at least change his ways."

"What you're telling me, this guy is a gangbanger. I'd say the likelihood of a meaningful conversation is somewhere south of zero."

"Then we'll just have to try something else, won't we?"

* * *

On a normal day, it would have taken about an hour to get from my downtown office to the Saint Bernadette campus in Franklin. Most days, except for rush hour, it's an easy drive down I-65 to the exit at Highway 96. The Interstate mostly follows the alignment of the old Louisville & Nashville Railroad, which wound its way through the hills getting out of town. Sixty years ago, the L&N, whose slogan was "The Old Reliable," dispatched a glamorous fleet of passenger trains through Nashville to destinations like New Orleans, Atlanta, and both the east and west coasts of Florida. Those days are gone, and today, the line belongs to a much larger company called CSX, which, among other things, moves countless coal trains between enormous open-pit mines in the west and any number of electrical generating plants throughout the southeast. Today, one of those trains suffered a minor derailment near the Thompson Lane overpass. And while the spillage did not constitute an environmental hazard, the attendant cleanup activity brought traffic in both directions to a near standstill as drivers crept through a near-mile-long backup to get a glimpse of the goings-on. As a result, I didn't arrive at the university until nearly four-thirty.

I found Phillip May seated behind his desk. Today, he was dressed in a smart-looking long-sleeved lavender dress shirt with a white band collar. An off-white linen sport coat was tossed carelessly across the back of the single visitor's chair.

"Just hang that on the back of the door, if you don't mind."

After I got settled, he said, "Terrible thing about Sarah Bergman. I saw on the news that she'd been murdered. It also said she'd been found by a family friend. Was that you?"

"Yes."

"I'm sorry. I suppose that's not an easy thing."

"No, it's not. It never is."

He hesitated for a moment. "I imagine you talked to the police. Do they have any leads, do you know?"

"They don't generally take me into their confidence, but if I were to guess, I'd say it's doubtful. It's too early. They'll go back and do a thorough search of the house and talk to the neighbors. If nothing turns up, they'll start tearing her life apart. Go through her emails, dump her phone, and track down people she might have been in contact with until they find something they can work with."

"Is that what they usually do? Tear her life apart, I mean?"

"Unless they're able to locate an eyewitness, or an image of the killer on home security video, or somebody confesses, that's about all they can do. I expect since you were friends with the Bergman's, they might get around to talking to you."

He sat up straight in his chair. "Do they have to do that? I mean, why would they want to talk to me?"

I said, "I wouldn't worry about it. They'll want to talk to everybody she knew. It's just procedure."

"Yes, but couldn't you tell them we talked and that I don't know anything that would be of any help to them finding the killer? I mean, they'd listen to you, wouldn't they?"

"Why would they? I'm not a homicide detective, and I'm not working on any murder investigation. Anyway, I don't think you have anything to worry about. I mean, you didn't kill Sarah Bergman, did you?"

It was a throwaway remark, but it seemed to rattle him. "What? No. Of course not. What reason would I have to harm Sarah?"

We were getting off into the weeds. I said, "Professor, it took me nearly two hours to drive out here this afternoon. I did that because you said you wanted to talk to me about something. If it was just to say you're sorry about being short with me the other afternoon, you could have done that over the telephone."

"No, that's not it. I mean, I am sorry, and I did want to tell you that, but that's not the only thing I wanted to talk to you about."

I made a show of looking at my watch. "Then what?"

"I want to ask you—no, that's not right. I wanted to tell you in person that I think it would be better for all concerned if you stopped looking for Isaac. After all, he's been gone all this time, and now Sarah is dead, so why does it matter anymore whether you find him, or even whether he's alive or dead?"

"Well, let me ask you. What difference does it make to you, unless you had something to do with it?"

There was a pause. "It's like this, and this is just between you and me. The last couple of years Isaac was here at the university, he was involved in some rather questionable activities. I'm not at liberty to say more than that, but I can tell you it's part of the reason why he wasn't offered tenure."

"And also, why he was being dismissed at the end of the term?"

"That, too."

"But you can't say what it was."

He shook his head. "No, and it doesn't make any difference any longer. He's gone, and it's over with. But the thing is, if what he was involved in comes to light, it would be a great embarrassment. Not just for him, but also for the university."

"And for you as well, it sounds like."

"I'm asking you to stop. You can interpret that any way you like. I know Sarah paid you, and I'm guessing you're the kind of man who is committed to finishing a thing once he's started it. But if you can see your way clear to do what I ask—for the good of the university, if it helps you to think of it that way—we can make it more than worth your while financially for you to let your investigation drop."

"Who is 'we,' Professor?"

"Does it matter? Let's just say there are other interested parties."

"This is an interesting situation, sir. You're the second person today to offer me money to drop the case. And you're right, integrity does have something to do with it. But now, I'm more interested than ever, because now I'm curious. I want to know exactly what Isaac Bergman did to cause the university to want to be rid of him and what happened to him after that. And if it turns out to be a black eye for the university, or anyone else who's hoping to see this go away, then I'm sorry, and that includes you. But Sarah Bergman paid me to find out what happened to her husband, and that's what I intend to do."

Chapter Fifteen

ince it was Friday, and since I had accomplished little or nothing during the week besides finding the dead body of Sarah Bergman, I decided that my meeting with Phillip May—another exercise in frustration—was as good a point as any to call it a day, and a week. But instead of calling first, I decided to surprise Maggie with a bouquet of flowers and then dinner at the restaurant of her choosing. On the way to her townhouse, I dropped into a florist shop and picked out an arrangement that I thought she would like. It cost sixty bucks out the door and was called "Wonderful Wishes." It included white roses, white clematis, and a contrasting blue flower called agapanthus. I had never heard of it, but Maggie had and wasted no time informing me that it was toxic if ingested, which meant she had to place it somewhere Stanley couldn't chew on it. I suggested she put it in his bowl, instead.

Then she told me about her day, the highlight of which was a visit from Detectives Spillner and Proctor at her office. Exhibiting their usual *politesse*, they badged their way past the receptionist at Children and Family Services and asked to speak with Ms. Margaret Totten.

"They wanted to know why I didn't wait for the officers when they responded to the call."

"And you told them?"

"I said I was upset seeing her like that and that I needed to get away."

"That was a reasonable answer."

"Not as far as they were concerned. They said I should have gotten in contact once I got settled down."

They were right, but I wasn't about to say so, particularly since it was me who had sent her packing in the first place. "How did they even know you were there?"

"A neighbor saw us show up at her home together. Then he saw me drive away. He told the officers he talked to what kind of a car I was driving and even wrote down part of my license plate number."

"And when they ran the partial, your name and the make of your car came up. And Lorraine Proctor knows who you are, and knows you and I are in a relationship."

"Yep." She got up, walked into the kitchen, and opened the refrigerator. "I'm going to make myself a drink. You want a beer?"

"Sure, why not? It's Friday, after all." I watched while she poured a double shot of vodka into a tall glass and then filled it the rest of the way with ice and cranberry juice. A double. Not good.

I waited until she came back into the living room and sat down again. "What happened after that?"

"They wanted to know whether it was me who referred Sarah to you. I said yes, and then I asked whether there was anything wrong with that."

"And they said?"

"Nothing. That Detective Proctor just made a note on a pad she had in front of her. Then, they asked me when was the last time I'd seen Sarah before the night she was killed. I told them Wednesday night. I said you and I had gone to see her and that when the subject of her husband came up, she got upset, so I stayed over with her, and you went home. I called an Uber and left Thursday morning."

I nodded. "Let me guess. They told you that as far as anybody knew, you were the last person to see her alive. After that, they started asking about your relationship with Sarah, and whether there were any problems between the two of you. That sound about right?"

"Almost word for word." She gave me a look. "Gamble, they think I killed her."

I shook my head. "No, they don't. What they do think is that if they can make you nervous enough, you might tell them something you otherwise wouldn't. It's a very common tactic used by cops everywhere. You'd be surprised how often it works."

Maggie finished her drink, and I had another beer. Then we went out for a late supper, and afterward back to her place to watch a late movie, and then hop into bed.

On Saturday, there was a follow-up article in the newspaper regarding the death of Sarah Bergman. In short, it said that, while the investigation was ongoing, the police were forced to concede that so far, there were no solid leads. Further, her body had been claimed by her family, and pending completion of the medical examiner's report, she would be returned to her home back east for burial. A bit further down, and on a related note, there was an announcement that a memorial service for Sarah would be held at the chapel on the campus of Saint Bernadette University the following week. I did not need Maggie to tell me that we would both be attending.

Chapter Sixteen

Monday morning, I was in the waiting room at the offices of Morse, Kaplan, and Jamison, the law firm where Luther Fanning, the lawyer whose name I found in Isaac Bergman's address book, was a partner. Luther was running late. The receptionist, whose name was Ariel Jenkins, informed me that Mr. Fanning was in a meeting with a client and would be with me as soon as they were finished. Yes, Mr. Fanning was aware I had an appointment, and yes, she had told him I was waiting.

"But sometimes these meetings to run long." She gave me a what-can-you-do smile. "I can offer you a cup of coffee while you wait. I'm sure he'll be just a few more minutes." I passed on the coffee and said I was fine. To pass the time, I thumbed through a worn copy of *Smithsonian* magazine. The cover story had to do with Westminster Abbey and the impending coronation of the new King Charles.

A few more minutes turned into half an hour before a red-faced man whom I would have put somewhere on the downhill side of seventy stalked out of a door behind the reception area and exited quick-step, slamming the door behind him. That got me another apologetic smile from the receptionist. A moment later, Luther Fanning appeared in the same doorway recently vacated by the irate client and invited me back to his office.

Just hazarding a guess, I put Fanning's age at sixty-something. At that, he looked fit and healthy, and I noticed there was no ashtray on his desk. So, not a smoker. He wore a blue three-piece pinstriped suit, black shoes polished to a high gloss, a light pink shirt, and a red tie. He had a thin face, a thick head of gray hair, and brown, almost black, eyes. On the wall behind him were several framed diplomas and awards, each lauding him for some noteworthy accomplishment or other.

After we got seated, him behind a massive oak desk and me in a burgundy leather visitor's chair, I handed him my card and showed him my identification.

"I'm working on a case," I said. "I have a couple of questions I'm hoping you can answer for me."

"Right, okay. You know the drill. What's the case, who's the client, and what're the questions?"

"Let's start with this. Isaac Bergman. Was he a client?"

"Is that why you're here?"

"Well, yes and no. I was hired by Mrs. Bergman to look into his disappearance. I found your name in his address book, and I thought…"

He held up his hand. "Let me stop you right there. Isaac Bergman has been gone for several years, and his wife, in case you haven't heard, died last week. From what I read in the papers, she was apparently murdered."

"I know that. It was me that found her body."

"Then I must be missing something. You said just now you were looking for Isaac. Are you also trying to find Sarah's killer?"

"No. I'm leaving that to the police. But Sarah Bergman paid me in advance, and alive or dead, I owe it to her to at least try to find out what happened to Isaac. It won't change anything as far as Sarah is concerned, but it means something to me that I earn the money I get paid."

He appeared to give that some thought. "Okay," he said at last. "Personally, I think you're wasting your time, and you're right. Even if you do find Isaac, alive or dead, it won't make much difference to anybody, except maybe to Isaac, and then only if he's alive." He allowed himself a small smile. "But what the hell? There's no telling what you might turn up, so if you've got some questions, let's have 'em."

Before I could say anything, he spun around in his chair and opened a small refrigerator. He took out two bottles of water, opened one, and handed the other to me. "It's important to stay hydrated," he said. "And I'm sorry, you were about to ask me something."

"Yes. First, I was wondering, did Isaac leave a will?"

"No. I always tell my clients they should take care of that, but Isaac never did anything about it. I guess, like a lot of folks, he figured he'd get to it when the time came. Far as I know, everything he and Sarah owned was held JTWROS—that's joint tenancy with right of survivorship. It's shorthand for saying Isaac wouldn't have to be dead, or even legally declared dead, for Sarah to have access to their assets. Same for Sarah, if she had died first. Bank accounts, stocks and bonds, whatever. Of course, now, assuming Isaac is still alive, and you do find him, then whatever they had jointly—the house, cars, bank accounts, whatever—is legally his. So, in fact, maybe what you're doing could make a difference, at least as far as he's concerned.

"On the other hand, if they're both dead, then they're intestate. That means there is no will. In that case, the estate will go through probate, and the court will attempt to locate relatives. Could be parents, or brothers and sisters, nieces and nephews, right down the line. Eventually, somebody will end up with the money. As I recall, Isaac has a sister somewhere."

"In Indiana," I said. "She's a pediatrician."

"Well, then, there you have it." He sat quietly for a moment, thinking, I supposed. "You said you had another question."

"Yes. I spoke with one of Isaac's former colleagues the other day, and he led me to believe Isaac was planning to initiate some kind of legal action against Saint Bernadette University. I was wondering, would you know anything about that?"

"Well, normally, I wouldn't be able to even discuss that with you, but under the circumstances, I guess now, the whole thing is more or less moot."

"Moot, how?"

He took a swallow from his water bottle. "Isaac Bergman wanted to sue the university for wrongful discharge. He claimed that not only was he being let go without cause, but also that Saint Bernadette should be compelled to grant his tenure."

"And you told him what?"

"That, first of all, tenure at the university level is not like tenure in the public school system, where you just have to hang around for a certain number of years and get satisfactory performance evaluations. Colleges and universities—hell, as far as that goes, even junior colleges—grant tenure entirely at their own discretion, based on whatever criteria they establish. I told Isaac that. I even looked at his contract. He didn't have a snowball's chance in hell."

"And what about wrongful termination?"

"That was a little different. Non-tenured instructors sign an annual contract that spells out the terms under which their employment can be terminated. But there's no guarantee, or even any implication, that contracts automatically roll over. And in any event, he was notified forty-five days before the end of the term, which was also spelled out in his contract. That meant Saint Bernadette could let him go without even having to explain why."

I said, "Do I hear a 'but?'"

"But, just to make sure there were no loopholes, I got in touch with the university's general counsel. As you might expect, he was a little vague on the reasons for Bergman's termination. But he did tell me that there had been certain allegations, and it was for that reason they had decided it was time for him to move on.

"What kind of allegations are we talking about, if I can ask."

"Sex," he said. "It was about sex. And that's all I'm going to tell you about that."

Chapter Seventeen

L a Vergne, Tennessee, is a community of around 35,000 mostly Christian souls, located on U. S. Highway 41, which was once known as the Dixie Highway. Situated on southeast edge of the Nashville metro area, La Vergne straddles one of the several routes of the infamous Trail of Tears, which got its name when, between 1830 and 1850, more than 60,000 Cherokee, Muskogee, Chickasaw, Seminole and Choctaw Indians—the so-called Five Civilized Tribes—were forcibly removed from their original lands and forced to walk some 700 miles to what was then designated as Indian Territory. Along the way, as many as 16,000 men, women, and children died from disease, exhaustion, and exposure to the winter weather.

In later years, La Vergne became known for being a gateway point to a nearby recreational lake called Percy Priest Reservoir, as well as a speed trap for motorists on their way to Chattanooga and Atlanta. Fast-forward to the present day and a more robust LaVergne boasts two nearby auto assembly plants, a Nissan plant that opened in 1983, and a GM facility that began operations in 1990. Today, however, I wasn't looking to snag a new Cadillac or a Nissan Rogue off the end of the assembly line. I was more interested in vehicles that had come to the back end of their useful lives. In particular, I wanted to know whether there was anything left of a red 2015 Dodge Challenger that once belonged to Isaac Bergman. That meant a trip to Long's Auto Salvage, these days operated by brothers Don and Ray Long.

Long's Auto Salvage has been a fixture in the La Vergne area for as long as anyone can remember. Don's grandfather, whose name was originally

Longeneckert, opened for business right after World War II, when a shortage of new cars sent desperate motorists to La Vergne in search of the parts they needed to keep their pre-war jalopies on the road. Later on, the yard became a haven for old car buffs and hot-rodders, scrounging for just the right radiator, carburetor, or transmission needed to restore or otherwise rehabilitate their cherished hobby cars and dirt-track racers. In the present day, thanks to insurance restrictions, browsing the yard is no longer permitted unless, of course, you were tight with one of the brothers.

Which I was.

The windowless yard office was a squat, one-story wood structure that appeared not to have received a fresh coat of paint since sometime during the first Reagan administration. Its outside walls were hung like a bizarre Christmas display with hubcaps from almost any car or truck make you could think of. The once-white walls themselves had long ago faded to gray in the places where the paint hadn't peeled off altogether.

When I walked inside, the first thing I saw was a large, mixed-breed black-and-tan dog named Sparky dozing in front of the counter. Sparky, I knew, was assigned the job of guarding the office after hours. I also knew that it would take a full-frontal attack on the big beast to get him to bite, but he could howl like the hound of the Baskervilles on the moors if he heard an unfamiliar noise, and that would be more than enough to frighten off any but the most determined of burglars. But for the moment, he just opened one eye, gave me a quick up-and-down scan, and went back to sleep to dream about whatever it is dogs dream about.

The guy working the counter today was Don's younger brother, Ray, who, for some reason, preferred to be addressed as Ray-Ray. Call him Ray, and he'd just stare off to one side and pretend he couldn't hear you. Call him Ray-Ray, and he'd smile and give you a handshake with a paw the size of a catcher's mitt. At one time, Ray-Ray had worked for the Rutherford County sheriff's department, but that was before he let himself go and started putting on weight, to the point where he now tipped the scale at better than three hundred pounds. He had a scraggly beard, long, unkempt hair, and today was wearing a denim work shirt, unbuttoned, over a grease-stained tank undershirt.

Over the years, I had gotten to know the Long brothers fairly well, thanks to my making semi-regular trips to their establishment to search for some oddball part or other to keep my geriatric Thunderbird running. The last time I was in, I bought a pair of hubcaps to replace the ones that had somehow gone missing after my car was towed on a night when I ended up in jail over a bogus claim of drunk and disorderly at a Nashville bluegrass bar. It was exactly the right place to come looking, too. Long's Salvage did not now, and probably never would have, parts of any kind for the Panamera. Their yard was filled to the fences with Detroit iron only. It was a point of pride with the Long Brothers, right along with the Confederate battle flag that flew just below the Stars and Stripes on the flagpole in the parking lot.

"Mister Gamble." Ray-Ray looked up from the crossword puzzle he was working on and gave me a gap-toothed smile. Then he let his eyes drift over my shoulder and through the open front door to the parking lot behind. "Please tell me you ain't driving no Yoo-row car." He made a face like he had just bitten into a green persimmon. "I thought we was friends."

"Borrowed it for the day from my lady friend," I lied. "The 'Bird's in the shop for an oil change and fresh plugs."

"Oh, well, I guess that's okay, then. I was afraid you mighta forgot what country this here is."

"Not a chance. And in fact, I'm here about a Dodge. A Challenger, red. Probably been here about four years if you haven't gotten around to running it through the crusher."

"You looking to take on a project, Mr. Gamble?"

I shook my head. "What little I know about that car, it's too far gone for me. I just want to get a look at it."

"Is there a problem with that car? Somethin' I ought to know about? On account of you know, there ain't much of it left anymore. We done stripped out and sold off most of the good stuff. You know, the engine, transmission, rear axle, shit like that, and whatever else we thought somebody could maybe use." He gave me a don't-blame-me look. "I guess you also know that car's trouble, right? I mean, the whole reason it's here is it got stole, and then it got wrecked. Or is that why you're so interested?"

"Something like that, Ray-Ray," I said. "I understand Metro PD towing service delivered it here not long after it was found wrapped around a tree. What I'm wondering is whether anybody besides me came looking for that car after it got here." When he didn't say anything, I said, "Is that a problem?"

"Mister Gamble, me and Don stripped out all the useable parts right after the car got here. Far as I know, that's been it. Now, if you know somethin' I don't, I guess you're welcome to go take a look." He paused for a moment.

"I got to take a piss. I'll be back in a few minutes. But in the meantime, if you was to walk on out through the yard, you might find that car what you're lookin' for, up close to the fence all the way in the back. 'Course, there's another hulk piled on top of it, so you want to be powerful careful 'cause, like the sign says, nobody's allowed back there, and if you happen to get hurt, well, all I know is we were talkin' and the next thing I know, you went off someplace on your own."

"I'll be careful, Ray-Ray. But when I get back, I'd like to see the paperwork you've got for that car." I paused. "Think you might be able to find it?"

Ray-Ray eased his considerable bulk off the stool he had been sitting on and disappeared through a doorway marked "Office." I waited until the door closed behind him and then walked back through the shop into the salvage yard. The first thing I spotted was a large dog run, surrounded by a ten-foot-high chain link fence, where a couple yard sentry dogs, Bert and Ernie, were confined during the daytime. I wasn't quite sure what breed they were, but they were very large, very shaggy, and had barks that sounded like somebody beating on a steel barrel with a pipe wrench. I also knew that, despite their fearsome appearances, they were completely harmless and were more likely to subdue a nocturnal trespasser by bowling him over in hopes of playing with him than by tearing him to pieces. I paused at the enclosure long enough to stick my hand between the gate and the fence post and pet Ernie—Bert was sleeping soundly—and got a handful of dog slobber as my reward.

Back to business, Long's inventory had grown considerably since the last time I had paid them a visit. There were rows upon rows of battered Buicks, ossifying Oldsmobiles, and crapped-out Chryslers, dating from the late 1950s right up to the present day. Some seemed able to be repaired and put back on the road rather easily. Others looked to be total losses, hit perhaps by a speeding freight train, or else rusted beyond the point of no return. But I knew that in every chrome-festooned cadaver, there were at least a few parts still in good working order that could be harvested and returned to service in some other, more roadworthy vehicle.

It took a bit of looking, but sure enough, there was the Challenger right where Ray-Ray said it would be, sitting on the ground underneath a white, late-model Chevrolet Malibu that appeared to have come out second-best in an encounter with a utility pole. And as Ray-Ray had indicated, Isaac Bergman's hotrod Dodge was minus its engine, transmission, differential, wheels, doors, hood, decklid, and rear window glass. The front bucket seats were also missing, as well as the radio and the front console.

It looked as though I had wasted my time. There was nothing left of the red Dodge for me to look at except inside the glove compartment, which was empty, and beneath the back seat, which apparently no one had found a reason to remove. Underneath, I found the paper broadcast sheet, a coded list of all the accessories that were ordered with the car, and which accompanies it down the assembly line. There were a few that I recognized, including Code DEC6, the six-speed manual transmission, Code J, the 6.4-liter V8 engine, and Code PR3, the dazzling "Tor-Red" paint, now badly oxidized and encrusted with grime. But when Don and Ray-Ray stripped the car after it arrived at the salvage yard, they missed what might have been the biggest prize of them all. Because underneath the back seat bottom, tucked in between the springs and the burlap protecting the underside of the vinyl seat cover was a large plastic sandwich baggie partially filled with something that looked like shards of broken glass, or maybe rock candy. But it wasn't either one of those things, I knew. It was crystal methamphetamine, or something a lot like it, and there was enough of it to dose an entire college dormitory. I removed the baggie and put it in my pocket. Then I walked back to the office to find out whether Ray-Ray had managed to come up with the paperwork I'd asked for.

* * *

The "paperwork" documenting the transfer of ownership from Isaac Bergman to Long's Auto Salvage that I'd asked Ray-Ray to dig up turned out to be nothing more than a half-assed bill of sale. It was written in longhand on a single sheet of Nashville Department of Public Works letterhead that read, "Delivered to Long's Auto Salvage, 2015 Dodge Challenger," followed by what looked like a VIN number. No dollar amount was indicated, and there was no signature by Isaac Bergman or anyone else. In other words, the transfer document was completely worthless. Not that I was surprised.

I said, "This is it? This is all you got when the car showed up?"

"Maybe." Then, "Promise you won't tell nobody if I tell you?"

"I'm going to be honest with you, Ray-Ray, just so there's no misunderstanding later on. This car is connected to more than just a case of grand theft auto. You and Don are good guys, Ray-Ray, and I don't want to jam either one of you up, but I found a bag of what looks like crystal meth hidden under the back seat. Now, I don't think that has anything to do with you, and so we're going to forget about that. But this car might also, and I really mean *might*, also be connected to a murder. Whether it is or not depends on who delivered the car here, so if you don't want to say anything, I understand. But depending on how this plays out, it might, and there's that word again, also turn out, you're withholding evidence in a homicide investigation. And if that's the case, well then, once more, you might be screwed."

He looked at me like he was seeing me for the first time. "Are you shittin' around with me, Mr. Gamble, or is all this for the God's truth?"

"I'm not shittin' around, Ray-Ray."

He gave a long sigh, and his massive bulk seemed to settle about a foot lower on his stool. "Well, there's this guy, works for the city. Sometimes, when there's a wreck like this, one that's been totaled, he uses a city truck to bring it out here to us. We give him some money for it, and a receipt, and he keeps half the money and turns the other half back to public works."

So, there it was, a dead end. Just another penny-ante flimflam on the part of some underpaid city employee. Nothing that would take me one millimeter closer to figuring out what happened to Isaac Bergman. If I had to guess, I would have said he left the car somewhere with the keys in it, hoping that either he could report it stolen or, in the event he really was on the run, the car couldn't be used to track him down. The other possibility was that he was dead and that whoever had boosted the car had done the same thing. Either way, I asked Ray-Ray to make me a copy of the bill of sale. Then I thanked him and headed back to town, feeling frustrated and, except for the finding the bag of meth—or whatever it was—like I'd wasted the better part of a day.

And I would have bet more than even money that, before the sun set on this bright afternoon, that Isaac Bergman's forlorn red Dodge Challenger would be fodder for the crusher near the back of Long's Auto Salvage Yard.

* * *

Later that afternoon, when I got back to the office, the message light on my phone was blinking. I took out a pencil and a piece of note paper and pressed the "play" button.

"Mister Gamble, this is James Gannaway. We met about a year ago, if you remember."

I did. James Austin Gannaway was the attorney of record for Red Cherry when he purchased the assets of a recording and producing company called Black Strap Music. At the time of the transfer of ownership, the owner of the record company, a man named Charles Lambert, had seen Black Strap's fortunes sink to rock bottom in the wake of changing musical tastes, followed by some dubious investments that did not pan out. Deeply in debt, Lambert obtained a highly leveraged loan from Red Cherry, only to gamble away that money in a last-ditch effort to save his business. In the end, Cherry gained control of the record company for next to nothing. Lambert died a short time later in an automobile crash that may or may not have been a suicide.

"I do indeed remember, Mr. Gannaway," I said when I returned his call. "What can I do for you?"

"Well, sir, I'll be brief, as I'm sure we're both busy men. However, it has been brought to my attention that a certain client of mine recently presented a business proposition for your consideration. From what I understand, it's a pretty good offer—hell, Mr. Gamble, it's a damn good offer. But the thing is, my client hasn't heard back from you, and he's getting anxious to know if you're fixing to go ahead and take him up on it."

I said, "First, tell me something. When your client came to my office a few days ago, when he made me, what shall we call it? An offer I *shouldn't* refuse? When he made me an offer, he seemed more than a little anxious that I should drop my investigation into the disappearance of Isaac Bergman."

"So? He wants you to work full-time on his proposition."

"To find Tommy Mack, you mean?"

His voice went up a few decibels. "Is that so hard to understand?"

"Not at all. But first, I have a question for you."

"And that is?"

"Just this. At the time Bergman went missing, the police contacted you. I'm wondering why that might be. Why did they do that? Did they have a reason to think you might have information that would help them find him?"

"I'm sorry, but I don't know what you're talking about."

"Okay, fine, thanks for calling," I said and hung up the phone. I got up from my desk and walked down the hall to the soft drink machine. I bought a can of Diet Coke and walked back to my office. When I got there, the phone was ringing.

"I can tell you this much," Gannaway said without preliminaries. "When Bergman went missing, they went through his office phone records. My name came up, so they called. I'm something of a known quantity, and I guess they wanted to know how Bergman and I were connected."

"And what was the connection?"

"My client and your runaway professor were considering a business proposition. As far as I know, nothing ever came of it, so that's all I can tell you."

When I didn't say anything else, he went on.

"Look, Mr. Gamble, I'm sure I don't have to tell you, my client is not someone who's accustomed to being ignored, if that's what you're doing. So, if you don't mind a small bit of advice, if I were you, I'd take the deal. After that, you can go back to doing whatever it is you were working on."

"I understand."

"My client thought you might. He expects to hear from you by the end of the week. Otherwise..." and here, he paused for effect, "...otherwise, he said to tell you he'd have to make other arrangements."

This time, he hung up, leaving me to figure out for myself, as if I didn't already know, what those other arrangements might be.

Chapter Eighteen

A t two o'clock on Tuesday afternoon, Maggie and I attended an informal memorial gathering to mark the passing, and celebrate the life, of Sarah Bergman. Sarah herself was not present except in memory, since the coroner's office had not yet released her remains, pending completion of an official medical examiner's report on her death. Also, as Maggie learned on Monday, Sarah's family in New Jersey had been in contact with the Davidson County ME's office and had requested that her body be returned directly home for burial in her hometown of Scotch Plains.

It took me a while to figure out what I should wear. On a normal work day, unless I need to make a court appearance, or I'm working security for some celebrity at an upscale event, I wear slacks, a button-down cotton dress shirt, and a jacket, which I primarily need to conceal the Colt .380 I carry in a shoulder rig. For today's gathering, I added a necktie and left the .380 at home. Maggie, on the other hand, had no problem selecting an outfit, which today consisted of a simple black dress, a delicate silver necklace, and a silver brooch, plus a .380 of her own, which she carries in her handbag.

The service for Sarah was held in one of the convocation rooms in the Saint Bernadette Student Union building. Maggie and I arrived a few minutes after the scheduled start time and found the room already filled with about fifty people. There were chairs arranged around the walls, along with a buffet table at one end and a podium at the other end for anyone who wanted to offer some kind of remembrance. There was also a table that held photographs of Sarah. Maggie and I took a moment to look at them. Some showed Sarah at home, some at work, and even a few that were taken during her teenage years. She was a pretty girl who had grown into a beautiful woman and whose life had been lost much too soon and much too violently. One way or the other, I knew, she needed to be avenged.

Looking around the room, I spotted Robert Levy sitting in his wheelchair alongside his housekeeper, Roseanne Burgess. I also saw Evelyn Ellis, Phillip May, and a woman I supposed might be May's ex-wife talking with another couple whom I did not recognize. For that matter, I had no idea who any of the other people in the room might be. I assumed they were a mix of some of her neighbors, friends from the university, and maybe a few folks from the high school where she and Maggie had both worked earlier in their careers.

Interestingly, Lorraine Proctor, one of the two detectives assigned to the investigation of Sarah's murder, was also in attendance. In deference to the somber nature of the gathering, she had put on a jacket to at least partially conceal the Glock .40 and handcuffs she had attached to her belt.

While Maggie wandered off to visit with some people she knew, I drifted over to where a small buffet table had been set up with soft drinks, cookies, and assorted pastries. I picked out a few plain sugar cookies, poured myself a cup of something that looked like lemonade, and found a chair near the door where I could stay out of the way and avoid interacting with Sarah's friends. Somehow, my being at the celebration of the life of someone whom it was entirely possible had been killed because she was my client didn't seem quite right. After a moment, Lorraine Proctor spotted me sitting by myself. Perhaps feeling as out of place as I did, she came over and sat down next to me.

"Mister Gamble," she said. "I wondered whether I'd see you here."

"I could say the same thing about you, detective. Or can I call you Lorraine?"

She said pointedly, "Detective will do. And it's a funny thing. You'd be amazed how often perps show up at funerals and memorial services for their victims. I guess maybe it has something to do with taking pride in their work." When I didn't say anything to that, she went on. "How goes your investigation?"

"Are you asking about Sarah, or Isaac?"

She raised her eyebrows ever so slightly. It was a look I'd seen before, and it meant that, despite her pleasant tone of voice, her question was a serious one.

She said, "I thought we agreed last time that you were going to leave the murder investigation to us. Your job was to try and find the husband, if he even still exists."

"A deal is a deal, detective. But to answer your question, it strikes me that our two cases are one and the same. We should be helping one another."

"How do you figure?"

"I think the reason Sarah Bergman was killed is that, when she hired me, she unwittingly reopened the investigation into her husband's disappearance. I think that, whatever happened to him is something that somebody wants to keep secret. And I think that her killer, whoever he is, believes that with Sarah gone, there is no reason for me to keep looking for Isaac."

"So. Is this like, you show me yours, and I'll show you mine?"

"That's one way to put it," I said. "But first, there's something I wanted to ask you. The other night, after you and Spillner showed up at Sarah's house, I noticed you bent down and whispered something into her ear."

"And you want to know what I said to her."

"If you're willing to tell me, yes."

"I told her I was sorry for what happened, and she didn't deserve to have her life ended the way she did. I said we would take good care of her and treat her with respect. And that my partner and I would move mountains, if that's what it was going to take, to find the person who took her life and make that person pay. It's something that I do. It just seems like somebody ought to have a kind word to say to a person who's just gone through the worst experience imaginable." There was a beat. "Now, you first. Have you made any progress tracking down the missing professor?"

I shook my head. "So far, I've got exactly nothing. I have a contact who was able to run a records check and even do a deep dive on social media without finding a single thing, except that he doesn't show up on any of them."

"Meaning?"

"Meaning I think he's probably dead and has been right along. There are a couple people from the university I still want to talk to, but if nothing pans out after that, then I don't know. Maybe we'll have to wait until your cold case unit decides to take a look. How about you?"

"Pretty much the same at this point. We canvassed the neighborhood and scrubbed her phone and her computer without coming up with anything particularly interesting. The next thing is to go through her client files to see if we come up with anybody who might either be holding a grudge, or who has a history of domestic violence.

"Sounds like a reasonable approach." I held out the plate of cookies I'd picked out earlier and invited Detective Proctor to help herself. "They look homemade."

"No thanks, I tried one earlier, and it was terrible. It tasted like whoever made these skipped the sugar and used some kind of artificial sweetener instead."

I took a bite. She was right. It tasted like sawdust. I dropped the half-eaten cookie back on the plate and took a drink of lemonade to wash it down. And then I had a thought. I looked over at Proctor, and she looked right back at me, as if the same thing had just occurred to her.

"Whoever baked these is either a terrible cook, or else diabetic."

* * *

The biggest problem Tommy Mack had was that, as a result of a lifetime of penny-ante crime, he didn't have a crew, not in Nashville, or anywhere else in the surrounding counties. That meant he didn't know a guy who knew a guy, and he didn't have any strings he could pull. He was on his own. And so, it took him the better part of the day to walk to the address he had written on the palm of his hand at the time he dropped off Abigail Crowley's Audi cabrio, which he was sure would soon be on the police hot sheet, at the parking lot where he had originally nicked it. It was a long walk from downtown, and it was nearly three o'clock in the afternoon when he finally got to what turned out to be a low-rise condo complex on the southwest side of the city. Too early, he figured, for anyone who worked a normal job to be at home. Normally, given Tommy's chosen line of work, an empty dwelling would have been exactly the thing he would be looking for. But today was different. And so, he wandered over to a Trader Joe's just up the road to have a cup of coffee and a sweet roll and to formulate a plan.

Chapter Nineteen

After Maggie and I left the memorial service, we drove to a sporting goods store near her condo that also has an indoor shooting range. Shortly after we met, I was worried that one of the individuals involved in a case I was investigating at the time might try to get me to stand down by threatening her. As a precaution, I loaned her one of my own guns, a Smith & Wesson .32 caliber revolver. At first, she didn't want any part of it, but I convinced her it was for her own good and that, as long as she had it, she might as well practice using it.

To my complete surprise, she took to shooting like an overserved frat boy gravitates to a pony keg. After that, there was no turning back, and within a short time, she bought two pistols of her own, the Remington .380 that she keeps in her purse, and a Ruger Max 9, that stays by her bedside. And although the state of Tennessee no longer requires one, she also applied for, and received, a concealed carry permit. It turned out that she had a talent for shooting handguns, and within a very short time, she became an excellent shot, much better than I am at close quarters. On this particular afternoon, she burned through eighty dollars' worth of .380 and nine-millimeter rounds, tearing up silhouette targets as if she was firing a Tommy gun. The only question that remained in my mind was not whether she was skilled enough to hit a human target, but under duress, did she have the will to try. It was a question I hoped would never need to be answered.

* * *

The next morning, I was back on the Saint Bernadette campus, this time finding a parking space that was a reasonable walking distance from the administration building. Lucky, since I had an eleven o'clock appointment with Caroline Feldman, the registrar, and I wanted to be on time. I found a spot in a public parking lot just down the block from administration and, with a little huffing and puffing, arrived at my destination at ten fifty-five. It made no difference, as Caitlin, the young receptionist I had met the previous week, informed me that Mrs. Feldman was in a meeting and was running late. Yes, Caitlin remembered me. Yes, Mrs. Feldman was aware I had an appointment, and yes, she was sorry she couldn't be there as we had agreed. But something unexpected had come up and it was absolutely necessary that she see to that first. Would I care to wait, or did I want to reschedule? I said I'd wait. I was tired of driving back and forth between the campus and the city, and, for the moment, at least, there was nowhere else I needed to be.

Since I had an appointment, Caitlin offered to let me wait in Ms. Feldman's office instead of a hard seat in the reception area. While I waited, I took a look around. Her office was spacious, with three leather armchairs for visitors and a large window that looked over a green area at the rear of the building. Behind her desk was a credenza that was home to a desktop computer and several framed photographs of people whom I assumed were her husband and her two children. In one of the photos, the kids were hugging a large dog, and in another, the family was grouped together. It was the kind of picture that you might see turned into a Christmas card.

With Ms. Feldman still tending to her business elsewhere, I thumbed through several outdated copies of *People* magazine, where I found out what would be the new *haute* look for the upcoming fall season. It made me think I should go home and clean out my closet from top to bottom so I could re-tool my wardrobe.

I also found out what all the most popular celebrities would be wearing at the upcoming Academy Awards ceremony, which, thanks to the magazine being six months past its display-by date, had taken place several months earlier. Another edition featured photos of some of the hottest new couples on the entertainment scene, none of whom I had any idea who they might be. There was also a retrospective on the career of Gary Oldman, who, it was thought, might be announcing his retirement from the motion picture industry. Too bad. He was as good as they come.

At around quarter to twelve, a breathless Caroline Feldman showed up carrying a briefcase, a white paper bag filled with what turned out to be chocolate eclairs, an oversized purse, and a cup of coffee bearing the logo of the Saint Bernadette University student union buffet. She was an attractive woman, medium height, in her mid- to late thirties. She was dressed in a gray skirted suit and a soft pink blouse. Her hair was dark blond with lighter highlights. I remembered seeing her at the memorial service for Sarah Bergman, sitting next to Robert Levy.

"Mister Gamble," she said, breezing into the room, "I apologize for keeping you waiting like this. Sometimes these meetings come up at the last minute, and then they run over." I waited while she put down the various items she was carrying and got settled behind her desk. She pushed the white bag and a paper napkin in my direction.

"Eclair? They were left over from the meeting. Fresh this morning, and I hated to see them go to waste." When I hesitated, she said, "Take two if you want. They're very good."

"One is fine." I took a bite. It was better than good, I and immediately wished I had taken two. I said, "Thank you, and thanks again for seeing me on short notice. Can I assume you spoke to Professor Levy about why I wanted to talk to you?"

"Well, I did, but he was a little vague on the telephone when I spoke to him. He just said you needed help with an investigation you were working on, and he thought perhaps I could help you. I assumed it had something to do with Sarah."

"Then let me bring you into the picture."

Between bites, being careful not to let the custard filling ooze out into my lap, I told her I had been retained by Sarah Bergman to try to locate her missing husband, and that it was my understanding that she was friends with Isaac and Sarah. For that reason, Robert Levy thought she might be able to point me in a direction that might help me find out what had happened.

"I'm not sure how I can help you," she said. "Sarah is dead. I know you know that, since I saw you at the memorial service. I guess I'm wondering what possible difference could it make now where Isaac is, or what might have happened to him? Or are you working on trying to find out who killed Sarah? You know, everyone here was shocked about her death. Something like that is just so far out of our normal range of experience."

"I'm certain it is. But to answer your question, no, I'm not working on solving her murder. The police are doing that, and I'm confident they'll find her killer. But I do think the reason Sarah was killed is connected to the fact that she hired me to try to find Isaac. The police have long since moved on from that investigation, but when Sarah hired me, she reopened the case. My guess is it struck a nerve somewhere."

She drummed her fingernails on the top of her desk. "Let me understand this. You think somebody out there doesn't want Isaac found, even after all this time. And that whoever that person is, he killed Sarah to make sure that doesn't happen. Do I have that right?"

"Maybe not actually found," I said. "Maybe just finding out what happened to him could present a problem for somebody. Depending upon the circumstances, that might be enough to make that person, or persons, want to see the investigation brought to a close."

"Assuming that's so, how can I help you?"

"I was thinking, first of all, that you could tell me a little about both Isaac and Sarah."

"Such as what?" She raised her eyebrows a bit.

"Well, for instance, would you say their marriage was a strong one? You know, did they seem devoted to one another, or were they just going through the motions of being married?"

"Hard to say." She started drumming her fingers again. "I knew Isaac a lot better than I knew Sarah. The only time I regularly saw them together was at university functions around the holidays, or when someone was hosting a dinner party, or some other hideous faculty gathering. When I saw them together at those times, they seemed to be getting along well enough."

I finished what was left of my éclair with one more bite. *Damn, it was good.* "Then, you never got any sense that things might not be quite right between them?"

"No…nothing that would have raised any alarms. But they weren't clingy, either, and it did seem as though Isaac tended to spend more time talking to the other wives, rather than his male colleagues, or to Sarah. But then," and here she paused, as if to find the right way to say what she had to say, "Isaac was a good-looking man, and it wasn't a secret that women were attracted to him."

I thought about that. "Was it possible he was having an affair? Say, with one of the other faculty wives? Or maybe one of his students?"

Another pause, longer this time. "Can I be frank with you, Mr. Gamble?"

I said, "I wish you would. Sarah is dead, and truthfully, I think it's highly likely Isaac is also dead. At this point, the only thing I'm trying to do is find out if that's so, or if he's still alive somewhere. I owe that much to Sarah."

"And if he's alive, you're wondering whether he somehow found his way back here long enough to kill his wife?"

"I hadn't really thought about that. I suppose it's a possibility, but I doubt it. And anyway, that assumes he's still alive."

"Well, then," she said, "to answer your original question, I don't know how strong their marriage was, but I can tell you that Isaac had a reputation on campus as being a bit too familiar with some of the women in his classes."

"Are we talking about sexual relationships?"

She hesitated. "I want to choose my words carefully, here. There were rumors that, yes, there might have been sex taking place. But none of his students ever came forward with an allegation, so without a formal complaint, there was no legal cause to investigate."

"Did Sarah know about any of this?"

"I don't know. One would think she must have, although some women seem not to be able to see what's going on right under their noses. In any case, she never said anything to me."

"But you were close enough that if she did suspect something, she would have told you."

"Probably not, no. We were friends. We were not intimates. And anyway, don't you think that the police will find the answers you're looking for when they find Sarah's killer?"

"Good question. I think we're working on the same problem, but coming at it from opposite directions."

"I don't follow."

"It's like this. I think if I can find out what happened to Isaac, that will tell us who killed Sarah. If the cops can figure out who killed Sarah, that will almost certainly be the same person who knows what became of Isaac."

"In other words, their respective fates are intertwined." She took a sip of her coffee. "Say for the moment that's true. How can I help?"

"Well, apart from what we've already discussed, I'd like to know what time Bergman's last class ended on the day he disappeared. His wife led me to believe it would have been sometime in the afternoon. Also, I'd appreciate it if you can give me class lists for the last year he was here."

"This will take a minute." She turned and fiddled with the computer on her credenza. "Ah. Here we go. Isaac's last class that semester ended at two-thirty. It was Latin III. With Roman numerals. As far as details concerning his students, I'm sorry. I can't help you there. Student records are confidential."

I said, "Ms. Feldman, I'm not interested in anything other than rosters. I'm just trying to establish whether anyone who took one of Professor Bergman's classes four years ago might have stayed in touch with him. Or whether he ever talked to any of them about running off with him to Fiji to spend the rest of their lives as beachcombers."

"That's it?"

"Almost. I'd also like to know whether there was anyone in any of his classes who was likely not to receive a passing grade."

She gave me a look of disbelief. "What, you think that somebody flunking his class would be upset enough to kill him? And then, what? Take an incomplete and hope for a D-minus from somebody else the next semester?"

I let the question slide and instead took Bergman's calendar book out and opened it to one of the pages I had noticed when I first looked at it. "Take a look at this. The night before she was killed, I visited Sarah Bergman at her home. She gave me a box of Isaac's personal belongings that she had collected from his office here at the college after he disappeared. One of the things I found was this appointment book. Most of it is fairly straightforward, but there are also notations like these." I showed her one of the pages that showed "MB/730/750," "SS/900/600," and other similar entries.

"What do you make of these?"

"I don't know. I guess they could be meeting times, and I guess the initials, if that's what they are, could match up with some of his students. But I have no idea what the other number would represent."

"Right. And you'll notice, whenever initials like this appear, if that's what they are, it's always on a weekend night, and there's always an entry for that same set of initials at the beginning of the week. That's why I was hoping to get a look at his class roster, to see whether the letters actually represent some of his students. If they do, then maybe I can locate one or two of them and see if they can give me an explanation as to what these are all about."

She took a pad of paper out of her desk drawer and began copying down some of the entries. "Okay. Let me do this. Before I go and violate all kinds of confidentiality rules, let me see if I can match up these initials, if that's what they are, with Bergman's class rosters. If they are—and it will take me a day or two—I'll give you a call, and then we can get back together and try to figure something out. Does that sound reasonable to you?"

I said that it did and that I would wait for her call.

* * *

On my way back to the office, I took a run by police headquarters. I was hoping I might catch either Lorraine Proctor or John Spillner before they left for the day. Spillner was nowhere to be seen, but Proctor was at her desk, shuffling through a stack of paper that reminded me all over again what I missed least about being a cop.

"You again," she said when she saw me. "This is getting to be a habit." I took a seat in a hard wooden chair next to her desk.

"What can I do for you, Mr. Gamble? As you can see, I've got a lot of work to do here."

"This won't take long. I was wondering whether anybody here has given any thought to reopening the other Bergman investigation."

"I thought that one was your problem. And anyway, unless you've found a body, that particular Bergman case still belongs to missing persons. In case you forgot, over here, we work homicide."

"Not a body, sorry. Not yet, anyway. But I did turn up this." I took the baggie filled with what I thought was crystal meth and dropped it on her desk.

She raised her eyebrows just a little. "The hell is this? And where did it come from?"

"Yesterday, I took a ride out to a wrecking yard in La Vergne. I wanted to take a look at what was left of Bergman's car. No particular reason, I was just curious. As I expected, there wasn't much left of it, basically just the body with no running gear."

"Or very much of anything else. As I recall reading in the file, it was stolen and then wrecked. Our guys went through the car pretty thoroughly when it finally turned up out there."

"Except that they missed this." I poked the baggie with my finger." I found it under the back seat. I think it's meth. And I can see how somebody would have missed it. It wasn't on the floor, where somebody would ordinarily look. It was tucked up between the seat bottom and the springs. You would have had to turn the seat all the way upside down to find it. I'm guessing your guys didn't do that."

"Apparently not." She held the bag up to the light and studied it. "So, assuming this is what you think, and not just a bag of rock candy, what do you want me to do with it?"

"I was thinking it might give you a reason to take another look at Isaac Bergman."

"Right, okay. Let me see if I can follow your thinking here. You now figure that this Bergman guy was somehow involved in either manufacturing or selling meth. Maybe to some of the students on the campus where he worked, maybe someplace else. And that his involvement in the drug trade ended up getting him killed and buried in a shallow grave somewhere, or else wrapped up in a towing chain and dumped into Priest Lake. Does that sound about right?"

Now that she said it out loud, I had to admit it sounded weak. "Maybe. I think it's at least worth looking into. For all we know, whatever Isaac was doing could also be the reason his wife was killed."

"Because whoever killed Bergman was afraid that you'd find out who that person was, and the only way to stop your investigation was to kill the woman who hired you. Wouldn't it have been simpler just to kill you? Not that all of us here wouldn't miss you, of course."

"You're not the first one to suggest that, and yes, there was a chance Sarah Bergman would have just hired somebody else. But then, how many PIs would somebody have to kill before you guys would figure out it wasn't just a serial killer targeting private investigators?"

She stared at me for a moment, as if trying to decide on a number.

"All right, I give up. But let's take things in order. First, we need to be sure what's actually in this bag. If it turns out to be meth, or some derivative of meth, then we can check with narcotics and find out whether we can tie it to anything they might be working on. Depending on what they come back with, we can decide whether any of this is worth pursuing, or if it's just some kind of an outlier. Does that seem reasonable to you?"

Chapter Twenty

That night, I picked Maggie up at her condo, and we drove to a restaurant that offered outdoor patio seating. It was a warm evening, and the air was fragrant with blossoming honeysuckle and mimosa. There was a light breeze, and the temperature was warm enough that neither of us needed a jacket. I made an effort to dress up just a bit, choosing a light blue button-down cotton shirt and my usual khaki wash pants. Maggie had on a light blue tunic top over what she called palazzo pants. I noticed she was carrying a new crossbody shoulder bag, and I recognized that the zipper pull was decorated with a medallion in the shape of a Smith & Wesson logo. This particular bag, I knew, was designed with a separate pocket for a handgun. As fashion accessories go, this one wasn't cheap.

I also noticed that something about Maggie was a little off, but I knew better than to ask. In the time we have been together, she occasionally slips into a mood, most often when something is bothering her. She will almost always get around to telling me what it is, but not until she's had a couple of cocktails to loosen her up. As she told me once, the liquor is not intended as a substitute for good judgment. It's for courage.

After we got seated, with a basket of sourdough bread and butter, silverware, and menus, a waitress came by the table to take drink orders and announce the day's specials, none of which sounded particularly appealing. I ordered a Stella, and Maggie skipped her usual appletini and went for vodka and cranberry juice instead. I raised an eyebrow.

"It's good for the digestion," she told me after taking a sip.

"What is, vodka?"

"No, cranberry juice. I read an article in a health magazine. It has a lot of fiber."

"You can never go wrong with fiber." Since I wasn't sure yet what was bothering her, I didn't want to say anything that might provoke a round of unpleasantness.

"It also helps prevent yeast infections." She was quiet for a moment. I wondered if I should say something about never having had a yeast infection, then decided that might not be such a good idea.

"I got a telephone call today."

I buttered a piece of bread and waited.

"Well," she said. "Aren't you going to ask?"

I never get this stuff right. "Okay. Who called?"

"Michael Pomeroy"

It took me a second, and then the gears inside my head stopped spinning and locked into place. Michael Pomeroy was the man Maggie was married to when she lost what would have been their first child after the incident at Woodcrest High School. The miscarriage, and her subsequent inability to have any more children led to tensions with her then-husband, which eventually ended up with them calling it quits. Since that time, to the best of my knowledge, they had not had any further contact. That had been more than ten years ago, and now Michael Pomeroy had apparently reappeared.

I tried to keep my tone neutral. "What did he want?"

Before she could tell me, our waitress came to bring a second round of drinks and to take our dinner order. Maggie ordered pan-seared scallops served with sweet corn puree. I went with beef tenderloin medallions and *kaesespaetzle*, and we split a jumbo shrimp cocktail appetizer.

"He didn't say what he wanted, specifically. I mean, he was sort of vague. You know, there was nothing about money, or getting back together, or anything like that. Just that it'd been a long time, and he'd like to see me."

"But he didn't say why." I dipped a shrimp into the cocktail sauce and ate it in one bite. "Did you agree to see him?"

I watched her take one of the shrimps and place it on her bread plate.

Then, she cut off the tail and sliced the remaining part in half. She used her fork to dip one of the morsels into the cocktail sauce before putting it into her mouth.

"You know that's supposed to be finger food, right?"

She raised her eyebrows a quarter-inch. "Did I say anything when you gobbled up a whole shrimp in one bite?"

"You're right," I said. "So, back to the question. Are you going to meet him?"

"Tomorrow, after work. He wanted to come by my place and pick me up, but I told him no. I said I'd meet him in the lounge at the Maxwell House."

"That's good. It's very public." I paused for a moment to let that sink in. "Do you want me to come with you?"

"I don't think so. But if you want to meet me after, we can grab dinner someplace and then make an evening of it."

"At the Maxwell House?"

"Why not?" she said. "Pack a bag, and be sure to bring clean underwear."

* * *

Tommy Mack waited at the Trader Joe's until seven-thirty, by which time he was reasonably sure that the person he needed to talk to would be home from work. It was a short walk, no more than ten minutes from the Trader Joe's, to the address written on the palm of his hand.

When he arrived at his destination, he hesitated, realizing that he almost certainly would not be welcome, and indeed, once he was recognized, might be met with a scream for help or a call to the police, or an angry husband. Worse yet, he might get shot. Still, with no other option available, he had no choice. He mounted the front steps and pressed his ear to the door. He could hear a television playing in the front room, but no voices, indicating, he hoped, that the individual he wished to see was home alone. So, with nothing to lose, he took a step back, rang the doorbell, and waited for whatever outcome he was about to face.

Chapter Twenty-One

Maggie's get-together with her ex-husband was planned for six-thirty in the cocktail lounge at the upscale Maxwell House hotel. From what she had told me, his request to meet with her had come straight out of the blue, and she had no idea what he wanted. However, having had some considerable experience with ex-spouses wanting to reconnect, and since Maggie had never talked much about Michael Pomeroy, I was worried there might be a problem. On the other hand, I figured that in a busy hotel cocktail lounge, unless Pomeroy showed up with two six guns blazing, Maggie would be reasonably safe. For that reason, I decided not to stow away in some remote corner of the room. Partly, my decision was out of respect for her privacy, and partly, it was because I was pretty sure Maggie could take care of herself.

I left my car in the hotel parking lot and walked into the bar at around seven-thirty. Time enough, I hoped, for her to conclude her business with her former husband and send him on his way. Sure enough, I spotted Maggie sitting by herself at a small table near the back of the room. The Maxwell Lounge, as it is called, seemed to be a good place to be if drinking your troubles away is what you wanted to do. Soft recorded music was playing, and the lighting was subdued. The room was about half-filled with customers, laughing, conversing, and, here and there, couples, married or otherwise, doing a little flirting.

Since she was alone and since it was an hour past the time she was planning to meet with her ex-husband, I figured it was okay for me to join her at her table. In the brief moment it took to begin making my way in her direction, a tall man wearing denim pants and a corduroy jacket walked quickly past me, brushing against my shoulder in a manner that seemed deliberate.

"The fuck out of the way."

He turned and glared at me, turned away again, and stalked angrily out of the room. Then, the moment passed. My first thought had been to say something, but since I didn't recognize him, and since I also wasn't there looking for a fight, I let it go as just a careless encounter with someone who'd had a few too many.

The table where Maggie was seated was intended to resemble the kind of white oak barrel distillers used in whiskey cooperage, with a larger circular top that held one of those point-of-sale devices that served both as a menu and a credit card reader. She was dressed very conservatively, in dark slacks, navy-blue low-heeled pumps, and a dove-gray blouse with white two-button, rounded cuffs. Her outfit, I guessed, was meant to convey to her former husband that, whatever the reason was for his wanting to meet with her, there wasn't a chance in hell that the evening would conclude with a roll in the hay for old times' sake. For that matter, even from halfway across the room, I could tell she was more than a little agitated. There were already three empty cocktail glasses sitting on the table in front of her, and the look on her face made it abundantly clear that, whatever Michael Pomeroy had wanted to talk to her about, it had not gone well.

I pulled up a chair and sat down across from her. "This seat taken?"

She gave me a sour look. "Enter at your own risk."

"Okay, I'm going to need a little bit of guidance here. Should I ask how it went, or would you rather not talk about it?"

"I need another drink first."

I motioned to the waiter. "I'll have a Stella and bring another of whatever the lady is having." When he gave us a curious look, I said, "We're staying the night."

After he left, Maggie said, "Why did he look at us like that?"

"Well, off the top of my head, I'd say he's got you figured for a pro."

"Excuse me?"

"Two men in an hour. In a hotel bar? What would you think?"

"I think I'll claw his eyes out."

Over the course of the several years, I have known Maggie Totten, I have learned that there are times when Maggie and alcohol in combination can yield some surprising and occasionally combustible results. Most of the time, she doesn't drink anything stronger than diet soda, sparkling water, or cranberry juice. And, when she does drink something stronger, usually with dinner in a restaurant, she quits after two. But if she's angry, or upset, she's prone to just keep them coming. Once, after a particularly bad day at work, she pulled her .380 on some mope in a crowded country roadhouse. The guy had asked her to dance, and after she said no, he tried to press the point by putting his hand on her arm. Nobody got hurt that time, but I was fairly convinced that if he'd tried to make an issue of it, she would have shot him right where he sat. Thankfully, I was able to get us both out the door and into the car before the place went up for grabs.

"So," I said after our drinks arrived. "How did it go?"

"Not well at all. You may have noticed he wasn't in a very good mood when he brushed past you."

"That guy was Michael Pomeroy?"

"All six feet, four inches. What did you make of him?"

"I didn't pay much attention. I thought he was just some drunk having trouble walking in a straight line." I waited, and when she didn't say anything to that, I said, "You know, in the entire time we've been together, you've never said much about him. If it's not opening any old wounds, what was he like?"

She gave a small shrug. "Sweet, at first, like you are now, only without the rough edges."

"Okay. I'll take that as a compliment."

"You should. It keeps you from being treacly. But then, after those boys threw me down the steps at school, he started to get more and more withdrawn. He never came out and said so, but I'm pretty sure he blamed me for what happened. And then he started drinking, a little at first. But after a while, it got worse, and eventually, he lost his job."

"Did he ever hurt you? Was he violent?"

She shook her head no. "Michael is—was—a very nice man. I've never known him to want to hurt anybody."

"Well, he seemed like he might have been looking for trouble just now. What did he want with you?"

"To tell me a tale of woe, I guess." She took a swallow of her drink. "After we split up, he remarried and then took a job someplace in Florida."

"He didn't say where?"

"No."

"Okay, what did he say?"

"That things didn't work out for the new job or the marriage, and now he's single again, unemployed, and angry. He's just now moved back to Nashville and wants us to get back together. He says he still loves me. He says he's learned from his mistakes and thinks we can make a go of it this time."

"And you said?"

"I told him I was sorry to hear things hadn't been going well for him."

"Tactful of you. Did you say anything else?"

"I said I hoped he'd be able to get things turned around soon. And that under no circumstances did I want to see or hear from him again, and that if I did, I would get in front of a judge and ask for a restraining order."

I took a swallow of my beer. "I don't imagine that's the response he was looking for."

"No putting one past you, is there?"

"Sorry to hear," I said. But truthfully, I couldn't have been happier. And so, we finished our drinks and walked to the front desk to see about checking into a room for the night. But not before I decided that I would run down whatever information I could find about the man named Michael Pomeroy.

Chapter Twenty-Two

I have never had much luck getting a good night's sleep in a hotel room. It doesn't matter whether it's a Motel Six, a tourist cabin, or a top-of-the-line property like the Maxwell House. The combination of an unfamiliar mattress, pillows that are either too hard or too soft, too thick or too thin, along with the general atmosphere of strange smells, sounds, and textures, means that most times, it takes me an hour or more to drop off, and I'm generally wide awake long before the sun comes up.

This particular instance was something different. After Maggie had sent her former husband, Michael Pomeroy, packing, with an admonition not to contact her again, we went to dinner at a restaurant she liked. She liked it so well that over the time we have been together we've become frequent customers, and the wait staff had gotten to know our drink preferences. So, by the time we got to our table, there was already an appletini for her, a bottle of Stella Artois, and a chilled glass waiting for me. Unfortunately, on top of the four cocktails she'd consumed at the Maxwell Lounge, the three more appletinis she hammered down with her supper meant that any hope for a night of wild and crazy sex once we got back to the hotel was out of the question. In fact, while I was in the bathroom brushing my teeth, Maggie had taken off her shoes—I found one each on opposite sides of the room—crawled fully dressed under the covers and was snoring raucously by the time I finished getting ready for bed.

* * *

That same evening, Abigail Crowley found the man she knew as Michael Emery standing on her front stoop. It took her a moment or two to recognize him, since the last and only other time they had been together, he'd abandoned her in a downtown singles bar after dosing her drink.

"Michael?" she said, after realizing who she was looking at.

"Actually, my name isn't Michael Emery. It's Tommy Mack. I'm here to apologize for what I did to you the other night. Also, I wanted to let you know I put your car back in the lot where you left it the night we met. If you'd like, you can call a cab or an Uber to take you there. I'll be happy to pay whatever it costs."

When Abigail didn't say anything, he went on. "There's not a scratch on it. I even paid extra to have the inside cleaned up."

She looked him up and down, as if trying to make up her mind about something. Finally, she said, "Mister Mack, are you a Christian?"

Tommy didn't have the faintest idea what it meant when committed churchgoers talked about being a Christian, except that he thought it had something to do with being "born again," whatever that meant. But he had a definite feeling he was about to find out.

* * *

The next morning, Maggie was up and out early and showing no ill effects from the night before. Today, she was wearing white slacks, a dark blue top, and a light blue blazer. Her hair and her makeup looked as if she had just spent the last hour with a skilled beautician, getting ready for a guest spot on a television talk show.

Lord, she could be stunning.

I rolled over. "You're leaving already?"

She bent down and gave me a quick kiss. "I have a job, in case you forgot. Also, I'm sorry about last night. I know I left my A-game in the hotel bar. I'll make it up to you tonight."

And so, with that to look forward to, she was out the door. That left me by myself in a cushy hotel room with a checkout time of eleven o'clock.

I decided, since the last day or so seemed to be a money-is-no-object proposition, that I would order a room service breakfast. In my case, that meant two buttered English muffins and a double order of bacon accompanied by two cans of Diet Coke. No use loading up on empty calories, I thought, congratulating myself on my sensible food and beverage choices.

After breakfast, I took a moment to catch up on the local Morning Show news programs. In only a few minutes, I found out that a couple of local colleges, including Saint Bernadette, would be forced, "for inflationary reasons after COVID," to raise their tuition rates for the upcoming fall semester. It also appeared that the Tennessee Titans were close to signing their first-round draft pick to a multi-year deal, and some country-western singer I'd never heard of would be featured in an extended interview during the next segment. Finally, late the previous evening, there had been a traffic accident of sorts on Lower Broad, where an intoxicated motorist drove his car into one of those roaming bicycle bars that have popped up all around the area. No one was seriously injured, but a couple thousand dollars' worth of liquor was spilled all over the street, forcing the fire department to hose the spillage down a storm sewer grate, no doubt to the delight of whatever fish were swimming around in the Cumberland River. Now feeling fully informed, I turned off the television and headed for the shower.

Twenty minutes later, I was sipping the second of my Diet Cokes and enjoying the view of the river out the window of my hotel room when my cell phone began vibrating on the nightstand. I didn't recognize either the name or the number displayed in the caller ID, so I sent it to voice mail. Ten minutes later, the phone began vibrating again and displayed the same name and number. This time, I answered.

"Mister Gamble," the voice on the other end said, "this is Tommy Mack. I need your help."

"Where are you?" He recited an address which I wrote down on the notepad provided by the hotel. "Call you back in ten minutes."

That gave me enough time to figure out a plan. It wasn't the best idea I'd ever had, and it may have actually been close to the worst one. But on short notice, it was the only thing I could come up with that might have a chance to save Tommy's life. I just needed the answer to one question. One whose answer, yes or no, might determine whether Tommy would live to see another day.

Chapter Twenty-Three

The one question—the only question—I had for Tommy Mack was, "Do you still have the jewelry you stole from Red Cherry?" When he told me he did, my next question was, "Are you ready to give it back?"

He was.

I told him I'd pick him up in an hour at the address he had given me. "And Tommy, you'd better be there. Otherwise, don't bother calling me again, because I won't lift a finger to help you."

The address he'd given me was the same as the one where he'd knocked on the door the previous evening. When I rapped on that same door, it was answered by a woman of about fifty years, attractive but not beautiful, wearing slim jeans and a loose-fitting cotton sweatshirt decorated with the "Big Al" elephant mascot of the University of Alabama. Perhaps indicative of the mid-morning hour and the fact that she was still at home, she wore no makeup.

"Can I help you?" she asked when she opened the door.

"I'm looking for Tommy Mack. Is he here?"

"And you are?"

"My name is Gamble. I'm a private investigator. Tommy called me earlier. He said I could find him here."

She gave me a look I'd seen before, lots of times on the faces of lots of people. "Can I see some identification?"

I showed her my ID and a copy of my license. "Okay?"

"I don't know," she said. We were getting nowhere.

I said, "Can I ask your name?"

She gave me a defiant look. "It's Abigail Crowley. This is my home. And Mr. Mack is my guest."

"Well, Ms. Crowley, I don't know how well you know Mr. Mack. From the look of things, I'm guessing well enough that you allowed him to spend last night with you. And if that's so, then you probably also know what he does for a living. You probably also know that right now, he's in the worst jam of his life."

"He told me," she said, letting her eyes drop. "He took my car. But he brought it back, and he apologized for what he did. That should count for something, shouldn't it?"

"If he were in a twelve-step program, I'd say yes, it should. But he's not, and since this is the address that he gave me when he called earlier, I'm going to assume he's still here, or at least that you know where he is. I'm also assuming that right now, your primary concern is to make sure that whoever comes knocking on the door next isn't here to put a bullet in his brain."

When she didn't say anything, I said, "Where is he, Ms. Crowley?"

She hesitated for a long moment. "He's at the Trader Joe's. It's right down the block. He said he'd meet you there because he didn't want anything to happen to me in case you weren't who he thought you'd be."

"You mean, in case I was actually coming to kill him?"

"Yes. That's what he said." She looked at me as if she was trying to read my intentions. "You aren't, are you? Here to kill him, I mean?"

"I'm trying to save his life, Ms. Crowley. Right now, I'm very likely the only one who can."

* * *

I found Tommy sitting by himself on a bench outside the Trader Joe's. When he saw me drive up, he got up and started walking toward the car, the whole time looking around cautiously as if he feared there might be a sniper on the roof of the CVS at the end of the parking lot, waiting for a clear shot to pick him off.

I ran down the window on the passenger side. "Get in, Tommy. We have a busy day ahead of us."

He climbed into the passenger seat and buckled his seat belt. "Are you going to take me back to jail, Mr. Gamble?"

"No reason to. As far as the court is concerned, you're still out on bail. Your hearing date isn't until next week."

"Then what?"

I said, "We're going to take a ride out to Mount Juliet, and you're going to return the jewelry you stole from Red Cherry."

He seemed to sink into his seat at that. "You're joking, right? I mean, he'll kill me the minute we walk in the door."

"No, I don't believe he will. He owes me a favor, and I think he's honorable enough in his own way to live up to his commitments."

And I don't think he'll kill you in front of a witness, I wanted to add—unless he kills the witness, too.

The favor I was referring to had to do with an investigation I was working on about a year earlier. At one point, I had made noises about wanting to talk to Cherry face-to-face. And so, Red had sent a couple of his goons to my office with instructions to deliver me to the man himself. In the process, they roughed me up a bit. To my amazement, he allowed how that was not something he had told them to do and that he owed me a favor if I ever needed one. And although I didn't feel any particular sympathy for Tommy Mack, in this instance, I also didn't think his getting clipped for having committed a simple burglary was an equitable price to pay. And since I also didn't think storing up favors from the head of a criminal organization was something that was apt to earn much compound interest going forward, I decided saving Tommy was as good a way as any to cash in my marker.

"You do have the stuff with you, right?"

He patted his jacket pocket. "Right here."

"Give it to me." There were several loose pieces wrapped in a woman's handkerchief. I looked at them briefly, then refolded the handkerchief and dropped the bundle into my jacket pocket. "Ready?"

CHAPTER TWENTY-THREE

"Does he know we're coming?"

I shook my head. "I thought the element of surprise might work in our favor. This way, there won't be so many guys shooting at us when we pull into the driveway."

"Okay, now I know you're just fucking with me, right?" He didn't sound sure, though.

"Yep, that's what I'm doing." At least, I hoped that was all I was doing. With a guy like Red Cherry, you can never be sure.

Tommy didn't have much to say on the drive out to Mount Juliet. I supposed he was thinking about how much trouble he was in trusting me not to lead him into and wondering whether I had enough juice with Red to keep him from blowing both our brains out the minute we walked through the front door. On the even-money chance that Tommy's fears were well-founded—that, to put it in his terms, I wasn't just fucking with him—I sent a text to Dick Dohrn at the *Times*, Lorraine Proctor at Metro PD, and Maggie, letting them know where I was going and who I would be seeing. That way, I figured if we didn't survive the encounter, at least the cops would know where to start looking for the bodies.

* * *

His celebrity status in Nashville notwithstanding, Red Cherry never attained the recognition nor the adulation in Mount Juliet enjoyed by the town's favorite son. Here, we're talking the late, great, country-western singer, composer, weapons-grade conservative Charlie Daniels, who died from a hemorrhagic stroke at age 83. At the time of his death, Charlie had an estimated net worth of around $20 million. Big money, for sure, in anybody's book, but nowhere near the wealth accumulated by his less-well-known neighbor, Robert Cherry. Of course, Charlie made his money playing by the rules, and making good music as well.

Cherry, his wife and teenaged son settled in Mount Juliet after departing New Orleans in the wake of Hurricane Katrina. Once settled in his new home in Wilson County, Tennessee, it didn't take him long to get his various criminal enterprises back up and running, and in the space of about three years, he had established himself as the criminal kingpin of the mid-south. His son, meanwhile, was carving out a career for himself in the United States Marine Corps, so in this instance, at least, the apple fell quite a distance from the tree. His wife, meanwhile, had reportedly fallen in love with life near the ocean and so had relocated semi-permanently to a lavish property on Captiva Island.

Of course, in the intervening years since Red was the head of the Gulf Coast underworld, the nature of organized crime had changed considerably. Unlike at his earlier venue, there were no shootouts in the street, no tourists getting mugged, and no overt corruption of county or city officials. Red's new *modus operandi* was more subtle and involved money laundering through the acquisition of legitimate businesses, Internet fraud, shakedowns of high-visibility personalities with gambling or other problems best kept secret, identity theft, and even televangelism. Last I heard, he was starting to dabble in cryptocurrency, although what he was doing might have actually been legal.

In any event, whatever he was up to these days had certainly paid off in spades. When Tommy and I arrived at his residence, we pulled past the mailbox into a short driveway entrance that ended at a pair of Indiana limestone gateposts that supported heavy, decorative steel gates. A row of tall arbor vitae privacy trees faced the road, and behind the trees was an eight-foot metal fence with vertical bars set too closely together for even an individual as small as Tommy to squeeze through.

Looking at the fence, I said, "How in the hell did you get in here, anyway?"

"Nobody ever says no to a pizza delivery guy."

"What?"

He took a deep breath. "I know a guy here in town who delivers pizzas, and sometimes a little dope, to make a little extra money on the weekends. He's not a bad guy, but he's always a little short, if you know what I mean.

"Anyway, one night, I rode along with him, you know, just for something to do and to maybe check out the neighborhood. Some of these places looked like they might have something I could use. So the next week I gave my friend a hundred bucks to borrow his car on a night he wasn't working. I picked up a couple of pizzas at another store and drove to this place. I didn't know who lived here. It just looked like the kind of place I should scope out."

"And?"

"And, I rang the buzzer on the gate there, and when somebody answered, I said 'pizza delivery.' The guy on the other end said, get lost. We didn't order any pizzas. I said, well, how about if you take 'em anyway, no charge, on account of this is my last delivery for the night, and I don't know what else to do with them. So, they opened the gate, and I drove in.

"When I got to the door, a big guy answered. There was a lot of noise inside, and I could see there was some kind of a party going on in the back, so I said, here's the pizzas, just take 'em. The guy looked at them and said, let me give you some money just the same. And I said, no, that was all right, but could I use the bathroom? I thought he was gonna tell me to fuck off, but then he said, okay, sure, right down the hall, just let yourself out when you're done. So then, he took the pizzas back to where the party was, and I went down the hall, but I went into the bedroom instead of the bathroom. I knew I didn't have much time, so when I spotted a jewelry box on the dresser, I just grabbed what was on the top and got the hell out of there."

"In other words, you stole the first thing you could put your hands on."

He gave me a look, like you-can't-blame-a-goat-for-being-a-goat.

"That's pretty much the size of it. I got a pair of earrings, a bracelet, a necklace, and a pin. They all matched, so I figured it was a set that I could sell for a good price. But before I could even try to sell the stuff, I got picked up on an old beef, and then you know the rest. And now, here we are. And the hell of it is, it turned out it's all low-quality stuff and isn't worth much of anything at all."

"Yep," I said, "and now, here we are."

I got out of the car and walked over to the gate. I saw right away that there were CCTV cameras mounted atop both gateposts. On the other hand, there were no armed guards and no snarling Dobermans behind the gate eager for the chance to chew off an arm or a leg. I took that as a plus.

When I pushed the button on the comm panel, a voice responded immediately.

"Help you?"

"Yes, please," I said, wanting to sound as pleasant and non-threatening as possible. "Jackson Gamble to see Mr. Cherry. Is he at home today?"

"Gamble," the voice said. "Is Mr. Cherry expecting you?"

"No, but I think he'll want to see me. I have someone with me I know he'll want to talk to. His name is Tommy Mack."

"Just a minute. I'll see if he's available."

I waited. And then I waited some more.

It took about ten minutes before the gate rolled back. "Go ahead and drive in, Mr. Gamble. Follow the driveway up to the front of the house. Somebody will meet you there."

* * *

If I had taken the time to look up Red Cherry's home address on Google Earth, I wouldn't have been quite as surprised as I was when I saw that his Mount Juliet home wasn't the Windsor Castle-sized residence I had expected. Instead, it was a pink brick ranch that would have been within the monetary reach of anybody earning a mid-six-figure annual salary—plus a hefty year-end bonus, of course. I guessed four bedrooms, or maybe five. A four-car garage, a tennis court and a swimming pool. Probably a media room. Altogether, the usual package for high-income types working both sides of the law.

As instructed by the disembodied voice from the gatepost intercom, I followed the long driveway for a hundred yards or so and parked next to the front steps. Not one, but two somebodies were there, waiting. They were doing their best to look like they belonged in a neighborhood like this one, dressed as they were in colorful golf shirts and khaki slacks. But between the gallons of jailhouse ink on their exposed skin and the poorly concealed sidearms they were packing, it was pretty clear that they were a couple of bodyguards working for Red. And although neither one of them presented a threatening appearance, there were no smiles all around, either.

"Okay, Tommy," I said to my passenger. "Let's go say hello to Red." I got out of the car, walked around to the passenger side, and opened the door. Tommy wasn't moving. I said, "Coming?"

"Are you sure this is going to be okay, Mr. Gamble?" Tommy's voice, and indeed, his entire self seemed to have gotten smaller, as if he was dissolving, like the wicked witch of the west, right into the upholstery of his seat.

"No, I'm not sure. But I am sure that this is the only real chance you've got to walk away from this mess and maybe get back to that lady who seems to have taken a liking to you."

The two bodyguards who met Tommy and me at the door escorted us through the house and out the back door to a large patio area that included a fair-sized swimming pool. But not before they patted us both down very professionally and very thoroughly. I expected to be frisked, and so left my Colt in its holster in the trunk of my car. I wasn't really worried about Tommy packing. In his entire career, he had never been known to use a weapon, although as frightened as he was—and for good reason—I probably shouldn't have ruled the possibility out.

Once outside, we waited alongside the pool while Red swam a few laps before climbing out. I had to admire his technique. He moved easily through the water with powerful strokes and well-coordinated movements. After he climbed out of the water, he toweled off his face and his hair and put on a short terrycloth robe. Then he walked over and stood next to Tommy and me. Red was, if anything, even fitter than I remembered: well-muscled, narrow-waisted, and broad-chested. For a fifty-odd year-old man, he could not have been in better physical condition.

"Mister Gamble," he said, without offering his hand, "you should have called ahead. I might have had company, you know."

"I do know that. And I'm sorry to show up like this with no notice, but I thought what I needed to talk to you about wasn't something that should wait."

He stepped into a pair of white, oversized New Balance sneakers. "And that is?"

"Brought your property back." I reached into my pocket and handed him the package I'd taken from Tommy. "I also did what you asked me to do when you came by the office the other day, although I don't expect any money for it."

For the first time since we'd walked in, Red turned his attention to Tommy. And in that instant, time seemed to stop dead in its tracks. I thought for a moment that I had made a serious mistake bringing Tommy with me. At a minimum, I pictured myself driving back to the city while Tommy stayed behind, never to be seen again, alive or dead. At worst, I thought, neither one of us would be driving anywhere, ever again.

"By doing what I asked, you mean you brought me this guy?" It took a beat or two until it sank in what I meant. Then he stiffened, and his eyes got narrow. "So then, this is the rat bastard that broke into my house? And stole my grandmother's jewelry?" He turned to face Tommy directly. The expression on his face was one that would scare the life out of a blind man.

"Is that right? Did you break into my home?"

"Wait a minute. You bailed him out, and now you're saying you don't know who he is?"

"Don't be stupid. I know who he is. I want him to admit what he did. So. Again. Did you break into my home and steal my property? Simple question. Yes or no."

Tommy stared at the ground. He nodded his head and mumbled something I couldn't quite make out. But Red heard all he needed to. He cocked his fist and hit Tommy squarely in the middle of his face with enough force that I thought for a moment the little man's head might come off. Tommy flew, more than fell, backward onto the concrete pool apron. He bounced once, and then he lay still. Red wasn't quite finished, though. He kicked Tommy viciously in the ribs, the impact solid enough to roll him over far enough to expose his back. Then he stomped down hard, once, and then a second time, between Tommy's shoulder blades. Finally, in an act of almost inexpressible cruelty and violence, he stepped down on Tommy's upper right arm and then yanked his wrist sharply upward. I could hear tendons snapping as his elbow gave way. Tommy screamed once and blacked out.

And then, just like that, Robert Edward Cherry's rage seemed to dissipate, and he was once again at his ease, in perfect self-control. He handed me back the handkerchief with the jewelry.

"You might as well let him keep this. It isn't worth much, and I never really knew my grandmother, anyway. For all I know, she bought it at a rummage sale." He shot a glance at Tommy, and for a second or two, I thought he was going to kick him again—or worse, break his other arm. But the moment, and his fury, had passed, almost as if it had never happened at all.

"Come on inside, and let's have a drink. I'll get my guys to get your friend cleaned up a little, and then you can have him back. He looks like he might need a doctor."

Not wanting to argue and not having any other choice, I followed him into the house.

* * *

Ten minutes and a double shot of George Dickel on the rocks later, I was back in my car, a little bleary-eyed, but anxious as hell to get as far away from Red Cherry as possible. Tommy was already there, seated on the passenger side. His eyes were closed, and he was swaying slowly back and forth, moaning softly to himself and cradling his useless right arm against his body with his left. Someone had been thoughtful enough to throw a beach towel over the seat, so that the blood that was still dripping from his nose and a nasty contusion on the back of his head where it had hit the concrete wouldn't get on the Porsche's leather upholstery.

Classy guy, that Red Cherry.

The sliding gate was already open when I got to the end of the driveway. I pulled partway out onto the street to check traffic, then turned right to head back toward Nashville. I got maybe a hundred yards when I saw an M8-series BMW coming toward me from the opposite direction. I didn't think much about it until it had already passed me. That was when I realized the driver was someone I'd seen before. The driver's name was Phillip May, and sure enough, when he reached the gateposts in front of Red Cherry's estate, he turned into the driveway.

So, Red was expecting company after all.

* * *

Three-quarters of an hour later, I dropped Tommy back at Abigail Crowley's condo. When she came to the door, she took one look at him, and the color drained from her face so fast that I thought she might faint. But then she pulled herself together and gave me a look that could have frightened Mother Teresa into admitting she knew where Jimmy Hoffa was buried.

After the two of us helped him inside and got him situated on the couch, she said, "I thought you were going to protect him." Her voice was harder than I would have thought possible.

"I did protect him. Otherwise, he wouldn't be alive. As it is, I'm pretty sure now that nobody is going to try to come after him again. Plus," I said, "he gets to keep the jewelry he stole. Not that it's worth much, but if nothing else, it should serve as a reminder of how close he came to today being the last day of his life."

I knew it was weak, but under the circumstances, it was the best I could do. But I also knew there wasn't much else I could have done. Red Cherry's predilection for violence had followed him north from the Gulf Coast to the mid-south, and seeing what he was capable of reminded me, as if I needed reminding, that Tommy and I were probably both lucky to get away with our lives.

"You call the condition he's in now protection?"

"I call it still being alive, Ms. Crowley. I know it's not pretty, but he's not dead, and he can tell you all about what happened when he's feeling up to it. But for now, I think you should put him in your car, which, as you say, he was kind enough to return and drive him to a hospital." I gave her my card. "Call me when you get him settled. We can talk some more then, if you'd like."

* * *

After I got home, I tried to think of a plausible reason why Phillip May would be paying a visit to Red Cherry's home. I could only think of two that made any sense. One was that May owed Cherry money, possibly the result of a gambling debt or a loan repayment, and he wanted to deliver the money personally. But that seemed unlikely. Organized crime bosses like Cherry are sometimes involved in loansharking, but the actual loan and repayment process is usually handled by some underling farther down the food chain. I couldn't imagine a college professor like Phillip May being deeply enough into hock to a mob boss to merit a face-to-face meeting with the big man himself. But then, I also couldn't quite imagine how somebody like Phillip May, working as an instructor at a small, private college, was able to swing the purchase price of an exotic German import costing upward of six figures.

Maybe the answer to that was that May and Cherry were partnered up in some kind of illegal enterprise that involved Saint Bernadette University. I supposed it was at least possible that May was selling drugs on campus. That would account for the extra income needed to swing the purchase of a high-end BMW. The other possibility was that May had engaged in a sexual relationship with a female student and was now being blackmailed. But a situation like that would seem to suggest that he would have less money rather than more. And even if that were the case, what would that have to do with Red Cherry?

And then again, maybe it was something else altogether, although I couldn't think what. It was hard to imagine, given the relatively small size of the Saint Bernadette academic community, that any kind of illegal activity on the part of a full-time professor could go unnoticed for very long. Still, on the premise that it was at least worth looking into, I decided I should get back in touch with Robert Levy to find out whether he might be willing to give me more information on Professor Phillip May.

And then there was the problem regarding what had just happened to Tommy Mack. Was there anything I could do to make up for the horrific injury he'd suffered? At the time, I was pretty certain that Red wouldn't kill him, and for that matter, have me killed, just to make sure there would be no witnesses. And I figured, now that it was done, whatever enmity that Red might still hold for Tommy was probably over with. I also knew that, at the time Red's attack on Tommy took place, there wasn't anything I could have done to prevent it. I could have tried to get between them, I supposed, but all that would have done was delay the inevitable. And in a perverse sort of way, I decided that my being there probably kept Tommy from an even worse beating, if not the end of his life. So, for now, at least, that would have to be enough.

Chapter Twenty-Four

When Maggie called at nine o'clock that night, I was well into my second six-pack of Stella. I was trying to forget what had taken place earlier, but my mind didn't seem to want to let go of the sound Tommy Mack's right elbow made when Red Cherry snapped it like a dead tree limb. Perhaps for that reason, I was pretty far down the road to getting knee-walking drunk. Maggie picked up on it right away.

"Bad day?"

"The worst so far this year. I was thinking of coming over."

There was a beat. "You don't need to be driving. Just stay put. I'll be there in twenty minutes."

It actually took her twenty-five. That gave me enough time to finish the beer I was drinking and open another. I was halfway through that one when she came through the front door. She gave a quick look at the empty green bottles lined up like soldiers in rank order on my living room cocktail table.

"Looks like you've got a little bit of a head start on me." She dropped her purse on a side table and went into the kitchen. When she came back, she was holding a vodka and cranberry juice in a tall glass. A very tall glass. It might be a very interesting evening.

"Okay," she said, taking a seat in one of the two occasional chairs I keep in my living room. "Do you want to talk about it? And I promise, if you want me to hold the questions until the end, I'll be perfectly happy to just sit and listen."

So, I told her about my day. How Tommy had called, and I had convinced him that the best thing he could do if he wanted to keep on breathing was to return the stuff he'd stolen from Red Cherry. My hope was that Red wouldn't have one of his hired hands put a bullet into Tommy's brain—and perhaps mine as well—and instead would give him a pass in exchange for getting his property back.

Maggie took off her shoes and folded her legs underneath her. "But judging from the state of affairs we're looking at here, I'm guessing that's not how it went down. And before you say anything, you never said I should hold my questions until the end."

I half-laughed at that. "No, it wasn't, although as you can see, I'm still alive and well." And then I told her what Red had done to Tommy. "And there wasn't a damn thing I could do about it. It happened so fast, I didn't even see it coming, but even if I had..." I let the thought trail off.

"Then what happened? No, wait. Let me fix myself another drink."

She disappeared back into the kitchen. I heard ice cubes clinking, and then, after another minute, she reappeared with a fresh drink. And I was amazed all over again how quickly Maggie can knock back a shooter.

"Okay, so what happened after that?"

"I had a drink with Red while his guys cleaned Tommy up a bit. Then I drove him back to the city and dropped him at his lady friend's apartment with instructions to take him to a hospital. I gave her my number and said to call me after she got him settled. I'm pretty sure the ER docs aren't going to buy a story about how he fell down a flight of stairs, or whatever bullshit Tommy makes up. Which also means my name is likely to come up, and that means I'm probably going to be talking to the cops before another day goes by."

* * *

In fact, I never heard from law enforcement, at least not with respect to Tommy Mack. I spent an hour and a half the next morning after Maggie left for work, nursing a hangover and then calling one Nashville hospital after another, trying to locate Tommy. When I finally found the right place, I asked to be connected to his room. However, I was informed that he was in recovery from surgery and would not be taking calls or visitors until later in the day. That gave me time to get cleaned up, eat a decent meal, and drive downtown to the office to check messages and make a few phone calls.

When I got to the office, the telephone was ringing. I was too late to catch it before it went to voicemail, but the call was from Caroline Feldman at Saint Bernadette University. I pressed the callback button and waited three rings before she answered.

"Mister Gamble," she said when she picked up. "I tried calling yesterday, but I suppose you were out of the office, and your cell wasn't answering, either."

"I'm sorry, Mrs. Feldman. Yesterday was a little bit of a bad day."

"Yes. I can see where someone in your line of work might have some rough patches." When I didn't say anything to that, she went on. "Anyway, as you requested when we spoke earlier, I went back through our enrollment records for the second semester of the year Isaac Bergman, well, what? Went missing? As I recall, you were interested in finding out whether there were any students who might have left the university around the same time. Now, there were about two dozen who were early graduates who left after the first semester, but I didn't think they would have been the people you were interested in, so I didn't put them on the list."

"So, not counting early graduates, were you able to come up with any names?"

"Well, of course, there was the rest of the graduating class, about six hundred in all, but I'm guessing that isn't what you were looking for, either."

"No," I said, wondering if she was ever going to get to the point. "I'm interested in students who left for no apparent reason, or at least, not because of graduation."

"That's what I thought. And in that case, I have four names for you. If you have a pad and pencil handy, I can give them to you."

"Go ahead."

"Very well. These first two individuals are both—were both—seniors, so, of course, it seemed odd that either of them would have dropped out such a short time before graduation, especially since they had enough credits. Their names are Roberta Eisley—that's E-I-S-L-E-Y, and Geneva Robertson."

I wrote those down.

"The others are James Paul and Madison Burgess, both juniors." I stopped writing when I heard that last name. And I felt the hair on the back of my neck stand up straight. I chose my next words carefully, not wanting to convey the uneasy feeling that was squirming around inside me.

"What can you tell me about these students, Mrs. Feldman? Anything at all would be helpful. I'm especially interested in their course loads and their grades. And whether they lived on campus, or did they live at home and commute to class?"

"Well," she told me, "Their personal information is confidential, so I can't really tell you anything about their grades, or whether they had any problems that might have come to the attention of the university's administration. I can tell you all four students were in good standing at the time they left school, and all of them lived in our residence halls. None of them were in danger of failing any of their classes. In fact, Roberta Eisley and Geneva Robertson were both awarded their diplomas even thought they were no longer inattendance at the university."

"So, you have no idea why they left? Or where they went next?"

"None that I can disclose, I'm afraid. But I can tell you they were all from local homes, so I don't imagine you'll have too much trouble running them down."

And with that, our conversation was pretty much over. I thanked Mrs. Feldman and hung up the phone. Not thirty seconds later, another call came in, and I knew from the caller ID it wasn't going to be good, so I let it go to voicemail. There was something I needed to do first, and I had to go home to do it.

Chapter Twenty-Five

On my way home from the office, I stopped at a Publix grocery store and picked up a few things I needed, including Diet Coke, a six-pack of Stella, a quart of cranberry juice, some chips, and a couple of frozen dinners. Once everything was put away, I took another look at the daily calendar that belonged to Isaac Bergman. When I went back through the notations for the months of February and March, in the year he went missing, I was able to match up the initials I found on the various dates in Bergman's calendar with the names of the students who had dropped out before the end of the semester. Sure enough, "RE" lined up with Roberta Eisley; "GR" matched Geneva Robertson, and "MB" matched Madison Burgess. There was no corresponding set of initials, "JP," for James Paul. There were other initials in Bergman's calendar, but whoever those students were had apparently finished out the semester or had graduated.

So, in each instance, Isaac Bergman had evidently met with MB, GR, and RE early in a particular week and then again at the end of the week. And the first set of numbers noted next to the initials likely corresponded to the time the meeting took place. But what the second set of numbers indicated was anybody's guess. Whatever was going on, though, it was clear that, for all three female students who left the university before the end of the semester, there had been some ongoing connection between them and Professor Bergman.

I felt as though I should be congratulating myself for having achieved a breakthrough, except that I had no idea what that breakthrough actually was—if, in fact, it was anything at all. Frustrated, I set the calendar and my notebook aside and went into the kitchen to warm up one of the frozen dinners I'd bought earlier.

I was in the kitchen, cleaning up after my supper, when I heard Maggie drive up and park in the driveway behind the Panamera. Most people would keep a car that expensive in the garage, but mine will only accommodate a single car, and since these days the Porsche is my daily driver, I leave it out so that I don't have to move my Beatles-on-the-Ed-Sullivan-Show-era Thunderbird out of the way every time I go out.

When the doorbell rang—it's a courtesy we extend to one another even though we each have a key to the other's home, I shouted, "Come," and she let herself in. She was dressed for work in navy blue slacks, matching shoes, and a light blue top, and she was carrying a purse and a briefcase, which she dropped on a chair in the living room.

"Tough day?" I asked.

"Easy day. I had three clients scheduled, but two of them didn't show up. One called to reschedule, and the other got into some kind of a fight with her husband and wound up in the emergency room, so I had the afternoon free to catch up on paperwork."

That last bit reminded me that I owed Wanda Beaudry a return call from the one I'd let go to voicemail earlier in the afternoon. Tomorrow, I thought, would be soon enough for that.

Maggie wandered into the kitchen and mixed herself one of her usual cocktails. Then she came back into the living room and sat down on the couch next to me.

"What's this?" She picked up the calendar book I'd found among Isaac Bergman's effects. I'd put it aside when I was working in the kitchen earlier and had left it on the cocktail table close to where she was sitting. I explained that I'd managed to match up the initials with the handful of Saint Bernadette students who had dropped out of their classes at about the same time Isaac had gone missing.

"Three of the four who dropped out are female students. A woman named Caroline Feldman, who is the registrar at the college, helped me put names to the initials. Tomorrow, I'll start running them down to see if I can figure out what was going on between them and Bergman. It looks like he met with the students early in the week and then on the weekend. I'm guessing one set of numbers is a time of day, but I haven't figured out yet what the other number indicates."

Maggie studied the entries for a moment, then flipped back a page or two. "You say these are all female students?"

"All but one. There was a guy who dropped out about the same time, but he doesn't show up in Bergman's calendar. I don't know; maybe he was trying to talk them out of leaving school."

She shook her head and gave me a look like a teacher would give to a slow student. "That's not what's going on here."

"No?"

"No. He pencils them in on Monday and then again on Friday or Saturday. Only the second meeting isn't with Isaac, and the other numbers are dollar amounts. Gamble, he isn't trying to keep them in school. That's not it at all. He's prostituting them out."

Chapter Twenty-Six

The next morning was Saturday, and even though it was the weekend, I was back in the office and on the telephone. My first call was to Wanda Beaudry, returning her call from the previous afternoon. As usual, I had to go through the routine of asking to speak to her, leaving my number, and then waiting for her to call me back. I waited maybe ten minutes before my phone rang.

"Nice of you to get back to me so promptly," she said, without preliminaries. "I thought I'd hear back from you yesterday."

"It's been a bad week," I told her. "I wasn't ghosting you."

"Then I'll forgive you this time, because I know how that goes and because I wanted to follow up on something that I'm going to need your help with. But not right away."

"Please tell me you're having a casino night as a fundraiser, and you need a dealer at your blackjack table. Something simple like that."

"I wish." There was a pause, and I knew she was working up to asking me to do something I wasn't going to want to do. "You remember that Victor Robles guy we talked about? The one who beat up his woman? I know I mentioned this to you earlier."

"You mean the guy who's a member of a murderous street gang? The one we don't want to get near for any reason? That guy?"

"That's the one. And unfortunately, he did a number on her again. This time, she's in the hospital, in a coma from head trauma. I spoke to one of the ER nurses there, a woman who lived here at the shelter for a while a year or so ago. She told me Rosaria—that's her name, you may also remember—that

Rosaria might be circling the drain."

"And what do the cops say?"

"Well, they picked him up for questioning, because, of course, the hospital contacted them as soon as Rosaria was brought in. But they can't do anything unless she files a complaint. And obviously, she can't do that until she wakes up, if she ever does."

"Then there's nothing you can do either. I mean, for all you know, this time, she really did fall down the stairs and hit her head."

"Yeah, I'm sure that's exactly what happened. And then, with her head cracked open, she got up and walked five miles from where she lives to Centennial Park, where she collapsed on the sidewalk next to the duck pond. That's where one of the groundskeepers found her the next morning. Mister Robles says he doesn't know what happened to her, or how she got there."

"Okay," I said. "What is it you want to do? And what do you need me for?"

"For the time being, nothing. As it so happens, when MPD went to interview Robles, it turned out he had a few outstanding warrants. No major weight, but there were a couple of assault beefs, so they hauled him in. And when he went into arraignment court, he found himself in front of a judge named Amanda McCracken."

"Ah," I said. I knew Judge McCracken by reputation. She had been elected and then re-elected a couple more times, running on a "get tough on repeat offenders" platform.

"So, she remanded him?"

"Toot sweet, as they say. Called him a menace to the community. But he does have a lawyer, and the guy has already said he plans to appeal the no-bail. So, if he does get out, we're going to need to pay him a call. But as far as you're concerned, this one will be easy. I just need you to drive the car. You won't even have to turn the engine off."

"Are you going to tell me the plan, or am I better off not knowing?"

"The second," she said. "I'll be back in touch when I hear how the appeal goes. Until then, think of this as a save the date."

"Right." But I remembered the last time I had helped Wanda settle accounts with a guy who had put a bad beating on his wife. It had been four years ago.

We tracked the guy down at his home, in the small hours of the morning after a late-night drinking bout with some of his shit-kicker buddies. Wanda tased him, and we dragged him into the house. Straight off, Wanda wanted to kill him, but I said nothing doing. He hadn't killed his wife, so she needed to leave the scales balanced. In the end, she gave him a shot of Ketamine and then snipped a quarter-inch off the end of the guy's penis. That seemed like a fair punishment for what he had done and one he wasn't likely to forget. And that's where it should have ended. But a week later, the guy got himself killed anyway, in a shootout with the police when he tried to break into another women's shelter where he thought his wife was staying; only she wasn't. Since then, my contacts with Wanda had been strictly social.

"If I'm going to do this," I said, "then I'm going to ask you to do something for me. I need another records check. The guy's name is Pomeroy, comma, Michael. LKA is somewhere in Florida. No idea where, but now he's relocated back to Nashville, so you might need to look in a couple of places."

"What am I looking for?"

"The usual. Arrest records, civil judgments, restraining orders. Also, does he own a gun? I don't think he's a hard case. I just want to know if he's been up to anything sketchy."

"Right. So, who is he, exactly?"

"Maggie's ex. He's back in town after a bust-up with wife number two. He says he's a changed man, and he wants to get back together with Maggie."

"Did he say he's found Jesus?"

"More like he found Old Granddad. I think he might be a problem."

"Well, Florida doesn't keep very close track of guns, but other than that, I should have something for you in a day or two."

After we hung up, I started thinking about what I had just agreed to do and what a stupid mistake I'd made. After Wanda's own experience with the boyfriend who had beaten her to within a heartbeat of killing her, and after many years of protecting and comforting the terrified women who turned up at her shelter, she had transformed herself by degrees into a one-woman vigilance committee. In a nutshell, the problem was an obvious one. Most of the women who came to Wanda for help were afraid to file charges against their abusers, either because experience had taught them the law could do very little to help them, or because, at some point, they had to return home. A few days, a few weeks, a month would go by, and then the cycle of abuse would start all over again. Wanda's self-appointed mission was to break the cycle, by whatever means necessary. And whatever she had planned for Victor Robles, it was not going to be good.

* * *

Next up, I wanted to talk with Robert Levy. I was curious about what was the legal trouble between Isaac Bergman and the university. I supposed that the simple answer was that he was planning to file—or maybe did file—a wrongful discharge lawsuit.

When I dialed Levy's number, his housekeeper, Roseanne Burgess, picked up. Just to be saying something while I waited for Levy to come to the phone, I asked Mrs. Burgess how her knee replacement recovery was coming along.

"Just fine, thanks for asking. 'Course, I still have some bad days where it hurts like the very dickens, especially after I go to therapy. I'm trying to get around a little more without using this blasted cane, and so long as I don't try to do too much, it seems to be gettin' stronger."

I told her I was glad to hear it and asked to speak to Professor Levy.

"Mister Gamble," Robert Levy said when he picked up. "How goes your investigation? Have you made any progress finding out who killed Sarah?"

"I'm not investigating her death, Professor. So, the answer is no progress whatsoever."

There was a pause. "Then I don't understand what it is you are doing."

I said, "Professor Levy, I'm not a policeman. There are capable detectives working on Sarah's case, and I have no doubt they will identify the killer. As I thought I made clear when we first talked, my priority is still finding out what happened to Isaac Bergman. If something falls out while I'm shaking that tree, then fine, I'll turn over whatever I discover to the police and let them do their job."

"I see. Then perhaps you can tell me why you're calling me at all."

"Shortly before she was killed, Sarah Bergman gave me a box containing various documents and other things that had belonged to her husband. One of those things was an address book, where I found the name of an attorney named Luther Fanning." I paused to see if that might get a reaction. When I got none, I continued.

"Fanning indicated that Isaac had contacted him regarding a lawsuit that he was considering filing against Saint Bernadette for wrongful discharge. I was just wondering whether you might be able to shed any light on that."

Another pause. "I'm afraid not. Isaac never spoke to me about anything like that, and I don't think such action would even be possible. Isaac didn't have tenure, so the university was free to terminate his employment for any reason at all. That would have been spelled out very clearly in his contract, which, in Isaac's case, would have had to be renewed every year. They don't automatically roll over."

"So, no job security at all."

"Nothing contractual, no. Evaluations of non-tenured faculty are made at the conclusion of the academic term. There are a number of factors considered, such as publishing history, student survey results, and observations by the chair of the department."

"Understood," I said. "But Fanning told me that he did investigate whether Bergman's suit was at least something he ought to pursue. So, he contacted the university's general counsel to be certain Saint Bernadette was within its rights to let Isaac go. After that conversation, he told Isaac he had no case."

"Then what are we talking about here?"

"When I spoke to Fanning, he said that the person he spoke with at the university intimated that Bergman's dismissal had something to do with sex. That was the way he put it. It was about sex."

"And you're wondering whether I knew anything about that."

"Yes, sir, I am."

"Well then, I will tell you. What I knew was that Isaac Bergman was a good-looking man whom many of the women on campus found attractive. And I have no doubt that there were more than a few liaisons that likely involved Isaac and some of those same women. I also know that Professor

Bergman was cautioned several times about his—what shall we say—his free and easy style where women were concerned. But I don't think it was the ultimate cause of his dismissal, although it certainly played a part. As I explained to you earlier, he simply didn't publish anything of any real consequence, and even in a small school like Saint Bernadette, that still counts for something."

"Okay, but when I went through the box of personal effects Bergman's wife gave me, I ran across a daily planning calendar that had some interesting entries. For instance, during some weeks, there apparently were meetings with certain individuals. No names, just initials, times, and a second set of numbers included as part of the second meeting."

"And what did you make of that?"

"Nothing, at least not at first, although I was able to match up the initials with some female students who left the university early. Before graduation, you see."

"Perhaps Bergman was trying to convince them to stay in school."

"No, sir, he wasn't. I wasn't able to see it, but my friend recognized it right away. I'm afraid that what Professor Bergman was doing, for lack of a more delicate term, was pimping these girls out. They were turning tricks for him, and he was probably splitting the money with them. And I think somebody else figured out what he was doing and killed him, either as retribution for the damage he was doing to these young women or else to keep his activities from becoming public knowledge. If not that, then one of the girls, or a parent or a brother, decided to put Bergman out of business.

"And?"

"And I wasn't sure before, but now I am. Isaac Bergman is dead, and his wife was murdered to make sure nobody would ever find out the reason why. So, with that in mind, my question to you is, were you aware of what Isaac Bergman was doing, or can you think of anyone else who might have known?"

Levy was quiet for a moment, as if in thought. Finally, he said, "So then, reading between the lines, what you're really asking me is do I know who killed him?"

Chapter Twenty-Seven

With nothing on either of our calendars, Maggie and I slept late Sunday and then took in a matinee movie at a local cineplex. During the years we have been together, I've learned that, regardless of whether or not the film she chooses is one that I would have selected, she never fails to pick a good one. The one she selected for today's outing was based on a best-selling novel about a young woman who lived alone in the Carolina swamplands. After fending off an unwanted suitor who later turns up dead, she is charged with his murder. Eventually, she's acquitted and becomes a noted wildlife artist. It was a much better choice than the one I wanted to see that had to do with some comic-book superhero saving the world from an inter-dimensional alien attack.

After the movie, we went to a fast-casual restaurant for drinks and an early dinner, and then back to Maggie's condo, where Stanley, her cat, was waiting close to the door, apparently wanting to be fed. Still in a good mood from the pleasant day we had spent together and momentarily forgetting Stanley's attitude toward me, I reached down to pet him. It took him just a fraction of a second to realize who I was before his paw flew out, claws extended, and hooked me on the back of the hand. Then he hissed and ran upstairs to Maggie's guest bedroom, where he hid out under the bed until I left the next morning.

* * *

Abigail Crowley did not just drop Tommy Mack at the Baptist Hospital emergency room and drive off into the night. Instead, she went in with him, and, then, waited several hours while the ER docs checked him over before reaching the obvious conclusion that it would be necessary to admit him. The first thing they did was administer a shot of morphine to relieve the pain, which, after the shock had worn off, became excruciating. Then, they took X-rays and an MRI before determining that surgery would be needed to repair the torn tendons and detached muscles in his damaged right arm. However, since it was late in the day and no orthopedic surgeon was immediately available, Tommy was taken upstairs to a room and scheduled for surgery first thing the following morning.

The next morning, I was in the office when Abigail Crowley called to update me on Tommy's situation. There were several cracked ribs, but no damage to his back where Red had stomped down. No bones in his arm had been broken, she said, but there was extensive damage to the bicep tendon, the two collateral ligaments, and something called the joint capsule, all of which work in tandem to permit movement and to join the bone and the muscle in the upper arm to the two bones that comprise the lower arm. In addition, there was nerve damage that might limit both the use of, and the sensitivity in, his right hand.

"I stayed here with him all night, and I was here when he came out of the surgery. He's not in any pain right now. Lord knows, he's so doped up, I'm surprised he can even talk. But he doesn't blame you for what happened. He told me about how he had gotten into that man's house and stolen his property, and he said he got all that was coming to him. And, he promised me he was going to change his ways."

"That would be a good idea," I said, not knowing what else to say.

"Also," and here she hesitated for a moment, "he wants me to buy him a gun. He said since he has a criminal record, he won't be able to buy one for himself. So, I was wondering. I don't know how to do that, so would you be able to help me do that? I'll pay you for your trouble, of course."

This time I knew exactly what to say. "Ms. Crowley, that would be a very bad idea."

In fact, Abigail didn't need my help at all to buy a gun. In Tennessee, buying a gun is simple. An individual goes into a gun shop or a sporting goods store, fills out a federal form, waits a minute or two while the information on the form is checked, and then pays for the gun and leaves. Except for the paperwork, it's just like buying a lawn mower, or a hamburger at a fast-food restaurant. On the other hand, it is a federal offense to make a "straw purchase" of a gun, meaning, a person cannot buy a firearm for the purpose of handing it over to another individual who is legally barred from owning it. For that reason, I wanted no part of obtaining a gun for Tommy Mack.

"Ms. Crowley, you seem like a good woman, and I think once Tommy gets past whatever is the charge he's facing at the moment, you can help him turn his life around. But putting a gun in his hands will not move his redemption forward one bit.

"Beyond that, Tommy has a criminal record, something you already know. Some of those convictions were for low-level felonies, and even though they were non-violent offenses, the fact that he is a convicted felon means he is not permitted to own a firearm. And if you try to obtain one for him, you are also committing a felony. So, my advice is to forget about Tommy getting a gun of any kind. If he's truly worried about his safety, I suggest after he gets his legal troubles cleared up here in Tennessee, that he should think about moving someplace far away, where nobody knows him, and nobody cares about anything he might have done in his past life."

"I understand," she said. But she didn't sound convinced, so I wished them both good luck and hung up. But it was only later that it came to me why he wanted to get his hands on a gun, and I also realized that I really didn't care.

* * *

With no appointments on my calendar, I tried running a computer search for the four dropouts who had taken leave of Saint Bernadette University at around the same time that Isaac Bergman vanished. As a first pass, I went to an online telephone directory and entered, one after the other, the names Roberta Eisley, Geneva Robertson, James Paul, and Madison Burgess. Not surprisingly, I got lots of hits for the names Robertson and Paul, although none of them had first names that matched the individuals I was looking for. And it didn't take long afterward for me to realize that, given the number of young adults who still were living at home with their parents, plus the fact that almost no young people have landlines anymore, I was probably barking up the wrong tree.

Digging a little deeper, I next tried an Internet search site that, for a fee, tracks down individuals by name, including current and previous addresses, landline and cell phone numbers, aliases, and criminal records. Again, I had no luck, except with James Paul. I found out he was now Staff Sergeant James Robert Paul, currently serving with the United States Army at Fort Sam Houston in San Antonio, Texas. I made a note of his telephone numbers as well as the main number for Fort Houston, which I learned is known colloquially as "Fort Sam," as well as the "Home of Army Medicine." I wasn't entirely sure what I was looking for with respect to Sergeant Paul, except perhaps that he might have been involved in recruiting girls for Bergman's prostitution ring.

A call to Fort Sam revealed that Sergeant James was, at the moment, assigned to the Brian Allgood Army Community Hospital in Seoul, South Korea. The information officer I spoke with could not give me any details regarding the exact nature of James's responsibilities, only that he was on active duty at the hospital. So, for the time being, at least, that was that.

Before calling it a day, I telephoned Marvin Calvert. We exchanged a few pleasantries before he informed me that he hadn't been able to dig up any information regarding Isaac Bergman beyond what we already knew. That officially made his disappearance a cold case, which meant that, as far as the cops were concerned, unless his remains turned up at a construction site excavation, or a hunter in the woods stumbled across his bleached bones during deer season, his whereabouts were likely to remain unknown.

I thanked him for the update and then asked whether he'd mind checking into one more thing for me. "Could you go back through your records for about the same time as Bergman went missing to see whether there were any criminal complaints or investigations having to do with Saint Bernadette University?"

"I could, I guess," he told me. "But it'd be simpler if I knew what I was looking for."

"Anything to do with either prostitution or drugs."

"You think your guy was involved in something like that?"

"Just a hunch," I told him. "We're talking about a college campus here. Lots of kids, lots of pretty girls, and maybe a popular professor who maybe saw an opportunity to make a little money on the side. I know it's a long shot, but I'm running out of ideas."

"I understand. But if you don't hear back, it's not because I'm blowing you off. It just means nothing turned up, okay?"

I said that was fair, and we hung up.

Chapter Twenty-Eight

Wanda Beaudry called me at home early that evening with a couple of updates. First, Victor Robles was still behind bars at the county lockup.

"My guy at the courthouse told me his lawyer's appeal of the remand order and the request for bail pancaked off the end of the runway. Apparently, the good Senor Robles is something of a known quantity within judicial circles, so he'll be sitting tight while the cops wait for his wife to come around and swear out a complaint."

"So, still in stir," I said. "Good to hear."

"Also, I was able to dig up some information on your Michael Pomeroy."

"And?"

"There's not a whole lot. He was married to somebody named Julianne Lynne Stapleton. Divorced after five years, citing irreconcilable differences, whatever the hell that means."

"It means they got to a point where they couldn't stand the sight of one another."

"Thanks for clearing that up. Anyway, no kids, she got the house along with the mortgage. They split the savings and the investments. He was working as a regional manager for a restaurant chain that took it on the chin as a result of COVID and got laid off. His LKA in Florida was an apartment in a town called Bradford, which is just north of Tallahassee."

"Doesn't sound like much, does it?" I said. "Any criminal record? Restraining orders, anything like that?"

"Couple of DUI's, including a six-month license suspension, except to drive to and from work. Also, he got pinched a couple times on domestic violence charges. I don't know, maybe that's what the irreconcilable differences were all about. I can tell you from experience, it's hell living with a drunk." There was a pause. "What's the story with this guy, Gamble? You worried he's going to give your Maggie a hard time?"

"No. I'm planning to make sure he doesn't."

* * *

It took me less than an hour the next morning to run down an address for Michael Pomeroy. It actually isn't that difficult to find somebody if you know the right people working in the right places. In this case, it meant getting in touch with a guy named Drew Logan at the license bureau. Drew was a guy I'd helped slither through a couple of very messy divorces several years back, no charge. That meant I could always count on him for DMV-type information when I needed it. I took a chance that, if Pomeroy was serious about relocating back to Nashville, he'd eventually get around to changing out his Florida driver's license and vehicle registration, and sure enough, he had. The address he listed on his registration, which was for a 2013 Ford Taurus, was a rented apartment in Madison, on the north side of the city. I thought about heading straight out to pay him a visit, and then decided to wait and see whether he made any further effort to contact Maggie. My hope was that her telling him that she had no wish to see him again would be sufficient to dissuade him from making a nuisance of himself.

* * *

When I got home that evening, I found Maggie's Volvo parked in my driveway. Normally, we don't do sleepovers except on the weekends, and since today was Tuesday, my first thought was that something either very good or very bad had happened. In either instance, I knew from experience, if there was something she wanted to discuss, she didn't want to do it over the telephone.

When I walked into the house, Maggie was sitting on the couch with one of her cranberry juice cocktails on the table in front of her. That meant it was bad.

"Michael showed up at my office today," she said, without preliminaries. "He just walked in and demanded to see me."

"Okay."

The Department of Family Services is located on the 10th floor of the UBS Tower on Deaderick Street. It's a fairly large space with a secure reception area, so nobody can just walk in off the street and demand to talk to a counselor. People with an appointment sign in at a front desk and then take a seat to wait until their name is called. At that time, someone, usually the counselor they are meeting with, comes out and escorts the individual into a conference area. In other words, nobody, Michael Pomeroy included—or me, for that matter—can simply barge into an individual caseworker's office unannounced and without an appointment.

I said, "How far did he get?"

"As far as Wellington."

"Ah," I said.

Wellington is a very large, dark-skinned man who is a former middle linebacker from Jackson State University, who is at present working on his dual master's degrees in psychology and social work. At DFS, he sometimes acts in the role of a security man, assisting caseworkers when clients are upset, or when they pose a threat to themselves or staff. The rest of the time, he holds down the reception desk. Because of his size and his ability to adopt facial expressions that are downright menacing, he is an invaluable member of the staff. The rest of the time, when he isn't looking scary, he is the kindest and most gentle man anyone could ever hope to meet.

Maggie said, "Wellington informed Michael, and I'm quoting here, that 'Ms. Totten has a full calendar for the next few days, and that he would need to make an appointment.'"

"And?"

"And Michael started shouting and demanded to see 'his wife'—that used to be me, in case you forgot—and tried to get past the desk. I'm not sure exactly what happened after that, except that Wellington escorted Michael back to the elevators. That was his term, 'escorted.' And then he came and got me and walked me to my car, and I came here since I'm pretty sure by now Michael knows where I live."

"Hold that thought." I went into the kitchen and took a bottle of beer out of the refrigerator. Then I sat down in a chair facing where Maggie was sitting. I chose that spot because I have an easier time reading her emotional state when I'm looking straight at her.

"Okay," I said. "So, we know you met with Michael at the Maxwell House cocktail lounge the other evening, and you told him to buzz off. That was after he telephoned you. And now, he's showed up at your office." I paused and took a swallow of my beer. "Have there been any other times he's tried to get in touch with you that you haven't told me about? More phone calls, or maybe emails?"

"No. Why?" Her voice went up half an octave. "Do you think I'm doing something to encourage him?"

"Of course not. But I did do some nosing around, and I believe your former husband has the potential to be more than just a nuisance. I don't know what he was like when the two of you were together, but I checked up on him, and his time in Florida did not go well."

She looked up sharply. "Checked up on him how? And why?"

"It's what I do, Maggie. You know that. I make my living looking into people's backgrounds. In Michael Pomeroy's case, he had some trouble with the law back in Florida." I gave her a quick rundown on what I had turned up. "Look. A guy loses his job. He gets upset. He starts drinking. Maybe he's not careful about where he does it, or how much, or how often. I can understand that. But beating up his wife, no. That's crossing the line."

I said, "You have never told me anything about your life when you were married, and I have respected that. I figured that was your business, and you'd talk about it if you wanted to. If you didn't, that was okay, too, because it was none of my concern, and it had nothing to do with who we are now. But I did feel that I needed to know if he represents a threat to you. Because if he does—"

CHAPTER TWENTY-EIGHT

She cut me off. "What?"

"Because if he does, I will not let that happen."

Because if he does, I will kill him.

181

Chapter Twenty-Nine

Because I was concerned for her safety following the near-confrontation with her former husband earlier that day, I suggested Maggie spend the night at my house. And rather than go to a restaurant, I quick-thawed a couple of small steaks in the microwave and then tossed them on my backyard grill.

While I tended to the outside cooking, Maggie whipped up a package of seasoned rice, plus a salad for herself and a plate of sliced tomatoes for me. Then, after dinner and dishes, we settled in on the couch with dessert and watched what turned out to be a "Gilmore Girls" marathon on one of the high three-digit cable channels. If it had been up to me, I would have chosen something else—almost anything, in fact—but she had a more stressful day than I did, so I figured for tonight, I would let her take command of the remote.

The next morning, Maggie had an early client meeting, so she was up, showered, and dressed before I had even gotten out of bed. And rather than make her wait around for me to get presentable before moving cars around in my driveway, since mine was still parked behind hers, I told her she could just take the Panamera, and I'd drive her car downtown later. Then we could have lunch together and swap cars back again. At least, that was the plan.

I pulled on a pair of gray sweatpants and a white T-shirt and walked Maggie to the front door. "Let's just move the cars," she said. "I don't want to drive that thing. I'm afraid something will happen, and it'll get damaged."

"It won't get damaged. It's just like driving any other car. There's nothing to it. Here," I said, taking the keys from her hand, "I'll even start it for you." I was showing off a little bit now, since the Porsche was equipped with remote start, something her Volvo did not have.

When I pushed the remote start button—twice, as the instructions indicate—instead of the engine turning over, there was a loud noise that sounded like *WHUMP*, followed instantly by a flash of light and then a bright fireball and a full-on explosion that lifted the 4,000-pound car completely up into the air and off the driveway onto the lawn. The accompanying shockwave blew out all the windows in the front of my house, as well as the back window and taillights of Maggie's station wagon. The Volvo was also shoved several feet forward despite the transmission and driveline being locked in PARK. The same shockwave, a force stronger and hotter than anything I have ever felt in my life, blew me backward into the house. Knocked nearly senseless, I stumbled into Maggie, who was standing several feet behind me, so that we both ended up on the floor. There was a noise in my ears that sounded like a tornado warning siren, and my face and chest burned as if I had spent an entire day standing in front of the open gates of hell.

Up and down the block, car alarms began howling, and I remember saying a silent prayer of thanks that it was still too early for any of the neighborhood children to be outside playing in their yards or riding their bicycles in the street. I tried to call out to Maggie, but nothing came out, and at the same time, I tried to sit up. When I did, my entire world started to spin, slowly at first and then very fast. And then there was nothing but blessed quiet and all-enveloping darkness.

* * *

When I finally woke up, it was several hours later, and I was lying in a bed, as I found out, on the fourth floor of St. Thomas Hospital. Somebody had removed my T-shirt and sweatpants and draped one of those hospital gowns on me, the kind that open in the back, so that anyone who cares to look can tell how much your middle-aged ass has begun to lose its muscle tone. Maggie, bless her heart, was sitting in a visitor's chair next to the bed. When

I began to stir, she looked up from the magazine she'd been reading and smiled.

"How are you feeling?"

"Like a boiled lobster," I said. "Where am I? And what time is it?"

"It's about five o'clock." She leaned over and gave me a soft kiss on my forehead. "When the EMT guys showed up, they asked me where they should take you. I told them you used to be a Catholic, so they brought you to St. Thomas. I guess they were worried you might be shaking hands with Jesus before the day was out." When I didn't say anything to that, she went on. "They'll be bringing your dinner around in a few minutes."

"No way." I shook my head no. "I'm leaving." I started to get up. It hurt like hell, and the world began to spin crazily around all over again. Maggie pushed me gently back down on the bed.

"Sorry, bub, you're not going anywhere." Her tone left no doubt where I would be spending the night. "Doctor said she thinks you can go home in the morning. She wants to keep you tonight for observation."

"Okay," I said, "How about you? Are you hurt?"

"Little bit of noise in my ears, and I landed on my butt when you crashed into me, but that's about it. But then, I wasn't standing in the open doorway like you were." She patted me on the back of my hand. "You're my hero."

"Right. So, what happened? And how did I get here?"

And so, she told me. After the Porsche exploded, in the process blowing out the windows in three more nearby houses, my across-the-street neighbor, Kline, showed up with a kitchen fire extinguisher that was of no use whatsoever in combatting the six-figure *freudenfeuer* in my front yard. He did, however, have the presence of mind to call 911, which brought the police and fire departments to my house on the double. After the EMTs got there, they clamped an oxygen mask over my face and strapped me onto a backboard, just in case I had suffered a spine injury. Then they lifted me onto a gurney and into an ambulance, and we were on our way in a matter of minutes, with Maggie in the back, holding my hand.

After a quick trip to the hospital, lights and siren all the way, I was examined by an ER specialist, who told Maggie that other than a few semi-serious burns on my chest, face, and neck and a punctured eardrum, he expected me to be fine in a few days. I was in luck, he said, after hearing Maggie's account of the events of the morning, because her car was parked between me and the explosion, partially shielding us both from what could have been a much worse outcome.

"Of course," she said, "your car is a total loss, and mine is pretty well fucked also, thank you very much."

"So, how…" I started to ask.

"After we got you settled in here, and it looked like you'd probably survive at least for a few hours, I called my insurance company, and they fixed me up with a rental. It's a Jeep something or other. You'll have to do the same when you're feeling better. Also, both the police and somebody from the fire marshal's office are going to want to talk to you. I guess they need to find out if this was some kind of an insurance hustle you were running."

Of course, they would. "Anything else?"

"Well, after I picked up the rental, I drove back to take a look at your house. All the windows in the front are gone, but the house didn't catch on fire, so you're good there. I called a board-up service, and they said they'd be out this afternoon, although I haven't gone back to check. But that old guy from across the street—Kline, right? He said he'd keep an eye on things the best he could."

"So then, I guess you didn't make your appointment this morning."

"Nope, and it looks like I also lost my car," she said, giving me a smile that was nothing short of wonderful. "But I've still got you, all things being equal, I'd say it was a push."

* * *

Maggie took off a couple hours later. I figured that was fair, since she'd spent her entire day either sitting with me, or else trying to mop up the mess that slopped over into her own life as a result of my car being blown to bits in my driveway. A short time after, I was visited by the hospital chaplain, a Catholic priest named Schmidt. He asked how I was getting along, and when

I said I was fine, he offered to say a prayer with me to thank God for saving my life. I didn't see the point in telling him it was actually a decade-old Volvo that had done most of the saving, so I took hold of his hand, and we said a prayer together.

After he left, a nurse and the hospital's doctor came by to check on me. They took my temperature, blood pressure, and a blood sample and told me to pee into a container so the lab could check for blood in my urine. Then they gave me a hydrocodone tablet and a tranquilizer and left, turning off the lights on their way.

After they were gone, I lay in bed trying to make sense of what had taken place earlier in the day. First, I tried to figure out who might be unhappy enough with me to want to blow me, and maybe Maggie as well, into an alternate universe. Over the years, given my line of work, I have made any number of enemies, including killers, embezzlers, unfaithful spouses, welfare chiselers, bail skippers…you name it. But for the most part, those people were now either dead, incarcerated, or have moved on to other cities or phases of their lives. That pared my list down to the people involved in the case in which I was currently engaged. Off the top of my head, I could think of five, as if that wasn't enough, who might want to see me come to harm. Those included Tommy Mack, Red Cherry, and, by extension, Phillip May, plus Michael Pomeroy, and whoever had killed Sarah Bergman.

Since I didn't have any better idea who killed Sarah than I did the night Maggie and I had found her body, I didn't see any point in dwelling on that possibility. As far as Tommy Mack was concerned, I was pretty sure he wasn't at all happy with me, especially since I had talked him into meeting with Red face-to-face, a visit that had resulted in Tommy nearly having his right arm ripped out of his shoulder. But I also knew Tommy was not by nature a violent man; he was a petty thief. And anyway, I doubted he would have the expertise to construct a sophisticated explosive device. I also didn't think, given his own medical problems, that he would be capable of crawling underneath my car to plant a bomb.

Then there was Michael Pomeroy. I couldn't be sure what to think about him. Obviously, he was anxious to get back into Maggie's good graces and, by extension, her life and her bedroom. But I didn't think he knew enough about me or my relationship with his ex-wife to want to kill me. For that matter, since I wasn't privy to the conversation he'd had with Maggie, I wasn't even sure whether he knew who I was. And also, how would a former manager of a restaurant chain know anything about building a bomb? I didn't know the answer to that, but I supposed I should make it my business to find out. Maggie had never said very much about him, so I didn't know whether he'd done any military service, and if he had, what was his MOS? Had he, for example, had any demolitions training?

All that left me with two remaining candidates. Red Cherry, I knew for certain, had the resources and access to the expertise required to rig up a car bomb. But for the life of me, I couldn't think of a reason why he would want to have me killed. I hadn't done anything to interfere with any of his business activities, illicit or otherwise. And I had also found Tommy Mack for him, and didn't ask for the money he had offered me to make the job a priority. Besides, I figured if Red wanted me offed, there were easier ways to do it than creating a spectacle that would inevitably lead to a major case-type investigation, particularly since the risk to innocent bystanders was so high.

And that brought me around to considering Phillip May. I couldn't have said just why, but the fact that I had seen him driving his car into Red Cherry's driveway on the afternoon I had delivered Tommy Mack made me feel sure that there was something more to May's visit than to take a dip in Red's pool. More than that, Phillip May taught physics and chemistry, a skill set that lent itself readily to constructing an explosive device. Beyond that, May was friends, and close friends at that, with Isaac Bergman, who was himself involved in an illicit enterprise. And while I couldn't be absolutely sure, it looked very much as though one and one and one made three.

I made up my mind that, the very first chance I got, I was going to pay Phillip May another visit.

Chapter Thirty

After two days in the hospital and three more days recuperating at Abigail Crowley's rented townhouse, Tommy Mack was starting to feel a little bit more like his old, upbeat self. His arm still hurt like hell, and he was tired of sleeping on his back, which was not his preferred position. But at least he was in comfortable surroundings, and he was relatively safe, since, as far as he knew, nobody was hunting for him. I had called Fat Wally Sadler to let him know that I had located Tommy, and that I would make sure he showed up for his court date, which was scheduled for the Monday morning after next. Wally grumbled a bit and then hinted that he might move to vacate Tommy's bail. If he did, I'd have to haul Tommy's ass out of Abigail Crowley's bedroom and return him to the city lockup, something I definitely did not want to do.

There was also the problem of Tommy slipping his electronic tether shortly before he stole Amanda Crowley's car and beat feet out of town, only to return later that same night. On that score, at least, I was able to convince Fat Wally that since I knew where Tommy was and had promised to make sure he showed up for his hearing, he'd square the issue with the cops.

On Wednesday night, the same night I was taken to St. Thomas hospital after seeing my hundred-thousand-dollar ride disappear in a ball of fire, Tommy finally convinced Abigail that it would be in both their best interests if they bought a gun for protection. After all, he argued, even though, as far as he knew, Red Cherry was done exacting his revenge for breaking into his home and stealing almost worthless jewelry, there was no guarantee that Red wouldn't change his mind and decide to clip Tommy and be done with him once and for all.

And so, the next morning, Tommy and Abigail drove to a Bass Pro Shop near the Opryland Hotel complex, where Abigail bought a Brazilian-made Taurus G3C 9MM handgun for slightly less than three hundred dollars. It's an ugly little gun that doesn't have the quality or the elegant look of, say, a Beretta M9A or a Kimber Micro 9, but then, it's cheap, and it holds twelve rounds. And as Tommy said, it only had to work once. And, anyway, he didn't want to break the bank—actually, Abigail's bank, since Tommy could not legally purchase a firearm. Another thirty bucks bought a box of fifty rounds of ammunition. That was more than enough, Tommy thought, to take care of the situation he was planning to deal with. And just to make sure his adventure would come off without a hitch, the first thing he did when he and Abigail got back to her apartment was to take a file and set to work removing the stamped-in serial number from the gun.

* * *

At about the same time, Tommy and Abigail were leaving Bass Pro on their way to enjoy a late breakfast at a nearby Waffle House, I got a couple of visitors. The first was somebody named Daugherty from the fire marshal's office. He had an accent thick enough to cut with a chainsaw and he made it clear he was going to need information so he could fill out a report about the "splosion" and the "fahr." I wasn't particularly worried about talking to him, since I hadn't been the cause of either one, plus I had Maggie to back me up. However, after we got the preliminaries out of the way—my name, address, the make and model of the car, my driver's license number, and a description as best as I could tell them of what had happened—Mr. Daugherty got down to what he really wanted to know.

"Did you all have comprehensive insurance coverage on your car, Mr. Gamble?"

"I'm feeling much better this morning, Mr. Daugherty; thanks for asking."

"Hospital's got plenty of doctors, Mr. Gamble. I'm a fire department investigator. But glad to hear it just the same." There was a pause while he scribbled something into a notebook. "So, back to the question. Do you have insurance for the car? And was it paid for?"

"Yes, and yes."

"Then I expect you'll be filing a claim?"

"Obviously."

"And just out of curiosity, can I ask why you would park an expensive car like a Panamera in the driveway rather than in your garage?"

"I already have a car in the garage."

"Right," he said, checking through several pieces of paper he had attached to a clipboard. "A 60-year-old Ford Thunderbird. Is that some kind of a hobby car you're restoring?"

And that was how the rest of the morning passed. Instead of simply filling out a report, it now seemed as if Mr. Daugherty was trying his very best to make a case that I had dynamited my own car in order to collect the insurance, never mind that if I had been any closer than I was to the Panamera when I pressed the remote start button, I would have blown myself, and probably Maggie as well, into molecules.

It took another forty minutes of him asking questions and me answering them before he finally decided that whatever had caused my car to explode, it wasn't an insurance caper. Neither was it a botched attempt at suicide. More or less, by default, that made it attempted murder, which meant that more cops would be calling on me soon.

My second guest of the morning showed up around the time I was finishing my green jello, which was the highlight of a lunch that also consisted of a cold roast beef sandwich, a cup of vegetable soup with a pack of crackers, and, at my request, a Diet Coke. I hadn't expected him, but even so, there he was.

Red Cherry. In the flesh. Again.

"Heard you had a little bit of trouble." Never one to stand on ceremony, he pulled the visitor's chair close to the bed and sat down. Today, he was dressed for the golf course with tan slacks, matching Louis Vuitton sneakers, a pink polo shirt, and a lightweight robin-egg blue narrow-lapel jacket. A wise choice, the jacket, considering the temperature in my room felt like it was somewhere south of sixty-five degrees.

"That was a shitty thing that happened to you." He looked and sounded genuinely sympathetic. "I heard your lady friend was with you. She's okay, I hope."

"Yeah, she's fine. She was inside the house when the car blew up," I said irritably. "Look, excuse me for being direct, but I'm not feeling my best just now, so, why are you here? You want to find out what went wrong so you can get it right the next time?"

His eyebrows shot up. "Me? You think I tried to blow you up?"

I shook my head, which immediately shot a spasm of searing pain that began at the base of my skull and ended up somewhere near the tips of my toes.

"As a matter of fact, I don't. But I think you know who did."

"And why would you think that?"

"Because I think the individual who did was someone that we both know, and first chance I get, I'm going to pay him a visit. See what he has to say."

He actually sounded hurt. "Gamble, if I wanted you to go away, believe me, you'd be gone, and not from some Mickey Mouse car bomb." When I didn't say anything to that, he went on.

"Too public, too noisy, too much collateral damage. I don't need that kind of trouble. There are much simpler ways to make somebody disappear. You were with the cops. You ought to know that."

"Then, what?"

"What else? I brought your money." He reached into his jacket and extracted a fat brown envelope.

"What money is that?"

"Twenty K, like we discussed. You remember, for finding that Tommy Mack guy for me." He dropped the envelope on the bed. "They're mostly hundreds, all non-sequential, but I threw in a few fifties and twenties, just in case you wanted to stop for lunch at Five Guys or someplace like that on your way home."

I sat up in my bed so that I was nearly at eye level with him. "I can't take your money. I'm not proud of what I did. I delivered Tommy that day because I thought it was the only way I had to save his life."

"How did you figure that?"

"Honestly? I didn't think you'd kill him in front of a witness." It occurred to me even as I was speaking that, at that moment, there was nobody in the room except Red and me, and for all I knew, no one else had seen him come in.

He gave me a look that I couldn't quite read, one that was somewhere between anger and amazement. Then he burst out laughing.

"I've got to hand it to you, Gamble. You might be the only honest man I've run across since I left Mississippi. Not necessarily the smartest, but definitely honest." He stood up to leave. "Look, keep the money. Take your lady friend on a nice vacation, someplace where there's a beach or a ski slope, or whatever the hell it is you like to do. Or better still, put a down payment on a car. I understand you'll be needing one."

"The old one was insured," I said.

"Then buy a better one. If it was me, I'd go for a Blackwing. The red one." And with that, he was gone.

* * *

The hospitalist discharged me at two-thirty that afternoon, with instructions to protect my punctured eardrum by keeping my ear dry and to avoid blowing my nose strenuously. The burns I had suffered were on par with a serious sunburn, she said, and that they would settle down after five to seven days. So, with those admonitions ringing in my good ear—my damaged ear had been filled with an antibiotic gel and plugged with a cotton wad—I called Maggie at her office and asked if she had time to come and scoop me up. Otherwise, I said, I could take an Uber.

"Not a problem. I'll be there in half an hour." By the time she rolled around to the front entrance, I had already been seated in a wheelchair and parked in the lobby to wait for my ride. Since the ER docs had cut off the clothes I'd been wearing when I arrived, the hospital was good enough to spot me a set of scrubs and a pair of shower shoes, so that I didn't have to leave the

192

building in nothing more than my underpants.

"That's a good look for you," Maggie said, eyeballing my new outfit. "Anyplace special you'd like to go? Maybe someplace where you can pick up a stethoscope?"

"Home, first, I think, so I can find something to wear and to pack a bag."

"What do you need to pack? You've got plenty of clean clothes at my place." When I didn't say anything to that, she said, "You are staying with me, right? I mean, at least until you get your windows fixed. You can call your insurance agent from my house."

"No, I am not staying with you. I'm going to stay in a hotel until I can sort out what just happened." She started to argue with me, but I said, "Maggie, think about it. Somebody tried to kill me, or maybe both of us and whoever that is, that person would have succeeded if we hadn't been lucky. I have no reason to think he won't try again, and I'm not about to expose you to that kind of risk."

Then, I decided to go for broke.

"Matter of fact, I think you should plan on staying at the hotel with me. You can even have your own room if you want privacy. I just don't want you getting hurt in case some lunatic comes busting through the front door with a Tommy gun blazing because he thinks he can find me at your place."

She didn't say right away, but I could tell she was mulling over what I had just said. When we got to my house, I saw that the lawn and the lower limbs of the sycamore tree in my front yard had been badly scorched. The grass would grow back eventually, but I'd need to have somebody come and trim the sycamore so it wouldn't look lopsided. On the plus side, if you could call it that, the board-up service had already been there and nailed sheets of plywood over the empty spaces where the front windows had been. Somebody had also cleared what was left of the Porsche and Maggie's Volvo out of the driveway, so I could get my other car out of the garage—assuming, that is, that it would start after sitting for the better part of a year.

Before the Panamera found its way into my driveway, my ride had been a baby-blue 1965 Thunderbird. And contrary to what Mr. Daugherty had suggested, the 'Bird was not a hobby car under restoration. It was, instead, my daily driver for the past several years before the Panamera showed up. The car had come to me by way of a client who found himself short of funds when the time came for him to pay my fee for services rendered. So, we made a handshake deal. I could keep his car until he paid up. However, shortly after I took possession of the 'Bird, the guy died, and since he had signed the title over to me, I decided to keep it until I could find a buyer and get something a bit more sensible for myself. But as it turned out, the old gal proved to be very reliable and very comfortable, even if it was a 12-mpg gas hog.

We used Maggie's key to get into the house through the front door, which had not been damaged since it was standing open at the time the Panamera blew up. Mine is not a big house. Like most of the other homes up and down my block, it has a kitchen with an eating area, a living room, two bedrooms, and a bathroom in between, plus a one-car attached garage and a basement. Taken altogether, it's no more than nine hundred square feet, not counting the basement and garage, and would probably be a tight squeeze for a family with more than two kids. However, most of my neighbors are older adults, and perhaps for that reason, the homes are all well-maintained with nicely kept lawns and mature trees. I try to do my part by keeping the grass cut and the outside trim painted. Today, though, the house didn't look very good, and neither did the three houses closest to mine, which had also had their front windows boarded over.

Inside, things didn't seem too bad. There was broken window glass, and pieces of the wooden window frames scattered all across the kitchen and living room floors. The few wall hangings I owned had also fallen onto the floor, along with table and floor lamps and my television set. Well, I figured, at least for the time being, the house was secure, and I could get busy cleaning things up in the next couple of days. For now, though, that could wait. I did, however, put in a call to my insurance agent to let him know what had happened, and that I would be filing claims for both the loss of the car and the damage to the house.

"Already on it," he told me. "As soon as I saw the story on the news, I got busy with the paperwork. Once we get the police report and you sign off on the claim form, you'll be receiving a settlement for the car in about a week. But you'll need to get an estimate on the damage to the house before we can process a claim for that."

I told him I'd get on it right away, thanked him, and hung up.

Maggie sat on the edge of my bed and watched while I threw several days' worth of clothes and toiletries, plus my phone and charger, and my Colt .380 and shoulder rig, into a small suitcase. And even though I am not particularly perceptive in certain circumstances, I could tell that in the time it had taken me to get myself organized, her mood had grown noticeably darker.

"No," she said, at last.

"No, what?"

"No, I'm not going to move into a hotel with you. I understand why you feel you should do that, and I also understand that you're worried about me. But we are not going to give in to some maniac and hide out like fugitives on the run in some old John Garfield movie. But..."

"But," I interrupted, "on the other hand, you think I should move in with you, at least until my house gets fixed."

"Yes," she said. "Absolutely. I think you should. And anyway, who's going to take care of Stanley?"

Oh, right, Stanley. I forgot. And so, I moved in with Maggie.

Chapter Thirty-One

The next day, Maggie went to work at her usual time while I spent the better part of the morning on the telephone. The first call was to follow up with my insurance agent. He informed me that he had already gotten a copy of both the police and fire marshal's reports and that I should have a check to cover the replacement value for the car via FedEx within the next day or two.

"I'll email you a copy of the claim forms, but just a heads-up. The car is four years old, so naturally, the settlement will reflect the depreciation over that period of time. Also, we're still going to need an estimate for repairs to your home. There's a guy we work with sometimes. He's very reputable. I can send him over if you'd like."

I told him his man would be fine and that unless there was a problem, he could go ahead and do the work. He went on to express his sympathies for my losses and the injuries I'd sustained. I thanked him for his efforts and his good wishes, and we said goodbye. In quick succession, after we hung up, I got two calls on my cell. The first was from Dick Dohrn at the *Times*.

"Congratulations," he said, without preliminaries, "You're a celebrity. You made the six and the ten o'clock news the other night. Are you okay? They said you were taken to a hospital."

"More or less. I have a punctured eardrum and some minor burns. No broken bones, though, and my hair wasn't burned off. Looks like I'll live."

"Well, we did a piece on it in yesterday's edition. We can do a follow-up, if you feel like there's anything more to the story."

"You mean, like, do I think I was the victim of a terrorist attack, or maybe a mob hit gone wrong? Something like that?"

He made a noise that was somewhere between a snort and a laugh. "More like, are you working on anything that might make somebody want to kill you? More than usual, I mean?"

When I didn't answer right away, he said, "I'm sorry, that didn't come out right. What I'm trying to ask is whether what happened might be part of a bigger story for down the road. I seem to remember the last time we talked you were trying to find out what happened to some college professor who went missing a while back. And then, right after that, his wife was murdered in her own home. And now, somebody tries to take you out with an explosive device."

"And you're hoping, what? That all this might be part of the crime of the century?"

"Well, it certainly doesn't seem like a coincidence, does it? An unexplained disappearance, a murder, and a car bomb, with just one guy as the nexus tends to get our attention. And, after all, we are a news organization. Matter of fact, I'm thinking about assigning a reporter to the story. See what he can come up with."

I thought about the last time I worked with a *Times* reporter on an unfolding story and how badly that had turned out.

"How about this?" I said. "Suppose you hold off on the reporter for a little while? Go ahead and work on the car bomb story if you want. I mean, when there's a major explosion in a residential neighborhood, nobody expects you to play it down. I'll even give you a pithy quote if you want. You know, something like 'The Good Lord was watching over us, sure enough, and me and my old lady, you know, we're both powerful grateful.' Just don't try to tie it together with Sarah Bergman's murder. Not yet."

"Does that mean you think the two are connected?"

"That's the theory I'm working on. But if you say so in print, all it will do is cause whoever's behind all this to run for cover. Right now, that's the last thing we need."

The line was quiet for a moment, and I could tell he was thinking. "Okay," he said at last. "For now. But when this is all wrapped up, I'm going to expect a complete core dump from you putting this together, start to finish. Nothing gets left out. Deal?"

"Deal," I said and immediately regretted it.

* * *

I took my time showering and let the water run a bit cooler than I usually like it since the skin on my arms and face was still tender from the rush of superheated air that had blown me off my feet when my car exploded. It made me think all over again how lucky I had been not to have gotten perforated by the various pieces of metal, glass, and hard plastic that wound up scattered across my front lawn.

When I stepped out of the shower, Maggie's cat, Stanley, was stretched out across the bed. However, instead of arching his back, hissing, and running off to hide somewhere, he just picked up his head and stared at me. It made me think that maybe he had finally decided that I represented no threat to him and that we could be, well, not best buds exactly, but at least able to tolerate one another. And then it occurred to me that perhaps the change in his attitude toward me had something to do with the fact that Maggie was not at home, and he didn't feel that I represented a threat to his mistress. To test my hypothesis, I reached out my hand to let him smell. He didn't growl, or hiss, or try to bite or scratch me. He just hopped down from the bed and ran down the stairs toward the kitchen, where Maggie kept his bowl.

So that was it. He wanted to be fed.

The second call of the morning came just as I was finishing ladling a generous helping of some kind of kibble into Stanley's bowl. Personally, I couldn't imagine myself eating exactly the same meal two or three times a day for the rest of my life. But then, I'm not a cat.

"Mr. Gamble, this is Detective Bert Sievers, with Metro PD. My partner and I, we were hoping you might have some time to today to come downtown and talk to us about the, well, what? The incident that took place on Monday. Do you think you might have some time to do that? Or if you want, if you're not feeling up to it, we can come to wherever you're staying. I mean, I guess you're probably not in your house, what with the damage and all."

I gave Detective Sievers an excuse about not feeling well enough just yet to drive downtown, but that I would try to come by police headquarters the next morning. He wasn't happy about the delay, but we settled on a ten o'clock appointment on Thursday morning. Truth to tell, although I didn't actually say so, I didn't particularly want to talk to the cops at all. I wasn't worried about them trying to turn the explosion into some kind of an insurance hustle. However, I also didn't want to get into a line of questioning that might make them want to connect what happened to me with the Bergman investigation. Things were already complicated enough without more cops getting into the act.

* * *

By afternoon, I was getting restless. There were only a few places on my body that didn't hurt in one way or another, but just sitting around the condo watching daytime television wasn't going to be the cure for that. So, to pass the time, I tracked down one of Stanley's toys and played with him until he got bored and wandered off to give himself a bath. After that, I scooped out his litter box, which made me think all over again, why it's better to be the cat than the cat owner. Then, I washed the dishes from breakfast and vacuumed the oriental rug in the living room. Still with nothing else to do, I scoured the bathtub in the guest bathroom and washed the bed linens.

Maggie called during a break between clients to ask how I was getting along.

"I'm bored," I told her. "I need to be doing something besides cleaning house and sitting here playing with the cat. I'm going to go and stir up some excitement."

"Wait, you've been playing with Stanley? All of a sudden you two are getting along? What happened?"

"He was hungry, so I fed him."

"And that's not enough excitement for one day?"

"Almost. But there's something else I need to do."

"Okay." There was a pause. "Is there any possibility that this 'something' is likely to wind up getting either one of us killed?"

"No. Nothing to it. I should be home before dinnertime."

"Okay, then I'll pick up some takeout on my way home. Do you want pizza or Chinese?"

"Surprise me."

"Will do. And please, I know how you operate. Don't do anything stupid."

I promised I'd do my best, and we hung up. Then I got on the phone to Professor Robert Levy. I explained that there was something I needed to talk to him about and asked if he had some time available when I could come over.

"As I'm sure you know, Mr. Gamble, my days are anything but busy. Drop by whenever you like. But if you're coming today, you'll have to let yourself in. Roseanne is off today. I'll leave the door unlocked."

Half an hour later, I was back at Levy's home, once again seated across from him in the three-season room. As it had been during my earlier visit, with the afternoon sun high in the sky and all the windows closed, it was at least eighty degrees, maybe more, in the space where we were sitting.

After we exchanged a few pleasantries, Levy said, "So, Mr. Gamble, I seem to remember reading something about you in the newspaper earlier this week. You had a bit of excitement, I believe. But then, I suppose that's all in a day's work for someone in your profession, is it not?"

"No, sir," I said, "it is not. I'm more used to people slamming doors in my face, or hanging up their telephone on me. Explosions in my front yard are a bit out of the ordinary."

"All the same, I'm glad you're still with us." He picked up a cup of whatever he was drinking and took a sip. "All right, then. You wanted to talk with me. I assume it has to do with the case you're working on. However, first, let me ask you. Are you making any progress finding out what happened to Isaac Bergman?"

"Some, yes. But I'm not quite ready to start speculating out loud. However, I'm more convinced than ever that somebody out there would prefer that, wherever Bergman disappeared to, he should stay there."

"I see. Then what can I tell you that will help?"

"Two things, actually. One, can you tell me what exactly was the relationship between Bergman and Phillip May? I mean, I understand they were friends, but was there anything more to it than that?"

"Such as what?"

"Well, for instance, did they have any kind of a business arrangement?"

He gave his head a small shake. "Mister Gamble, both Bergman and May were non-tenured teachers here at Broadview at the time Isaac went missing. Non-tenured staff rarely have any time to do anything other than worry about getting their annual contracts renewed and making sure their lesson plans meet the guidelines set by the university. And anyway, I can't think of anything Isaac Bergman might have been doing that would have any commercial value outside of academia. May, yes, I suppose so. He is a chemist and a physicist, and I'm certain his earnings potential is far greater in the private sector than it is at a small college. But I can't imagine what sort of an enterprise the two of them could cook up that would yield a profitable collaboration." He closed his eyes for just a moment, and I thought perhaps I had overtaxed his stamina.

"Or are you about to tell me something I'm not going to like?"

"Quite possibly, yes. But before I do, I'd like to ask whether you know anything about three female students who dropped out of school about the same time that Isaac Bergman left. Their names are," I paused to check the list in my notebook, "Roberta Eisley, Geneva Robertson, and Madison Burgess. Can you tell me anything about any of those girls? Why they might have dropped out, for example?"

"I don't know about the first two girls. For all I know, they might have gotten married, or transferred to another school, or left for any number of other reasons. Students drop out all the time. As far as Madison Burgess is concerned, she didn't drop out. She died. It was a suicide, I'm afraid. A drug overdose. It was a terrible thing. And before you ask, yes, she was the daughter of Roseanne Burgess, the woman who keeps house for me now."

He paused to take another sip from his cup. "But then, you didn't need me to tell you that, did you?"

Chapter Thirty-Two

Although it might have been the farthest thing from his mind at the moment, Tommy Mack was in a fix. His court date was coming up in less than a week, and, despite my assurances that I would have him in court for the opening of his trial, Fat Wally had gotten tired of his disappearing act and had decided to withdraw Tommy's bail after all. The beef that had gotten him busted in the first place was a penny-ante charge of falsifying state IDs and then selling them to underage college kids so they could buy liquor. Ordinarily, a charge like that wouldn't have resulted in more of a sentence than sixty days, ninety days, and a fine at most, and that was county time. But after more than thirty years as a frequent fuckup, both as a juvenile and as an adult, the Tennessee criminal justice system had seen just about enough of Tommy's act.

That spelled trouble on two fronts. One, he was being charged not only for the bogus IDs, but, as it turned out, an even older warrant that had turned up for fencing stolen property, mostly knock-off Rolex watches and other jewelry heisted earlier from a Nolensville Road pawnshop. But, two—and this was his real problem—he had also been tagged as a predicate offender.

Like many other states, Tennessee has a "three strikes" law, meaning that certain classes of offenders can be given life without parole, also known as the "Big Bitch," after being found guilty of three violent offenses. Typically, these include crimes such as first- or second-degree murder, aggravated kidnapping, and sexual assault, including pretty much anything involving minor children.

In Tommy's case, since he had never done physical harm to anyone, the three-strikes law did not strictly apply to him. However, the circuit judge he was facing this time, The Honorable Sheldon "Ship 'em Over" Robbins, had sentenced him on several earlier occasions, and the odds were, this time, Tommy would draw at least a five-year jolt. And even with time off for good behavior, he would likely end up serving three and a half years, probably at Hardeman County Correctional in Whiteville. That was almost certainly harder time than Tommy was prepared to do, especially now that he had Abigail Crowley in his life.

Then there was the matter of his injury, suffered only a short time earlier, when Red Cherry dislocated his arm and his elbow. The ER docs at the hospital where Abigail took him were able to get him fixed up—to a point. But there were more surgeries that would be needed and then months of physical therapy before he was back to being in good working order. But, as a lifelong petty criminal, Tommy had no medical insurance of any kind. And even if he took it on the lam again and didn't wind up behind bars, there was the problem of how he was going to pay for the various treatments he would need going forward. Medicaid was perhaps an option, but that meant he would have to register for it, and then stay out of the hoosegow in order to receive the benefits. And it was a sure bet that once his name hit the applicant list, it would trigger a fugitive warrant for his arrest, another obstacle, since penitentiary inmates did not qualify for state assistance. And as everybody in the system knew, medical care for inmates was far from the best.

And so, despite the fact that he had never been more than a two-hour drive from the place he'd been born, he knew that this time, he was going to have to run a lot farther. But first, there was something that he desperately wanted to take care of, and he only had a few days to get it done. Problem was, he couldn't figure out how. And then he saw an item in the newspaper that might be just the answer he was looking for.

* * *

There were a few more questions I needed to ask Robert Levy, mostly because I was hoping to confirm a somewhat shaky hypothesis that I had cooked up during my overnight stay in the hospital. My thinking went something like this:

Thanks to Maggie's insight into the cryptic dates-numbers-initials entries in Bergman's datebook, it seemed reasonable to assume that the good professor was running a small string of co-ed prostitutes out of the sorority houses and dormitories of Saint Bernadette University. Looking at how the notations laid out, it appeared he would meet with the young woman early in the week to set her up for Friday or Saturday evening. Then he met with her again on date night to make sure she connected with her trick. So far, so good, but then, how would he be able to persuade a young woman, a student at a nominally faith-based college, to go along with his plan? Maybe money would be enough, but somehow, that seemed like less than a sure thing. What if she got cold feet at the last minute and failed to show up to connect with her john? Then I thought that maybe he had a standing offer to turn a failing grade into an "A," which could be an important consideration for a student who needed every possible credit to receive her diploma on time.

And then I remembered reading a magazine article about a novel designer drug that, when dissolved in a liquid, creates a cocktail known as "happy water." The new drug is a complex mix of caffeine, diazepam, ketamine, MDMA, methamphetamine, and tramadol. Put them all together in just the right way, and you've got a drug that leaves the user, as the article indicated, "dreamy, hyperactive, and energetic." Other reports suggested that this so-called "super-drug" could provide an extended sense of sexual pleasure lasting five or six hours. Altogether, it seemed to be the perfect blend if you were looking to induce an otherwise normal young woman to enter into a sexual encounter with a strange man, or even more than one man. And who better to cook up such a drug than someone holding a doctorate in chemistry? That strongly suggested someone like Phillip May. And if he could produce it for his friend Isaac Bergman, could he not also earn another payday, turning it out in greater quantity for a customer like Robert Edward Cherry?

By itself, however, a business association between Phillip May and Isaac Bergman did not explain what went wrong for Madison Burgess. Robert Levy had said it was a suicide. But was it? Or was it just an accidental death resulting from an adverse reaction to the drug, or perhaps an early, hit-or-miss version that May hadn't quite worked all the kinks out of just yet? I knew that without solid proof, my scenario was thin soup that wouldn't have stood a chance of supporting a police investigation, let alone an indictment.

And then it hit me. Even if Isaac Bergman was pimping out coeds and Phillip May was mixing up designer cocktails to ensure that the girls would be compliant, neither one of those circumstances could explain why Bergman had vanished into thin air, or where he had gone, or who had murdered his wife. But I thought Robert Levy might be just the person to ask about that, and I also thought it was time to quit pussyfooting around. Maybe if I applied a bit more pressure, I could get him to tell me something approximating the truth.

Just to get the ball rolling again, I said, "Professor Levy, a few minutes ago, you were wondering whether I'd had any luck finding Isaac Bergman, and I told you I hadn't. But I do have a pretty good idea of what led up to his disappearance, and I'd like to share my thinking with you because I believe you can fill in some of the blanks."

"We've been over that, Mr. Gamble. I don't know why you keep asking me about it."

"Yes, sir, we have. And I know I'm going out on a limb a little bit here, but with respect, I think you know a lot more than you're letting on. I think Bergman is dead, and—hear me out on this, because you're not going to like it—I also think either you killed him or you know who did. And I think he was killed because of what happened to Meredith Burgess. So, how about if we quit fucking around here, and you tell me which one it is?"

For a moment, he didn't say anything. And then, he opened his eyes wide and made a coughing sound, like a cat hacking up a hairball.

I said, "Professor?"

He leaned forward in his chair and said something that sounded like "bad apple." And then he slumped over in his chair and lost consciousness.

Perhaps if she had been there, Roseanne Burgess would have known what was wrong and whether there was a medication on hand that might have snapped Professor Levy out of whatever distress he was experiencing. But since she wasn't, and since I had no idea what was happening, I had no choice except to get on the phone and call for help.

Chapter Thirty-Three

I t only took about ten minutes for the ambulance to show up with a police car in its wake, both code three. The EMTs, first through the door, made a quick check of Levy's vitals and then slapped an oxygen mask over his face, lifted him onto a gurney, and carried him out of the house. I followed them as far as the curb, and I saw that by the time they were set to close the ambulance doors, Levy was starting to come around. I could tell he was trying to say something, but with the oxygen mask over his face, it was impossible to determine just what.

Before the ambulance drove away, I asked one of the attendants where they were taking him. "Vandy," was the answer.

I started toward my car to follow, but one of the uniformed officers asked me to wait a moment so they could get some information.

Did I know the patient's name? Yes, Robert Levy. How old is he? Don't know. Was I a relative? No, just visiting. As far as I knew, had he had a similar experience in the past? No, I had no idea, although I did know his overall health had been in decline for quite a while. Had he taken any medications or consumed any food or drink during the time I was there? No. Anything else I could tell them for their report? No. Then they asked me for my name and contact information and let me go on my way.

* * *

By the time I arrived at the Vanderbilt Hospital emergency entrance on 22nd Avenue and found a place to park, Levy had already been taken to triage. I spoke to a woman at the admitting desk who informed me that Levy was being examined, and if I would just take a seat in the waiting area, she'd call me when they knew something definite. And so, I sat for the next hour, thumbing through a stack of month-old magazines and today's Nashville *Times*, waiting to find out whether the only man who might be able to provide the answers I needed to solve my case would live or die.

One item in the newspaper caught my eye. The Middle Tennessee Center for the Performing Arts was planning to host a black-tie-optional reception on Saturday night to celebrate the opening of a newly refurbished wing of the building. Among the guests of honor named in the article was Robert Edward Cherry, whose generous support over the years had helped to fund many of the Center's performances and activities. The article went on to say that admission to the event, including *hors d'oeuvres* and an open bar, was three hundred and fifty dollars a couple. Pricey for most folks, but pocket change for the crowd this event would be likely to attract. Idly, I wondered if an event like this might be something that would appeal to Maggie. And then I remembered that I hadn't worn a tux since my senior prom, and moved on to the sports page.

At about four-thirty, the woman working the admissions desk I had spoken to when I arrived came over to give me an update.

"This is just preliminary, Mister…"

"Gamble," I finished for her.

"Thank you. This is just preliminary, but the doctor says it appears Mr. Levy has had a TIA. A transient ischemic attack. It's a kind of mini-stroke. That means there has been a temporary blockage of blood to his brain. Usually, the symptoms pass within a few hours, or a day at most."

"He told you his name? He was able to talk to you?"

"He was able to tell us his name, yes. He wouldn't have needed to tell us anything else, because he's been with us on other occasions, so we have a pretty complete history for him."

"Does that mean he's okay? Or that he will be?"

"Well, for the moment, yes, he's stable, and yes, he should be fine. The trouble is, sometimes a TIA is a precursor of a more serious stroke that could follow in the future."

"The future," I said.

"Could be tomorrow, could be a week, a month, or never. However, given your friend's advanced age and the overall condition of his health, we're going to keep him overnight, just for observation. If he seems okay after that, you can take him home."

"Can I talk to him now? Just for a minute? I have a couple of questions I need to ask him. It's very important."

She shook her head. "He's still a little bit shaky. It would be better if you came back in the morning. Unless something else happens, he should be able to talk to you at that time."

I thanked her and decided that I might as well head for home, figuring there wasn't anything more I could do until at least the next morning. But then, as I got up to leave, I saw Roseanne Burgess come through the front door and stop to talk to one of the other women behind the admissions desk. I couldn't hear what was being said, but Roseanne was moving her hands animatedly and appeared to be in some distress. After a moment, the admissions lady nodded her head and then pointed to where I was sitting. That got Roseanne limping as fast as she could in my direction, her heels clicking loudly on the tile floor of the waiting area.

"Mrs. Burgess," I said. "Glad to see you're getting around without your cane. Your knee must be better."

"Yes, thank you, it is." Then, "What happened?" she demanded. "They said he had a stroke."

I pointed to the empty chair across from where I was sitting and waited until she got settled. "I think you might have misheard. I was told it was a TIA, if you know what that is."

She didn't, so I explained. "Not necessarily serious by itself, but possibly serious trouble down the road. They're doing a workup now, and then they're going to keep him overnight for observation. I imagine after he gets checked in, you'll be able to go and see him."

"Oh," she said, her face brightening, "I can't tell you what a relief that is. And, thank you for being here, Mr. Gamble. That means a lot. But how did you know? I mean, why are you here?"

"I was visiting with him earlier today. We were having a conversation, and partway through, he just collapsed in his chair. I called 911, the ambulance came, and here we are. And by the way, how did you find out what had happened? You were off for the day, as I recall."

"Professor Levy has been in the hospital here a couple of times before. After his wife died and I started keeping house for him, he listed me on his medical forms as his emergency contact. I would have been here sooner, but I was out shopping and left my phone on the kitchen table at home. It was stupid, I know, because I always have it with me. It's a good thing you were there." Then, a thought seemed to cross her mind, and her eyes narrowed. "By the way, if you don't mind my asking, what were you talking about? Did you say something to upset him?"

I said, "Maybe you can tell me. I was asking him about Isaac Bergman."

"Isaac Bergman. Again." Her voice got suddenly cold. "No matter what his wife may have told you, Isaac Bergman was a bad man, Mr. Gamble. An evil man. You don't know the whole story."

"Then why don't you tell it to me, Mrs. Burgess? Did Bergman have something to do with the death of your daughter?"

"That," she said, "is something I have no wish to discuss with you, Mr. Gamble. Not with you or the police or anyone else who might be looking for that horrible man. Not now, and not ever. As far as I'm concerned, I hope he's in hell."

The intensity of her reaction surprised me. I said, "I apologize, Mrs. Burgess. It wasn't my intention to reopen any old wounds. I realize this must be very painful for you."

If she heard me, she didn't show it. "Furthermore, you should know that Professor Robert Levy has devoted his entire adult life to Saint Bernadette University and its students." She leaned forward in her chair and gave me a hard stare.

"And I know you think you have a job to do, but understand that I will not allow you or anybody else to tarnish Professor Levy's reputation. Not as long as I am alive." And with that, she got up and limped away, leaving me to wonder just how far she would actually go.

I sat for a moment, trying to make sense of what I had just been told. Certainly, my question about Bergman had struck a nerve with Roseanne Burgess. And putting her reaction together with what I had learned from my brief conversation with Robert Levy, a picture of what might have happened four years earlier was beginning to take shape in my mind, except, of course, that I had no way of proving any of it.

* * *

Before I left the hospital, I called Maggie to let her know where I was and that I'd be home within the next hour. Also, if she wanted, we could go out someplace for dinner. My treat, since I suddenly had twenty-K that had literally dropped into my lap.

"Busy day?" she said.

"Pretty much from the get-go. I'll tell you about it over drinks."

"Sounds exciting. Anything I can do to keep it going?"

"Wear something sexy. Oh, and I have a stop to make on the way, so no hurry."

On the assumption that Roseanne Burgess had come straight to the hospital from her home, I stopped back by Levy's house to make sure all the doors were locked and the house was secure. While I was there, I thought I might as well help myself to a bottle of water, or, if I was lucky, a Diet Coke from the refrigerator. And while I was searching for my soft drink, I saw a package on one of the shelves inside the refrigerator door. It reminded me of something else I had encountered week or so earlier, and just like that, the picture in my mind became clearer.

Back in the car, I got on my phone and called the main number at Saint Bernadette University. When the receptionist answered, I asked to be connected to Philip May's extension. Turned out, he had a direct number, so I thanked the young woman I had spoken with and dialed that number. I got another receptionist, who informed me that Professor May had gone out around lunchtime and hadn't returned. Did I want to leave a message, or if I wanted, she could give me his cell number. So. Another call, another miss, as this time I went straight to voicemail. Whatever Phillip May was doing, he apparently didn't want to be interrupted by the telephone.

My last option was a call to Evelyn Ellis, who, as luck would have it, was in her office. I reminded her who I was, and of our recent meeting, and then handed her a made-up story about how Phillip May and I had made an appointment for later that afternoon at his home, but that he wasn't answering his phone.

"I know I wrote his address down somewhere, but now I can't find it. I wonder if you'd be kind enough to look it up for me."

"Just a minute," she said, and I heard her tapping away at the keyboard of her computer. "Here it is," she said, and rattled off a number and the name of a street that I knew to be just a couple of blocks from where Robert Levy lived.

Traffic was light, and I turned down the street where Phillip May's residence was located twenty minutes later. My first thought was that all the homes up and down the street were pretty much like all the other houses in that part of the city, which is to say, it was a close match to both Robert Levy's and Sarah Bergman's places. And since May's up-market Beemer was parked in the driveway, it looked as if the professor was still at home. And then, just as quickly, I realized I would not be meeting with him today. Not today or any other day.

There were two blue-and-white Metro police cars parked in front of the house, as well as a van from the medical examiner's office and an unmarked detective's prowler. A sizeable crowd had gathered on the sidewalk, taking in the scene that appeared to be mostly unfolding inside the house. A couple of uniforms were talking with some of the people outside, fishing for information that they might be able to pass on to the detectives for follow-up interviews.

My first thought was that I ought to just keep going. Whatever had happened inside that house was none of my doing, and there was no useful purpose to be served by my getting involved. But then, my curiosity got the better of me, and I decided to take a look. I parked my car three doors down from May's residence and walked to the front door, where a uniformed cop stopped me.

"Sorry, sir," he said, placing a firm hand on my chest. "This is a crime scene. I'm going to have to ask you to step back onto the sidewalk."

I took out my wallet and showed him my identification. "I'm a licensed private investigator. I am also acquainted with Phillip May, if that's who you've got in there. And if it is, I have some information that may be of value to your detectives."

He eyed me for a moment and then said, "Wait here."

A minute later, the uniform returned with a detective I knew from my days on the force. His name was Bill Merlin, and he was a detective sergeant from Central District homicide. We had crossed paths most recently a couple of years back on a case that turned out ugly and complicated, that had left several people dead.

He hadn't changed much since that time. He was a big man, brown-skinned, fully a head taller than me, and a good seventy-five pounds heavier. Sit him down on a piano bench, and he could have passed for Fats Domino, or maybe Big Twist, although I had no idea whether he could actually play a keyboard. He was wearing a tan suit, a pink shirt, a red-and-yellow tie pulled loose at the collar, and a wide-brimmed Panama hat.

"Jackson," he said when he saw me. "My man says you've got something for us."

"I might," I said. "First, can I take a look?"

He shrugged his massive shoulders. "Sure, why not? This guy ain't going anyplace."

He led me inside through a sparsely decorated living room and an equally sparse kitchen into a room at the back of the house that was set up as an office. There was a wooden desk with a couple of chairs parked in front and a credenza behind, a built-in bookshelf crammed with books and file boxes of all sizes, and a small refrigerator off to one side. Just the thing, I supposed, for a man who was too busy to stop what he was doing and walk into the kitchen for a glass of water or a can of Coke. But none of that interested me. What did interest me was the man named Phillip May, seated at his desk with a bullet hole in the right side of his head. His eyes were open and his face held a look of surprise, as if he had been struck by a bolt out of the blue. CSI officers were busy photographing the body and dusting the room for prints. May's right arm was hanging loosely at his side, and on the floor underneath his chair was a Ruger .22 caliber target pistol.

"How long?" I asked.

"Body's still warm; rigor hasn't set in yet. ME says maybe a couple of hours, no more."

"Suicide?"

"It's supposed to look that way, but it doesn't seem quite right. If you notice, all the stuff on the desk, his stapler, his phone, all that shit, it's all on the left. Also, you can see the varnish on the desk is worn on the left side. I'm thinking, why would you answer the phone with your left hand but shoot yourself with your right?"

Another shrug. "I'm betting somebody offed him and then tried to make it look like a suicide, although I wouldn't be surprised if we don't find GSR on his right hand. 'Course, we don't use paraffin no more, we got better stuff. But even so, the department just sent around a study that claimed a GSR test is only about fifty percent reliable. Just the same, though, we'll bag the hands. You know, procedure and all."

He turned to face me. "Okay, let's get back to you. You told my guy you've got some information. You really got something, or were you just bullshitting your way in here for some reason?"

I led him off to the side, away from where the others were working, so we couldn't be overheard. "Truthfully? A little bit of both. I don't know how far your guys have gotten searching the house, but I'm willing to bet that if you look hard enough, you're going to find some kind of a chem lab, either in the basement, or the garage, or maybe in a rented space somewhere."

"We already did, Jackson. Down in the basement, but so what? The way we got it, the guy teaches chemistry at some college."

"Saint Bernadette, yeah. But you should get your forensics team to take a look at the chemicals he's got down there. I think you'll find that what he's been cooking up is some kind of a date rape drug. Happy water, maybe, or

Rohypnol. Maybe some other stuff as well."

I went on to tell him about the daily planner I found among Isaac Bergman's personal effects and what I believed was Isaac Bergman's involvement with Phillip May in running a string of co-ed prostitutes at Saint Bernadette, with Bergman recruiting the girls and May supplying the drugs to keep them compliant.

"I think after Bergman disappeared four years ago, Phillip May kept right on producing and selling his chemical cocktails, only he found himself another partner. And I think both May's killing and Bergman's disappearance are connected to the murder of Bergman's wife a couple of weeks ago. I also think, if you go back four years or so, you'll run across a suicide case involving a young woman named Madison Burgess. I don't know what it says on the inquest report, other than 'drug overdose,' but I'm betting that the drug that killed her was probably cooked up by our late departed friend sitting behind the desk over there."

He didn't say anything, but I could tell he was thinking. "It's a package, Bill, as sure as we're standing here. Figure out who killed May, and you'll clear all three cases at the same time."

"And you think you can prove all this, right?" When I didn't say anything right away, he said, "Oh, wait. You can't prove anything, can you?"

I needed to be careful here, because I wasn't quite ready to tell him the rest of what I believed, which was that Phillip May's new partner might very well be Red Cherry. That was a bigger adversary than I was ready to take on, even if I had the entire Metro police force backing me up. And besides, I also wasn't quite certain that Phillip May hadn't gotten what was coming to him.

"No, I think I can," I said, "But I need to tie up a couple of loose ends first. Meantime, I suggest you have a conversation with Spillner and Proctor. See if they've turned anything up on the murder of Sarah Bergman. Depending on what they've got, I'm pretty sure we can wrap this whole thing up in a couple of days."

At least, that was what I hoped.

Chapter Thirty-Four

When I got back to Maggie's condo, my home-away-from-home, until the contractors finished replacing my front windows and door, I smelled something cooking in the oven. That meant Maggie had decided that tonight, she would be domestic, something she only occasionally did when we dined together.

"It's just a batch of cookies I baked for a birthday party at work tomorrow. Chocolate chip, without walnuts. If you're a good boy, I'll let you have a couple."

"How good do I have to be?"

"Well, considering you've had a few days to rest up, I'd say later on, you'll need to be on top of your game."

After she got the last batch of cookies out of the oven, we headed out to get something to eat. Once we were seated, with our drinks ordered—a bottle of Rolling Rock for me and something called a double-berry mojito for Maggie—she got around to asking the questions that I knew were coming.

"You had a busy day. What were you doing?"

I filled her in on everything that had happened, beginning with my phone call to my insurance agent and continuing through my conversation with Dick Dohrn, spending a few minutes of quality time with Stanley, stiff-arming Detective Sievers from the arson squad, and finally, my visit and subsequent trip to the hospital with Robert Levy. I skipped over the part about Phillip May's maybe/maybe not suicide and my subsequent conversation with Bill Merlin. I couldn't see anything to be gained by getting into a discussion with Maggie about finding another body, at least, not quite yet.

"I thought for sure Levy had had a heart attack, the way he just stopped talking and slumped over in his chair. But it turned out to be a TIA—kind of a mini-stroke. So, after the ambulance carted him off, I followed, just so there'd be somebody along who could at least tell the doctors what happened."

An expression of concern flitted across her face. "Will he be okay? Were you able to talk to him after he got to the hospital?"

Before I had a chance to answer, the waitress showed up at our table to drop off a basket of warm cornbread muffins, buttermilk biscuits, and two ramekins of butter and to take our meal orders. Maggie chose something called "simply glazed salmon," while I went for Cajun shrimp and crawfish with pasta. For dessert, we decided to split a slice of six-layer, multi-colored "bakery rainbow cake," which, when it showed up later, looked something like a Gay Pride parade banner with a scoop of vanilla ice cream on the side.

She spread the minutest bit of butter on half a muffin. "You were telling me about your conversation with Professor Levy," she reminded me. "What did you want to ask him about?"

"Well, pretty much, I accused him of killing Isaac Bergman. I was hoping I might catch him off guard and get him to admit to it."

"Always a good way to get a conversation started," she said, giving me just the barest smile. "What did he say about that?"

"He didn't say anything. He made a noise and then tried to say something that I didn't quite get. Then he just conked out. I didn't know what else to do, so I called for help, and that was the end of our discussion. Although later, I did run into his housekeeper at the ER. Apparently, she's listed as his emergency contact. After she got there, I talked to her for a minute, and then I called you."

"And now, here we are, having a wonderful evening together."

"We are," I said. "But there was something else. After I left the hospital, I went back to Levy's house."

"Because?"

"Because after he had his episode, we left in a hurry without anybody making sure his house was locked up. So, I thought maybe I should go back and check. You know, just to be sure, so that he didn't end up getting cleaned out while there was nobody at home."

"And?"

"And, while I was there, I helped myself to a Diet Coke from his refrigerator. I figured, what the hell, he owed me that much."

"And was that it?"

"Nope. When I went looking in his refrigerator, I found a carton of vials of insulin. You know it needs to be kept refrigerated, or it spoils after a few weeks."

I took a swallow of my beer. "Maggie, Sarah Bergman didn't die from a blow to her head, no matter how hard somebody hit her. She died from hypoglycemia. Insulin poisoning. Do you understand? If I'm right, Robert Levy not only killed Isaac Bergman, I think he also killed Sarah. He committed a second murder to cover up the first one." I walked her through the scenario I had worked out while I was flat on my back in the hospital, beginning with Bergman's date book and his subsequent disappearance, continuing with the death of Meredith Burgess, the murder of Sarah Bergman, and concluding with finding the cache of insulin in Levy's refrigerator.

"So, what do you make of it?" I said when I was finished. "Does any of that make any sense to you at all?"

"Not sure yet. Can I ask a couple questions?"

"Go ahead."

"Okay, everything you've said makes sense from a thirty-thousand-foot level. But the police are going to want to know, first of all, is there a body? I mean, do we know for an absolute certainty that Isaac is dead and not just shacked up with some dreamy-eyed coed on a beach in the Caribbean? And second, assuming everything you've said is a hundred percent correct, can you prove any of it?"

The answer to all three of her questions, I had to admit, was no, no, and no, and that was without adding Phillip May's death to the mix. But even so, I knew I was right. I would just have to dig a little deeper.

* * *

After we finished our meal, Maggie and I drove into the city and parked the car at a public lot near the Country Music Hall of Fame and the night spots on Lower Broadway. We didn't have a particular destination in mind, other than it was a nice evening and a chance to do something different. We spent the next hour or so walking up and down Broadway, holding hands like moony-eyed teenagers and occasionally stopping into one nightclub or another to have a drink and just look around. Maggie said she wanted to stop in at Tootsie's Orchid Lounge, a landmark honky-tonk located across the alley from the old Ryman Auditorium. In years gone by, on Saturday nights, performers from the Grand Ole Opry would frequently drop in after the radio show so they could sit in with the house band for a song or two, or maybe a set. Over the years, Tootsie's reputation grew to the point that these days, it is almost always packed with both tourists and regulars. Unfortunately for us, tonight was a Friday night, date night, and by the time Maggie and I got there, there was already a line out the door. So, rather than stand on the sidewalk and wait to get in, we decided to call it a night and head for home.

Chapter Thirty-Five

Saturday was the day all hell broke loose. And it started first thing in the morning.

I am not normally an early riser, especially on the weekends. And so, when my cell started buzzing on the nightstand in Maggie's upstairs bedroom, I naturally looked at the display to see what time it was. Six-thirty. That meant it was unlikely that whoever was calling had good news.

"Is this Mr. Gamble? Mr. Jackson Gamble?" the female voice on the other end asked after I picked up. I said it was.

"Mister Gamble, this is Janine Masterson at Vanderbilt Hospital." I threw my covers back and sat up straight in the bed, forgetting in the moment that I was completely naked.

"I'm calling to let you know that Robert Levy suffered a serious stroke during the night. Also, I'm sorry to have to tell you that he passed away at three o'clock this morning." There was a pause, then, "I'm calling you because I was told by admissions that you were the one who brought him to the emergency room yesterday."

"Yes," I said. "That's right." By this time, Maggie was awake and giving me a questioning look.

"I know this must be difficult, especially this early in the morning, but we were wondering since you were with him when he arrived yesterday, whether you know if he has any relatives we should be getting in touch with. We tried calling his emergency contact, a Mrs. Burgess, but there was no answer, and yours was the only other name we had."

"I understand, and I'm sorry. Professor Levy and I were acquainted, but we weren't close friends. I'm afraid I have no idea whom you should contact. He mentioned one time that he had a daughter, but I wouldn't know how to tell you to get hold of her. I wish I could help, but I can't. However," I said, as the fog of sleep and late-night sex began to clear inside my head," Professor Levy may have left final instructions with someone at Saint Bernadette University. Maybe someone there could give you that information."

"Well, that's helpful," she said, "and thank you. I'm sorry to be calling you so early on a Saturday morning."

"Not a problem. But before you go, can I ask you, was anyone able to talk to him before he died? I mean, even if it didn't make any sense. Did he say anything at all?"

"I'm sorry, but I'm afraid I wouldn't know. I wasn't with him. I'm not a nurse. I work in patient information. You might try asking one of the night nurses."

I said I would do that and hung up. At the same moment, Stanley hopped up onto the bed and started purring. He wanted something to eat.

* * *

The Tennessee Center for the Performing Arts is located in downtown Nashville, close by the state capitol building, the First Horizon Bank Building, and, across a wide-open plaza, the Sheraton Nashville Downtown Hotel. Over the course of the year, the Center hosts a number of mostly music-related events, including plays such as *Les Miz*, *Hamilton*, and *The Lion King*, plus the Nashville Ballet and Symphony, and performances by C&W artists like Blake Shelton and Kenny Chesney. And although there would certainly be background music, the gathering that was scheduled for Saturday night was not a performance. This evening's event was a cocktail and finger-food reception honoring several of the Center's principal financial supporters. A moderately large crowd was expected for the event, and along with the regular pedestrian and automobile traffic generated by the surrounding hotels, eateries, and night spots, the area around the reception venue figured to be bustling. Plenty of places to get lost in a crowd, if that's what a person wanted to do. And that is exactly what Tommy Mack had in mind.

The event was scheduled to kick off at 8:00 P.M., which, in Tommy's mind, meant the early arriving guests would begin showing up around 7:30. To mitigate any difficulties with parking, several valets were stationed in front of the building so that guests who wished to do so could simply drop their cars at the curb and proceed straight into the Center's lobby. The valet parking option, which was included in the price of the ticket for the evening's festivities, was a nod to the ladies attending who would be inconvenienced by having to walk from a public parking lot to the event venue wearing three- or four-inch heels.

Tommy, of course, didn't own a black-tie rig and wasn't about to rent one, although, he thought, it might have been fun to dress for the occasion. But in the end, it just didn't seem practical. And anyway, his plans did not include actually going inside the Arts Center lobby. Instead, he was content to wait near the drop-off area where the ticketed attendees would hand over their car keys to the valets or else exit from their taxis, Ubers, or limos.

Seven-thirty ticked past, and then 7:45 and finally 8:00, and Tommy figured, well, maybe tonight wasn't going to be the night after all. And then, when he was just about to give it up as a bad job and head back to Abagail Crowley's apartment, a gray-green BMW XM rolled to a stop in front of the Arts Center. Red Cherry climbed out from behind the wheel and handed his month-old, $160,000-dollar ride over to one of the blue-vested valets to be parked somewhere off-site. Red's wife was not attending this evening's event, as she was vacationing with some of her gal pals at a resort on Sanibel Island. That was good news for Tommy, as he was a little unsure of his aim since he would be shooting with his off-hand, and he didn't want to inadvertently injure anyone else.

And so, as the valet drove off, Tommy took three steps toward Red Cherry, took aim the best way he could, and fired six shots, after which the Taurus jammed, making it effectively useless. Five slugs found his victim, including one in the upper back, one in the right shoulder, one in the left arm, one in the left thigh, and one more in the right buttock. The sixth shot was wildly off target, shattering one of the big windows in the front of the Arts Center and setting off an intruder alarm loud enough to drown out the shouts and screams of panic from the two hundred or so people entering the Center or gathered on the sidewalk in hopes of spotting and photographing a celebrity.

As Red fell to the ground, Tommy turned and began running for all he was worth toward the public parking lot where he had stashed Abigail's Audi. At the same time, a half-dozen security people, as well as several armed citizens, also began firing, one or two in Tommy's direction, but also seemingly at one another, as nobody was quite sure who the original shooter actually was. By some miracle, or just plain poor marksmanship, no innocent bystanders were hit, and Tommy escaped uninjured. Within minutes, he was in the car headed for the I-40 entrance ramp at Broadway before the first sirens could be heard approaching the scene of the shooting.

In fact, Tommy had been planning his revenge for several days, ever since he had read the article in the *Times* about the Arts Center gala. And he was meticulous in how he went about it. Drawing upon years of experience watching *Law & Order, Major Crimes, Blue Bloods* and the various *NCIS* iterations, he knew to wipe his ammunition as he loaded it into the clip, because, on television, perps always got caught by leaving fingerprints on spent shell casings. With a revolver, of course, that wouldn't be a problem, but with an autoloader like the Taurus, the brass is ejected each time the action cycles, and Tommy wasn't about to hang around long enough to pick them up off the ground. He was also careful to wear surgical gloves, so that, in the event he was subjected to a GSR test, there would be no residue on his hands. He'd thought far enough ahead to bring a clean, shirt as well, which he immediately changed into after disposing of the long-sleeved shirt he wore at the time of the shooting.

Finally, on the way back to Abigail's apartment, he stopped at a boat launch on Old Hickory Lake and threw his budget-priced 9MM roscoe as far out into the water as he could. There was a small possibility that it might reappear later in the year when the Army Corps. of Engineers drew the water level in the lake down to winter pool, but by that time, Tommy figured he'd be long gone.

* * *

Later that same night—I wasn't sure what time it was. It might have been two in the morning, and it might have been later. Either way, I was having trouble getting to sleep, so I decided to go downstairs and try to find something on late-night television until I felt tired enough to go back to bed. At the same time my feet hit the bedroom floor, I heard a loud crash downstairs, like something heavy falling off a table or a counter and then shattering on the floor. Maggie heard it, too. She sat up straight in the bed and began fumbling for the Ruger 9MM she keeps in her nightstand drawer.

I said, "Sounds like the damn cat knocked something over. Wait here while I check, and try not to shoot me while I'm down there."

I threw back the covers and headed for the staircase. Thinking that whatever was going on was nothing more than Stanley chasing a moth and raising a ruckus, I didn't take any precautions going downstairs other than being careful not to step on the cat or the shards of whatever he had broken. I had just reached the bottom of the staircase leading up to the second-floor bedrooms when I sensed, more than I heard or saw, something moving in the darkness. Expecting to find Stanley playing around with whatever he had knocked over, I turned toward the living room to see what he was up to. In that same instant, I heard someone take a sharp breath behind me, and then something hard and heavy hit me on the back of the head. I dropped to my knees and instinctively reached my hands back to protect myself from another blow, which came, this time, on the side of my head. I didn't find out until later that what I had been hit with was the shovel from Maggie's fireplace set. In retrospect, I guess I should have been grateful he didn't use the poker.

A voice said, "There, that'll keep you quiet," and then my attacker started moving toward the stairs. With what little fight I still had left in me, I reached out and grabbed at an ankle, which, for my trouble, got me a hard kick in my shoulder before whoever it was stomped down hard in the middle of my back, sending a spasm of pain down the length of my spine.

"If you move again, I will fuck you up."

Maybe five seconds passed, ten at the most. The intruder started up the stairs toward the bedroom where Maggie and I had been sleeping, and then I heard three shots fired in quick succession—pop-pop-pop—and whoever had taken me out a moment before fell on the floor not ten feet away.

I was informed by the crime scene investigator who showed up right after the two uniforms, the Metro PD night detectives, and the EMTs who arrived at about the same time that Michael Pomeroy was almost certainly dead before he hit the floor. He took three nine-millimeter slugs, center-mass, in the heart and lungs. That answered my question about whether Maggie had the will to use her weapon on a live target. She absolutely did.

Chapter Thirty-Six

As expected, the next day's morning newspaper, television news, and talk radio were all stuffed to the margins with coverage of Saturday night's shooting in front of the Performing Arts Center. Among other things, readers, viewers, and listeners alike were informed that the attempted assassination of Robert Edward Cherry was—take your choice—a botched gangland hit, an attempted mass shooting by a deranged, unidentified shooter, or a clear demonstration of the inability of our elected officials to ensure public safety. Nobody seemed to know for certain, since, according to the handful of witnesses who actually saw the incident, the shooter had immediately fled the scene on foot, and nobody had been able to identify him, or even come up with a description. Of course, I knew it was Tommy, and I knew why he did it. And I couldn't say that I blamed him.

After that, it got interesting.

According to one talk-radio gasbag, what had taken place the night before was nothing less than divine retribution, as God himself reached down from heaven to punish an individual who represented the mortal incarnation of Satan himself. However, as it would turn out, Satan, in the person of Red Cherry, did not succumb to his wounds. Instead, as later a report would reveal, despite internal injuries and massive blood loss, he had a better-than-average chance to make a full recovery. Not surprisingly, one or two television analysts used their air time to call for stricter gun control. Others, meanwhile, advocated for an ordinance that would require all adult citizens be armed at all times, because, as everyone knows, the only person who can stop a bad man with a gun is a good man with a gun.

Which begged the question, considering the shooter and victim, which one was Tommy Mack?

Meanwhile, it wasn't until the next day, Monday, that the media had a single word to say about the death of a home invader armed with a fireplace shovel who had been stopped by a good woman with a gun. Also, not until Monday were there any reports regarding the death of a respected university professor who had been found dead in his home, the apparent victim of a self-inflicted gunshot wound. That article, which appeared on page three of the front section of the *Times*, did mention, however, that investigators found no suicide note. Further, associates from the university who were interviewed indicated that Professor May had seemed in good spirits and that he had given no indication that he might be suffering from depression. In light of that and other inconsistent evidence, police were treating May's death as "suspicious," and the investigation was ongoing.

* * *

When the cops and the paramedics arrived at Maggie's condo following her 911 call in the small hours of Sunday morning, several things happened in quick succession. The police verified that Michael Pomeroy was, indeed, Michael Pomeroy and that he was dead as the result of three gunshot wounds from bullets fired by Margaret Totten, the homeowner. They also determined that he had entered the condo by way of a lower-level window, which had been taped over and then broken, so that there would be no noise when the glass shattered. After a cursory examination by the first responders, the scene was photographed, and Maggie's Ruger Security 9 was confiscated by the police with the promise that it would be returned later, following a ballistics test and the completion of the coroner's report.

A couple of graveyard-shift detectives whom I did not know took a statement from Maggie. Shaken to the core, but with her wits firmly about her, she told them in exacting detail the series of events that led to Pomeroy being shot and killed, including their two previous encounters, first at the Maxwell House and then again at her office. They tried to get a statement from me, which wasn't of much use, since I had not been present at any of the events leading up to the shooting, and since I was semi-conscious at best at the time of the shooting. The fact that Pomeroy was Maggie's ex-husband had the potential to be a complication. However, his misadventures in Florida following their divorce, plus the fact that he had been out of Maggie's life for ten years, supported the notion that Pomeroy was indeed a home invader intent on bodily harm and not the victim in some half-assed love triangle that included Maggie and me.

By the time the police were finished with their questions, a guy from the medical examiner's office showed up, looking irritated at having been rousted out of a sound sleep at four-thirty in the morning. However, he went about his business quickly and efficiently, confirming the cause of death and that the TOD was approximately one-to-two hours earlier. Next, he arranged to have Pomeroy's remains transported to the ME's office for a complete autopsy. The paramedics gave me a quick once-over and determined that the head injury I had suffered was neither life-threatening nor cause for hospitalization. They did, however, suggest strongly that I should see my own doctor the next day.

And so, by the time the sun was coming up, the cops, the EMTs, the coroner's man, all had vacated the premises, taking with them the remains of the late Michael Pomeroy. That left Maggie and me without the first idea of what to say or what to do next.

* * *

A year or so back, I was the overnight guest of a police captain named Purvis, who ran a force in a small town outside Nashville. I was tracking a young woman who had gone missing, and in the process, got crossways with the local LEOs and wound up spending the night in the city lockup. During the conversation I had with Captain Purvis the following morning, while he was trying to figure out whether to charge me with something, he told me a story about how he had once shot a perp in Ocean City, New Jersey, and then cradled the dying man in his arms until he bled out from his wound.

"It's tough," I remembered telling him. "But it isn't personal. It's just the worst part of the job, taking a life, but it isn't personal."

But I was wrong. Taking the life of another person is very personal. For most people, it's a bridge too far. And once you cross that bridge, you can never cross back over. Not tomorrow, not in a week, or a month, or a lifetime. Even though the world and everything in it may look the same as it did on the other side, you're no longer the same person, and you can't cross back over. Unless you are a complete sociopath, killing another person is an act so final, it stays with you forever.

That was the message that was rolling around inside my head , as I thought about what to say to Maggie now that she had crossed that bridge. And, worse, she didn't just shoot some random home invader. She killed a man she had once loved, a man with whom she'd shared a marriage bed, a man who joined with her to create a child and then mourned with her through the heartbreaking loss of that child.

Later, that same man abandoned her, perhaps because the loss was too great for him to bear. And finally, after a decade, a man who had returned, wanting to reenter her life as if nothing had happened. And at the end, when he pushed too hard and broke into her home uninvited and unrecognized in the small hours of the morning, she shot him as he was climbing the stairs leading to her bedroom.

* * *

After we were finally alone—Maggie sitting on the couch, her knees drawn up and her arms wrapped around them, and me, seated across from her in one of her occasional chairs, a bag of ice against my head—she said, "Aren't you going to say something?"

"What would you like me to say?"

Her eyes began to fill with tears. "Tell me I'm not a horrible person. Tell me I didn't kill Michael just because he was Michael, and I hated him because he left me."

Before I could say anything, Stanley, bless him, hopped up on the couch and snuggled next to Maggie. He seemed to understand that something wasn't quite right, even if he had no clear idea what it was. She reached over absently and scratched him behind his ears, causing him to close his eyes contentedly.

I glanced out her front window, where the crowd of neighbors who had gathered when the fire truck, the EMT van, the ambulance, and two police cars first arrived, had dispersed. It was seven o'clock in the morning, light outside, and people had church services to attend, appointments to keep, or any of a hundred other places they needed to be. Their curiosity would pass. Bit by bit, the story would come out, first in the media, and then gossip and speculation would fill in the blanks. After that, maybe a few of the neighbors would drop by to see how Maggie was doing, and in a week or two, things would get back to normal, like nothing ever happened.

With nothing more insightful to offer, I said, "It was a righteous shoot, Maggie."

She looked at me with dull eyes. "Isn't that something police tell one another when there's been a shooting? What does that even mean?"

"It means that no matter what else is going through your head right now, you did what you had to do, and nobody is going to blame you for it."

"Won't they?"

I took a deep breath. "Look, I know nothing I can say to you right now is going to make one bit of difference, or make you feel any better, but just the same, let me ask you. When you saw me on the floor and someone coming up the stairs toward you, in that split second, did you recognize who that person was?"

"No. I should have, I guess, but no, I didn't. The stairway was dark, and the only light was behind him."

"So then, as far as you could tell, this was just some random home invader who'd broken into your house to do…what? Rob you? Rape you? Kill you? Kill both of us?"

She nodded. "I know." I got up from my chair and sat down next to her on the couch. After a moment, she leaned into me and began to softly cry. Not knowing what else to do, I put my arm around her and held her close until she finally dropped off to sleep.

* * *

Three days later, the ME's office completed its necessary examination of Michael Pomeroy's body. In addition to the obvious cause of death, three nine-millimeter slugs that tore up his heart and right lung, the toxicology screen revealed a BAC of one-point-eight, enough to stagger a full-grown water buffalo. Add that to his frustration over being unable to reconnect with Maggie, and it was easy to understand why he might have thought breaking into her home was a good idea.

Given the circumstances under which he had died, Maggie decided that it would be inappropriate for her to claim the body, and no one from his family was willing to step forward, either. Perhaps for those reasons, I couldn't help feeling sorry for the guy, particularly since if his body went unclaimed for more than ninety-six hours, he would be buried at government expense at the Davidson County cemetery. And so, because I couldn't shake a nagging feeling that Maggie's relationship with me might have been what pushed her ex-husband to resort to violence to get her back, I used some of the money I'd gotten from Red Cherry to pay for a proper burial service for Michael at Mount Olivet Cemetery. And I promised myself that one day I would tell Maggie what I had done.

Chapter Thirty-Seven

Sunday afternoon, I got a call from the Metro police detective Maggie and I had met earlier in the day, asking whether it would be convenient for both of us to come by police headquarters on Monday to answer a few more questions and make formal statements regarding the events surrounding the death of Michael Pomeroy. I agreed for both of us that we would be there by ten the next morning. We spent the rest of Sunday reading the newspaper, watching old movies on television, and doing our best to avoid talking about the elephant in the room, namely the shooting death of Maggie's former husband. Around six o'clock we went out for supper, then went back to Maggie's condo and, after a short night on Saturday, went to bed early. I offered to sleep in the guest bedroom to give Maggie some space. But she didn't want to be by herself, so we curled up together to grab a few hours of restless sleep.

* * *

Early Monday afternoon, after Maggie and I finished giving our formal statements at police headquarters, I dropped her back at home and then drove to a funeral parlor on West End Avenue, not far from two synagogues located in the same area. I was surprised to find the parking area was nearly full, and I wound up having to drive halfway down the block to find a space. Apparently, Professor Levy had a great many friends.

An attendant dressed in a black suit, white shirt, and black necktie directed me to the parlor where Professor Levy's closed coffin was positioned at the head of the room and invited me to sign the registry located just outside the door. Then he handed me a yarmulke to wear while I was in the room "as a sign of respect."

Since I had never attended a Jewish funeral before, I'd checked online the night before to find out how I should dress, and it was a good thing I did, since everyone in the room was attired in dark clothing, black or navy-blue suits on the men, black, blue or gray dresses or pantsuits on the women. I hoped I didn't stick out too much with dark gray slacks and a navy jacket. I did have the presence of mind to wear a tie. Looking around the room, I recognized a few people I had met during my visits to the university, including Evelyn Ellis and Caroline Feldman. I also spotted Roseanne Burgess seated by herself near the back of the room. Like all the other women, she was dressed in a black dress, black shoes and stockings.

At two o'clock sharp, a man named Webber, whom I supposed was a rabbi, entered the room and announced that, following the recitation of prayers, Robert Levy's earthly remains would be transported to Temple Cemetery for the *kevurah*, or burial. Then, the rabbi invited everyone in the room to stand while the cantor sang *El Maleh Rachamim* in Hebrew. However, the funeral parlor was thoughtful enough to provide an English translation:

Oh, God, full of compassion, who dwells on high, grant true rest upon the wings of the Divine Presence, in the exalted spheres of the holy and pure, who shine as the resplendence of the firmament, to the soul of Robert Levy, son of Jacob Levy, who has gone to his supernal world, for charity has been donated in remembrance of his soul; may his place of rest be in Gan Eden. Therefore, may the All-Merciful One shelter him with the cover of His wings forever, and bind his soul in the bond of life. The Lord is his heritage; may he rest in his resting-place in peace; and let us say: Amen.

Since I was not a member of Professor Levy's religious community, nor was I a close friend, there was no reason for me to go to the cemetery to attend the *kevurah*.

It was time to go home.

Chapter Thirty-Eight

Tuesday morning, Maggie headed off to work at her usual time. I told her I thought it might be a good idea to take the week off, but she said she needed to get back to her normal routine. Listening to other people's troubles, I supposed, helped her take her mind off her own. I was having trouble taking my mind off my own troubles when my phone began vibrating. The caller ID showed it was Wanda Beaudry. I almost let it go to voice mail and then decided since the week had already gotten off to a shitty start, I might as well go ahead and see what she wanted.

"Back in the news again," she said for openers. "With all that publicity the last few days, you should be running for office."

When I didn't say anything, she went on. "Seriously, how are you getting along?"

"I have a little bit of a headache. It's getting better, though."

"And your lady? How's she?"

I sighed. "Hard to say. I mean, let's face it. When somebody gets killed, it's hard to come up with a pep talk to smooth things over."

There was a pause. "Yeah, well, yeah. That brings me around to why I called. You remember we talked about that Victor Robles guy? The one who beat up his girlfriend that we were going to need to pay a visit?"

You were going to pay the visit, Wanda. I was just the driver, remember?"

"Okay, sure. Anyway, as they say, what goes around. It seems Senor Robles's girlfriend is the sister of another banger named Manuel Herrera, who by pure coincidence happened to be in the lockup at the same time as our Victor Robles."

"Coincidence. And?"

"And, it appears the two crossed paths in the recreation yard, and Robles somehow came away with his carotid artery punctured with a homemade shiv. Somebody heated the end of a toothbrush and drew it out to a point. Robles bled out right there on the basketball court. And, of course, nobody saw anything."

"They say justice is blind."

"Guess so. Anyway, I wanted to let you know."

And that was that for Victor Robles.

* * *

After Wanda hung up, I made a couple of my own calls, got the information I needed, and then drove over to Vanderbilt Hospital, which is the primary Level 1 trauma center in the city. I stopped at the reception desk to get the room number, then took the elevator up to the intensive care floor, where Red Cherry was in a private room. A very large man dressed in a tan tracksuit with red stripes down the legs was seated in a folding chair next to the doorway, thumbing through the current edition of *Guns & Ammo*. Copies of *Sports Illustrated*, *The Atlantic*, and *Outdoor Life* were on the floor next to his chair. Clearly, here was a man of eclectic tastes.

I stopped, expecting to be patted down. The man looked up at me, but remained in his chair. I said, "How's he doing?"

"You are?"

I showed him my ID. "I was hoping I could talk to him for a moment."

"You carrying?"

I held my arms out at my sides. "You can check if you want."

"Nah, it's okay. I know about you. Matter of fact, for some reason, he's kinda expecting you. But you should know, I am armed. And if any shit starts to happen, well, you know how it'll end up."

When I started to walk past him, he said, "I gotta hand it to him, he's one tough son of a bitch. But just the same, keep it short, and don't upset him."

For a man who by all reasoning should have been dead, Red Cherry looked pretty good. From his general appearance, instead of having major surgery to remove five nine-millimeter slugs , he could have just as easily been recovering from an appendectomy or gall bladder removal. He was propped up about halfway in his bed and connected to a heart and respiration monitor, a blood pressure cuff, and an oxygen cannula. When he saw me come in, he managed a small smile.

"Why did I think you might show up?"

"Returning the favor. Plus, I read in the newspaper you were indestructible. I wanted to see for myself."

"I don't feel so indestructible right now. How'd that little shit get his hands on a gun, anyway? He couldn't just go into a store and buy one."

"You're talking about Tommy Mack?"

"Of course, Tommy Mack. You think anybody else would try to take me out like that? Where the hell did he get a gun?"

"Line of work you're in, you have to ask a question like that?

"I guess not." He started coughing raucously. I waited, wondering if the racket might bring the big guy seated outside in to come check whether I was choking his boss to death. When he didn't, I guessed the noises Cherry was making must be a regular thing, given his condition.

After a minute, he settled down again. "So, you see that I'm still alive, but then, you already knew that. What's the real reason you're here? I mean, I appreciate your concern, Gamble, but it's not like we're best pals or anything."

"Okay, and I was told to keep it short, so I'll just get to it. I wanted to ask you what's your connection to a guy named Phillip May?"

"Who?"

"Right. Phillip May. A guy who, up until the other day, taught chemistry and physics at Saint Bernadette University. A guy who, from what I hear, had a pretty elaborate chem lab in his basement and who apparently committed suicide not long after my car exploded in my driveway."

He gave me a blank look, so I said, "A guy I saw pull into your driveway the same day I was there with Tommy Mack. Which, by the way, I haven't mentioned to the cops, if you take my meaning." I paused. "You do take my meaning, don't you?"

Another pause. "What is it you think you know?"

"I don't know anything for sure, but what I think is, that up until the time that he died, Isaac Bergman and Phillip May were running a string of coed hookers out of the college where they both taught. I think Bergman recruited the girls—they seemed to be attracted to him—and May cooked up some kind of a proprietary drug cocktail to make sure they were compliant. After the girls met with their dates, they either got paid in cash by Bergman and May, or else they made sure the girls got top grades at the end of the semester.

I took a breath. "I also think it's at least possible May was doing a little business with you on the side. I don't know for sure all the enterprises you're involved in, but it seems reasonable that the happy water May was brewing up would be something that would interest you, either because you, or one of your associates, was running some kind of escort service, or else you were reselling the drugs to somebody who was."

Cherry started to reach for the nurse's call button. "I'm getting tired here. I think it's time for you to go back to whatever it is you do when you're not pestering innocent citizens, because I don't see where any of what you've said so far has anything to do with me."

"Then give me just one more minute here, and I'll tie a ribbon around it for you." I grabbed the visitor's chair and pulled it up close to Cherry's bed.

"It's like this. One of the girls working for Bergman and May was a young woman named Madison Burgess. Her mother works for a retired professor, an old guy named Levy, who died the other day from a stroke. Levy was Bergman's dissertation advisor. Madison Burgess committed suicide, or else died of a drug overdose shortly before Bergman disappeared under suspicious circumstances."

"And you think, what? I took him out?"

"Not at all. But when Bergman's wife hired me to find out what happened to her husband, one of the people I talked to was Phillip May. Now, I'm guessing a little bit here. But if May and Bergman, or maybe just May, was doing a little business on the side with you, both of you would have had an interest in keeping that quiet. And when May found out I was looking into Bergman's disappearance, he came to you to see if you could help him out by getting rid of me. Or maybe you could pay me off to drop the case. I mean, the twenty K you offered me is a lot of money to get me to do something I was already doing. Unfortunately, he chose the day I was at your home with Tommy Mack to come and see you. That connects the two of you."

I had his attention now. "And then what?"

I said, "I think I've done enough talking. I can't prove any of this, but just the same, I think now it's time for you to fill in the rest. On the other hand, I could take what I just told you to the cops and let them take it from there."

"That would be a mistake on your part. A very big mistake."

"Yeah, but it wouldn't be anything new." I said, "Look, I don't have any axe to grind with you. I know what you do for a living, and I know if you weren't doing it, somebody else would be. I don't like it, but I also don't particularly care. I'm not looking to jam you up. I just want to know what actually happened to Isaac Bergman."

He said, "Show me your phone."

I took it out of my pocket and showed it to him. The screen was dark. "It's off. No recording."

"Okay." He took a deep breath. He was starting to get tired, for real. "Everything you've said so far is pretty much correct. May was cooking up some stuff for one of my, what? My associates, to use in his own business. Me, I don't run hookers, but I don't have a problem with guys who do as long as they remember me on the fifteenth and the thirtieth of the month.

"And you're right. When you started looking into this Bergman business, some people started to get nervous. After you talked to May, he came to me to ask what I could do for him. I told him, nothing, since I wasn't involved in what he and Bergman had been doing. For that matter, I wasn't directly involved in what May was doing on his own. It was him that rigged that bomb to your car. Something like that is easy enough to do, especially if you know your way around chemistry like he did." Here, he started coughing, and I thought for a moment I was going to have to run and find a nurse, but then he settled back down again. After a swallow of water, he went on.

"Well, when that happened, I knew for sure the cops would be on it. I mean, you can't set off a bomb in a residential neighborhood and not get serious attention from the police. I wasn't ready to risk May getting caught and then rolling over on my guy in exchange for some kind of a deal."

"So then, what, you had him clipped and tried to make it look like a suicide?"

"I didn't say that. Sometimes, things just happen."

"They do, but in this instance, the cops are going to want a better answer than that. Because, whoever did the job didn't realize May was left-handed, so the suicide angle isn't going to hold up." I said, "I hope whoever did it knows how to cover his tracks."

"If he's any good, chances are he's a thousand miles away by now. Fishing in the Caribbean."

I shrugged. "Okay, then, let's call it a public service killing. What about Isaac Bergman? You know anything about that?"

He shook his head. "No."

"Or Sarah Bergman?"

"I never met either one of them. I don't know anything about Bergman or his wife."

"Okay." I got up to leave. "Then we're done here. I could make up some bullshit about having everything we've talked about written down to be sent to the police in case anything happens to me, but the fact is, I don't care about Phillip May. He tried to kill me and might have killed my lady friend in the process, so as far as I'm concerned, whoever killed him saved me the trouble of doing it myself."

He looked at me. "You sure?"

"Absolutely. We're all square." I reached out to shake his hand. "Get well soon, Red." And I meant it.

Chapter Thirty-Nine

When I got back to Maggie's condo after my visit with Red Cherry, she was already home. Her last client for the day had called and cancelled her appointment, so she took the rest of the afternoon off. I offered to make supper, which turned out to be a pork sausage and egg scramble with diced shallots and green peppers. Not fancy by any means, but tasty and easy to prepare.

Partway through our meal, after telling me about her day, she got around to asking about Robert Levy's funeral.

"It was different," I told her. "Apparently, in the Jewish faith, it's considered dishonoring the deceased to actually display the body, so the coffin was closed. The body, as I understand it, is washed, dressed in white, and not embalmed."

"So then, nobody can look at the dead person and say something like, 'He looks so natural?' Were there a lot of people?"

"Quite a few. University people, like at Sarah's memorial service, and friends, I guess. At the end, there was a prayer, and then off to the cemetery. I skipped that and drove over to the hospital instead to talk with Red Cherry."

She put down her fork and gave me a look. "Why would you do something like that? Isn't that kind of risky? And why would you think he'd be interested in talking to you?"

"Not much of a risk, really. He's flat on his back, and I haven't done anything to annoy him. Plus, I was counting on all the painkillers he's been taking to keep him more or less docile."

"And I suppose he found you utterly persuasive and confessed to killing

Sarah."

"No. But he did tell me a couple of things I needed to know."

"Which were?"

I shook my head. "I hate saying this to you, but I can't tell you." She started to say something, but I held up my hand to stop her. "I gave my word, Maggie. That has to mean something. And anyway, none of it had anything to do with you, or us, but it would be beyond dangerous for you if I were to repeat what he told me."

She sat for a moment, thinking. "Okay, then I have something to tell you. I've decided to sell the condo and find someplace else to live."

"What? Where?"

"I don't know. I was thinking maybe in one of those new high-rises downtown. There've been two break-ins and two killings here since I met you. That's a lot of bad stuff. I've already contacted a realtor. I'm meeting with her tomorrow to start looking at listings."

"Maybe it's not the condo you need to get rid of. Maybe it's me. You know, I haven't exactly made your life an oasis of serenity."

"No. This last thing with Michael, you had nothing to do with that. That one is strictly on me. You're a keeper. And before you say anything else, so is Stanley."

* * *

Since I did the cooking, I cleaned up my mess in the kitchen while Maggie went upstairs to take a shower. After that, she announced that she was tired and was going to bed early. I told her I'd be along shortly, but that there were one or two things I wanted to do first. In fact, what I wanted to do was sit outside on Maggie's back deck and think about what had taken place since I had been hired by Sarah Bergman to locate her missing husband, to try to make sense of it.

It took a while, because facts and faces were spinning around inside my head like a ceiling fan running at top speed, and I still couldn't say for sure what had happened to Isaac Bergman, or why. But then I remembered something Robert Levy had tried to say to me just before he lost consciousness. And just like that, I knew exactly where Isaac Bergman had gone and also the name of the person who had murdered his wife.

Chapter Forty

The next morning, I was up and out early. My first stop was at a nearby McDonald's for my usual breakfast. Then, I swung by my house to see whether any progress had been made in replacing the windows and the front door. There was a sign in the front yard announcing to anyone interested that the Mid-South Home Improvement Company was on the case, but from what I could tell, the only work done so far was somebody placing the sign. I took down the telephone number so I could give the company a call to see if I could get things moving along a little faster. Not that I minded sharing quarters with Maggie—to say nothing of her bed—but like me, she was used to a certain amount of privacy, and I had the distinct impression she was starting to miss it.

My next stop was the office, where I picked up a few messages, none important, and paid some bills, including the next month's rent. Then I put in a call to the police, and spoke with John Spillner for about ten minutes. After that it was time to get back to work, for real. I checked the online telephone directory for Roseanne Burgess and, finding none, remembered that she had a cell phone and so was unlisted. And since I didn't know where she lived, I played a hunch and drove to the home of the late Professor Robert Levy. Not surprisingly, there was a car in the driveway.

I parked my own car at the curb and walked up to the front door. It was unlocked, so I let myself in. I found Roseanne Burgess sitting in the chair I had occupied in the three-seasons room in the back of Levy's home. There was an open Bible in her lap, and her purse was on the floor beside her. She looked up when she saw me come into the room. I took a seat in the chair across from her.

"Mrs. Burgess. How long have you been here?"

"Since the funeral service yesterday."

"You sat here all night? Why?"

She gave a small shrug. "The professor and I were very close. I can't believe he's gone. I suppose I'm having a hard time letting go."

"I understand. But old age is a fatal disease, Mrs. Burgess And Robert Levy was not in very good health. It was his time."

"That isn't true," she said hotly. "He had many good years left to live. It wasn't 'his time,' as you put it." She closed her Bible and placed it on the table next to her.

"You killed him. You dragged him into your stupid, pointless investigation about that horrible man, that Isaac Bergman. If you hadn't come through that front door the first time, Professor Levy would still be alive, still doing important work."

I thought about asking what important work that might be, but let it pass.

"Mrs. Burgess, I'm not going to justify what I do for a living to you. But I will tell you what is going to happen within the next twenty-four hours and why. And it's very important that you listen carefully."

"Just go ahead and say what you've got to say, Mr. Gamble. No matter what, it won't bring Professor Levy back."

"No, it won't. But I think by the time I've finished, you'll agree that it's just as well, because if he were still living, he would be arrested and charged with murder. And I'm very much afraid that you're going to be charged with the same crime."

"What are you talking about?"

I said, "The last time I spoke with Professor Levy, I accused him of killing Isaac Bergman. I didn't really believe it, but I wanted to see how he would react."

"You saw, all right. You upset him enough that he had a stroke."

"Yes, he did, and certainly that wasn't my intention. But right before he passed out, he said something that didn't make any sense in the moment. He said, 'bad apple.' Or at least, that's what I thought he said. But after I thought about it, I realized what he was actually saying was 'crabapple.' As in, the crabapple trees in the back yard. How long have they been there, do you know?"

"Several years. I don't know for sure. What difference does it make?"

"Well, I think you know exactly how long they've been there, and I also think you know it makes a great deal of difference. Because, unless I am very wrong, Isaac Bergman is buried underneath them, and Robert Levy put him there." I paused and waited for a reaction. Getting none, I said, "Isn't that right, Mrs. Burgess? Robert Levy killed Isaac Bergman and buried him beneath those crabapple trees there in the back."

Still nothing. "You're not disagreeing with me, Mrs. Burgess. That tells me I'm right."

She seemed to shrink back into her chair. "It seems like you already worked it out, so what do you want from me?" There was resignation in her voice.

"I need to be sure. I want you to tell me what happened. Maybe there's something I can do to help."

She sighed. "Well, they're both gone now, so I guess it don't much matter anymore. And anyway, I don't see where either one of 'em need any help from you."

"It's not them I'm thinking about. It's you."

"Me? What kind of help do I need from you?"

"In a minute. Let's keep things in order, if we could. First tell me about Isaac Bergman. How did he die, exactly?"

"I couldn't rightly say."

"No good, Mrs. Burgess, so let me just fill you in a little bit here. Before I drove over here this morning, I called the police. I talked to a detective there named John Spillner. He and his partner are investigating the murder of Sarah Bergman, and I told him what I'm telling you now. It's going to take them a few hours to get a warrant, so they might not get here until late today, or maybe not even until tomorrow morning. They might show up with ground-penetrating radar, or they might just start digging. Either way, they're going to find whatever is left of Isaac Bergman. After that, they're going to want to talk to you, and my guess is, sooner or later, you'll break down and tell them the whole story. So why don't you try it out on me before you have to tell it for real?"

Again, nothing. I said, "Mrs. Burgess, I believe you're a good woman. Otherwise, you wouldn't be sitting there with that book in your hands. But I don't have to tell you, murder is still murder, and you're going to have to answer for it. Either in this life, or if you believe that way, in the next one."

She sat for a moment, quietly before her eyes started to tear up. She reached down to retrieve something from her purse, and I thought for just an instant that she might take out a gun and shoot me. Purely as an instinctive reaction, I slid my right hand inside my jacket, gripped my .380 and cocked the hammer back. False alarm. She wasn't going for a gun. Instead, she took out a handkerchief and wiped her eyes.

"You're right, Mr. Gamble. There's no running away from it now. Where would you like me to start?"

"Take it from the beginning. What happened to Isaac Bergman?"

"Well. Around about the time my Madison died, Professor Levy got wind of what was going on with Isaac Bergman and those girls. He found out about the drugs, but he wasn't sure just where they were comin' from, so he asked Professor Bergman to come to the house for a conversation." She shrugged.

"Maybe he was hoping Professor Bergman could explain, or maybe convince Professor Levy that he didn't have anything to do with my Madison's death. I don't know. And I'm not sure what he said to him to get him to come, except he said to tell his wife there was a meeting. I was here, just finishing cleaning up after the professor's supper, when Professor Bergman showed up.

"I guess they didn't want to talk in front of me, so Professor Levy said they ought to go outside and leave me be. On the way out, Bergman said to me that he'd heard about Madison, and he was sure sorry for my loss. That's what he said, 'sorry for my loss,' like it had nothing to do with him. I tell you, right then, I had my hands in dishwater, and there was a big kitchen knife in the sink, and I'd just as soon cut that man's throat right there and then, only Professor Levy had already said he wanted to hear Bergman's story, and then he'd decide what to do. I guess I figured he was going to turn him over to the police.

"Anyway, they went out back, and they walked around the yard and talked like everything was fine, and then Professor Levy pointed to something back near where the crabapples are now, except that then the trees weren't planted, so there were just some holes in the ground with a big pile of dirt and a shovel. Then, when Bergman turned to look, Professor Levy took the shovel and hit him in the back of the head. He hit him with the edge of it and split that man's head near in two.

"After that, I helped him wrap the body in a couple of big trash bags, and we made the hole bigger and threw him in. Then we stuck them trees on top of him and filled in the hole. And that's where he is today, and look how big them trees have grown. That man that wasn't good for anything else, he made good fertilizer."

"What about his car? How did you get rid of that?"

"Professor Levy drove it into town and left it. He took all the keys, except for the one to start the car, and threw 'em away so nobody'd find 'em and try to get into his house and maybe hurt his wife. I followed him to where we dumped the car, then drove him back home. Next day, I went back to look, and the car was gone."

"And then what?"

"That was it, except a week later, Professor Levy had a heart attack, and after that, he never really got better. He was already near to ninety and shouldn't have been doing that kind of heavy work. Seemed like he just went steady downhill after that. And now he's gone."

I sat for a moment, not knowing what to say. After four years and counting, it turned out Isaac Bergman may have disappeared, but he hadn't gone very far at all. Just a few blocks away from his own residence, buried in the ground underneath a cluster of flowering shrubs and ornamental trees. I wondered whether Sarah Bergman had ever been a guest in Robert Levy's home and whether she had ever wandered outside to admire his garden, never knowing that she might have been standing no more than a foot or two away from her husband's grave.

I wondered, too, what the good people at Saint Bernadette University would think when the whole story came out. Maybe they would feel that justice, however slowly and however haphazardly, had been done. Or maybe they would feel ashamed that such a situation had been permitted to go on for as long as it did. But in the end, I knew, they would offer their thoughts and prayers, and life would go on, as it usually does.

And that brought me to my last point.

I said, "Mrs. Burgess, there's just one more thing. I'd like you to tell me why you killed Sarah Bergman. She didn't have anything to do with any of this, including the death of your daughter." When all I got in response was a blank stare, I went on, "Or should I tell you?"

"Why don't you tell me? I'm tired of talkin', and it seems like you're better at it than I am anyway."

"Okay. I think you killed Sarah because you were afraid my investigation might actually result in me finding out what had actually happened to her husband. You were here the first time I met Professor Levy. You knew the case I was working on. And you realized that, if I actually did learn the truth, both you and Levy would have to face the consequences. Levy as his killer, and you as an accessory after the fact.

"You probably heard me tell Levy, or maybe he told you afterward, that, come hell or high water, I wasn't going to stop looking for Isaac Bergman. So, what did you do? Go to her home to try to persuade Sarah to have me drop the case? And when she refused, then what? You hit her in the head with that cane you were using for a while, and then you injected her with a massive dose of insulin. Is that how it went?"

When she gave me an empty look, I said, "After I left the hospital the other day, I came back by the professor's house to make sure it was locked up. While I was here, I looked in the refrigerator for something to drink, and I found the insulin. It was your name on the prescription vials, not Levy's. That's when the whole case started to come together."

She said, "You're right. I did go to her house. I told her who I was and that I might be able to give her some information about her husband, but that was just to get in the door. I needed to find out whether she was really serious about finding that man.

"When she made it clear she wanted him back, I begged her to let it go. I told her what I knew about what he had been doing with those girls whose lives he had ruined and that it would be best to just leave things the way they were. Nobody else would have to get hurt. I begged her, but she just got angry and told me to get out."

"Then what did you do?"

"She started walking toward the door. She was going to throw me out. I wasn't sure if she'd tell anybody I'd been there, but if she did, I thought people would get suspicious, and I didn't want that, so I just—I just hit her, and she fell. And then I hit her some more."

"And then you injected her with insulin."

"Yes, but it was because I panicked. I didn't know what else to do."

"I don't think that's true. I think you knew exactly what to do."

"What do you mean?"

"Mrs. Burgess, I'm not a diabetic. I don't know how much insulin is sufficient to kill someone who doesn't actually need it, but I bet I could find out, and I bet you already knew. And I'm also betting you had that much, and probably more, with you when you went to Sarah Bergman's home. If that wasn't your plan all along, it was at least what you figured you'd do if she didn't go along with what you wanted. And that's the story I'm going to tell the police."

"And now you think, what, that I should drive down to police headquarters and turn myself in, like some common criminal?"

"At this point, it doesn't matter what you do, because I'm going to do it for you. You can turn yourself in or wait for the cops to come and get you. You've also made some terrible choices, and you're going to have to face the consequences." I got up to leave.

"I suppose I should feel sorry for you, Mrs. Burgess, but somehow, I don't. You're a hundred percent correct that Isaac Bergman got what was coming to him, but Sarah Bergman did not. She was a good woman who missed her husband, and she simply wanted to know what had become of him. That did not merit a sentence of death. So, whatever happens to you now, you deserve every bit of it."

Chapter Forty-One

When Tommy Mack got back to Abigail Crowley's apartment after putting five bullets into Red Cherry, he was surprised to find her packed and ready to go. But where? Tommy had never been more than a couple hours away from Nashville in any direction, and, truth to tell, he hadn't given much thought to where he needed to be heading now. And Abigail, though she was more widely traveled than Tommy, had never ventured west of the Mississippi River, so the conclusion they reached together was, why not head west?

It was a warm evening, and so they put the Audi's top down and headed toward Memphis on the old two-lane highway rather than Interstate 40. They checked into a Comfort Inn near the airport before cabbing it downtown to Beale Street for a late supper and an evening of nightclubbing. And although Tommy didn't say it out loud, he was as sure as he could be that before the sun rose the next morning, the police would be breaking down their motel room door with an arrest warrant. Maybe for Abigail, too, for aiding and abetting a fugitive. However, when that didn't happen, Tommy and his new best girl continued west across the Hernando De Soto bridge connecting Memphis, Tennessee, to West Memphis, Arkansas, and just kept going.

The next day, Monday, two days after Tommy shot Red Cherry and then high-tailed it out of town with Abigail, he was scheduled for a 9:00 A.M. court date for what the county prosecutor thought would be a slam-dunk bench trial followed by a quick-march to the county lockup. When Tommy didn't show up, the judge, understandably annoyed, issued a bench warrant for his arrest. That prompted an immediate telephone call to me from the police, who knew I had been looking for Tommy and thought I might be able to give them some idea about where they should start looking. I could have told them about Tommy and Abigail and let them put out a BOLO on Abigail's Audi, which probably would have gotten them pinched before they got to Texarkana.

But I didn't. I figured just this one time, Tommy needed to have something good happen in his life, so I kept my mouth shut. And I hoped Tommy wouldn't fuck up this golden opportunity.

* * *

After my telephone call to John Spillner, it wasn't until the next day, Wednesday, that the police were able to get a warrant to search Robert Levy's house and property. It didn't take them any time at all to figure out that if there was a body to be found buried anywhere in the back yard, the logical place to start looking was the berm where the crabapple trees were planted. It took a little bit of digging, but within an hour or two, and with the assistance of half a dozen cadets from the Nashville Police Academy eager to earn a few attaboy points, they located the mostly skeletal remains of what dental records proved to be those of Isaac Bergman. Confirming what Roseanne Burgess had told me, his skull had been cleaved nearly in half from a heavy blow struck with the edge of a garden spade. The medical examiner said that death was almost certainly instantaneous. Interestingly, there was enough of the clothes he had been wearing to indicate that he'd had on a corduroy sport coat with what looked like suede elbow patches.

Following the discovery of Isaac Bergman's remains, Spillner and Proctor, accompanied by a couple of uniforms, drove the short distance from Levy's residence to the home of Roseanne Burgess. They had a warrant in hand for her arrest on suspicion of the murder of Sarah Bergman. As it turned out, however, they weren't able to arrest her.

Arriving at her home, and following a search of the house, one of the uniforms took a look in the garage, where he found Roseanne seated in the front seat of her car, a twelve-year-old Mercury Grand Marquis. On the seat next to her was her Bible, open to Psalm Twenty-Three. A framed, five-by-seven photograph of her daughter, Madison, was propped up on the dashboard.

The Mercury had run out of gas several hours before the police arrived, but not before Roseanne had drifted off to a peaceful and painless death. As a matter of course, an autopsy was performed, but Roseanne's distinctly reddish complexion left the examiners with no doubt that the cause of death was carbon monoxide poisoning. And although she did not leave a suicide note, based on the information I was able to provide them, the police were able to mark the investigations into the deaths of Isaac Bergman, Sarah Bergman, and Roseanne Burgess closed.

The following week, there were three funerals: One was for Phillip May, whose body was released by the coroner's office after the cause of death was ruled inconclusive.

The second was for Roseanne Burgess, officiated by a minister from the Pentecostal church where she had been a congregant for many years. Understandably, given the manner and the circumstances under which she died, the service was sparsely attended.

The third was for Isaac Bergman, held at the same funeral home that had handled the service for Robert Levy a week or so earlier. However, as the story of how Bergman died and his remains subsequently recovered was made known, once again, it was a thinly attended event. There was a rabbi on hand to recite the funeral prayer, as well as a few people from Saint Bernadette University who showed up to sign the memorial register. Except for the rabbi, Bergman's sister, Leah, and an attendant from the funeral home, no mourners were present at the *kevurah*. But none of that mattered to me. Because when all was said and done, I had finished what I started out to do for a woman who wanted her husband back in her life.

I found Isaac Bergman.

Acknowledgements

Long Time Gone is the fourth installment in the Jackson Gamble series, and, as with the first three volumes, my thanks go first to Verena Rose, my primary editor at Level Best Books. She is a joy to work with, and is always ready to provide both inspiration and encouragement. In that same vein, I would like to also thanks Shawn Reilly Simmons, who, together with Verena Rose, make up the Dames of Detection, the brains and driving force behind Level Best Books. Without their support and dedication, PI Gamble would still be buried deep inside the confines of the hard drive of my computer.

Thanks also go to the many "Besties" with whom I have become acquainted through LBB, including Skye Alexander, Wendy Sand Eckel, Kerry Peresta, Lori Duffy Foster, Linda Lovely, William Ade, Cathi Stoler and Gerald Elias. You guys are all pals and amazing writers, and I'm grateful for your support over the years. Special thanks must also must go to Mark Levenson, author of *The Hidden Spirit*, and Level Best "Bestie," who schooled me in the finer points of Yiddish terminology. In that same vein, thanks to Karen Uban, a member of the Heartland Writers Guild here in southeast Missouri; and "Bestie," beta-reader, and LBB author of the Leah Contarini series, Libi Siporin. These two friends went beyond the call of duty to educate me about Jewish funeral practices. I was coming from zero on this subject, and even in a work of fiction, it's important to get the details right. Thanks, guys! Thanks also to April Roe, with Mercy Healthcare, who talked me through some of the finer points regarding hospital practices. Finally, a big shout-out to my wife Carol, who provides valuable proofreading and critical input, and who puts up with my disappearing act and sometimes foul mood while I'm squirreled away struggling to put words on a page. I am beyond blessed!

Sources

Even in a work of fiction, it is important to get the details right, particularly in areas where some technical expertise is necessary. In this book, there are references to hospital and medical care procedures, Jewish funeral customs, the history or organized crime in the southeastern United States, and certain elements of law enforcement technology. Failure to pay attention to the small things can distract the reader from the essence of the story, something all authors strive to avoid. To help ensure I had my story straight in this instance, I relied on the Internet sources listed below as well as input from several friends whom I have listed in the acknowledgements.

https://pubmed.ncbi.nlm.nih.gov/17721163/

https://www.vice.com/en/article/epzgvm/happy-water-drug-cocktail

https://news.yahoo.com/happy-water-cocktail-6-psychoactive-221855594.html?fr=sycsrp_catchall

https://www.myjewishlearning.com/article/text-of-the-mourners-kaddish/

https://funeralfundamentals.com/what-to-wear-to-a-jewish-funeral/

https://en.wikipedia.org/wiki/Ground-penetrating_radar

https://allthatsinteresting.com/dixie-mafia

https://www.mussenhealth.us/carbon-monoxide/autopsy-findings.html

https://www.tn.gov/content/dam/tn/health/documents/officeofthestatechiefmedicalexaminersoffice/resourcesforthemedicalexaminer/OSCME_CME_Handbook2017.pdf

https://my.clevelandclinic.org/health/diagnostics/22689-blood-alcohol-content-bac

About the Author

Greg Stout is the author of *Gideon's Ghost*, and *Connor's War*, both young adult novels set in small-town America in the mid-1960s, and *Lost Little Girl*, a detective novel set in Nashville, Tennessee, which received the 2022 Shamus Award for best first novel. His second detective novel, *The Gone Man*, was released in December, 2022 and his third, *Woman in the Wind*, was released in November 2023. A complete listing of Greg Stout's published works can be found at www.gregorystoutauthor.com. Greg resides with his wife, Carol, and two cats, Wallace and Gromit, in Cape Girardeau, Missouri, where he is a member of the Heartland Writers Guild, the Southeast Missouri Writers Guild and is a member of the board of directors for the Missouri Writers Guild.

AUTHOR WEBSITE:

www.gregorystoutauthor.com

SOCIAL MEDIA HANDLES:

https://x.com/GregStout16
https://www.facebook.com/greg.stout.560

Also by Gregory Stout

Gideon's Ghost (Beacon Publishing Group, 2019)

Connor's War (Beacon Publishing Group, 2022)

Lost Little Girl (Level Best Books, 2021)

The Gone Man (Level Best Books, 2022)

Woman in the Wind (Level Best books, 2023)

22 nonfiction titles (White River Productions and Morning Sun Books)